BOSSY

N.R. WALKER

COPYRIGHT

Cover Art: Cormar Covers
Editor: Boho Edits
Publisher: BlueHeart Press
Bossy © 2021 N.R. Walker

All Rights Reserved:

Warning

Intended for an 18+ audience only. This book contains material that maybe offensive to some and is intended for a mature, adult audience. It contains graphic language, and adult situations.

Trademarks:

BLURB

Michael Pietersen isn't up for complications. He's one of Sydney's fastest-moving career-focused corporate realtors, and the only thing he has time for is one-night stands with zero fuss.

Bryson Schroeder's back home from two years overseas with plans to leave his family's hotel empire and begin his own business ventures. Out with friends to celebrate his return, he sees a gorgeous blond man across the bar, and with merely a smile and a raised eyebrow, they leave together for a night of incredible chemistry.

The rules are clear: no names, no details, no complications.

But one night becomes one *more* night, and eventually the arrangement suits them both for weeks . . . until their professional and personal worlds collide. With their hearts already on the line, Michael and Bry need to decide just how complicated they want to get.

N.R. WALKER

BOSSY

CHAPTER ONE

MICHAEL

SO, before I tell you how this all began, I want to explain something real quick.

Sex for the purpose of just-sex is a thing that happens. Uncomplicated, no-strings-attached, mutual-physical-gratification kind of sex. As long as it's consensual, safe, and satisfying for all involved, everyone wins. Right?

Not everyone needs an emotional connection to enjoy sex. Sometimes said emotional connection just complicates matters, and who needs complicated in their lives?

I certainly didn't.

I was a busy twenty-eight-year-old gay man living in an amazing apartment in Darling Harbour, Sydney, with an amazing career, living an amazing life. I was a corporate realtor. I worked ridiculous hours under ridiculous pressure. I earned big money because I lived a high-stress, high-demand life. I was very good at my job. I got shit done and I got it done well.

I had neither the time nor the inclination for complications.

And I know what you're thinking.

You're thinking he's sooooo gonna get blindsided and fall head over heels in love and it's gonna be both gloriously and spectacularly bad.

Well, I'd just like to say in my defence, I didn't see it coming. And yes, that would be the definition of blindsided. I know what that word means. It just means something different when it happens to you.

I did *not* see this coming . . . Much like driving a car onto train tracks and getting stuck and looking out the window to see a train thundering toward you, getting closer and closer, and you know you're gonna hit and you're gonna hurt, and you're completely incapable of stopping it.

That's what it's like.

Highly traumatic and life-changing. With a dash of possibly wonderful.

Not that I think being hit by a train is wonderful by any stretch. But the impact and the aftermath would be similar, I'd imagine . . .

God.

See what it's done to my brain?

See what my high-IQ, tenacious, driven, hyper-focused brain is like now?

Mush.

A steaming pile of gooey mush.

Lord help me.

I swear, last-year-me wouldn't even recognise today-me. Well, he'd recognise the expensive clothes and perfectly styled blond hair, but probably very little else.

So, how did the derailment of my life begin? Let me take you back . . .

IT WAS FRIDAY NIGHT, the bar on Sydney's George Street was busy, the music loud, the vodka and limes were going down a little too easy. There were so many suits and egos, it was hard to tell where the corporate world ended and the supposed night off began.

It was Friday night, for God's sake, and all around me were conversations about commissions, clients, contracts, cases, and codes.

I mean, I loved it.

It was what I did. Corporate deals, high-end clients, prime real estate. Fast-talking, smooth and savvy, high-pressure, high-stress. Location, location, location.

But after an excruciatingly long week, I wanted to leave work behind, if only for a few hours. I wanted to not talk about business.

I wanted to let it all go, just for a night.

I wanted to find some guy who could make me forget. A guy who could take me home, forgo all manners and small talk, and take me to bed. I wanted to destress and detangle.

I just wanted uncomplicated sex.

But not just any sex. Oh no. I wanted really, really good sex. I wanted to get dicked so hard and so completely, I couldn't remember my own name.

So, while some Friday nights I did come here to network like most of the other suits, tonight I was looking for a different kind of working relationship. A physical relationship with mutual benefits.

A lot of the faces were familiar. This was the finance district after all and we all moved in the same circles. I'd been with a few of these guys as well, and yes, sure, I could have given Brad a nod or Hunter a smile, and I knew damn well how the night would end.

But I wanted something new. Something fresh and exciting and someone I didn't have to ever see again.

And that's when I saw him.

Tall, dark hair, solid build, dark eyes, and a nervous smile. The way he looked around the bar told me he was new here, and he wasn't sure he fit in. Call me superficial, but I could tell by his T-shirt that he didn't fit in here.

Don't get me wrong. Don't misunderstand. I wasn't judging him. But in my line of work, I could spot money when I saw it. Or when it was missing. Like telling the difference between a thousand-dollar suit and a ten-thousand-dollar suit. Or real Italian leather shoes. Or the difference between a Canali and a Charvet necktie.

It's what made me good at my job. I could tell the serious buyers from the players by the way they walked.

Like the four guys he'd walked in with. They were just four more suits and egos, but this guy was different. And his T-shirt was cool, as was the way he wore it. But in a room full of Armani, Brioni, and Gucci, he wore a vintage The Clash tee, black skinny jeans, and— Wait . . . Those were Alexander McQueen boots.

I liked it.

I liked it a lot.

Maybe I stared one too many times for a touch too long while he drank his beer, because one of his friends nodded toward me and shoved his arm. He met my gaze and I held it until he smiled and looked away. One of his other friends laughed and said something, giving him another shove, and after replying something that made them laugh, he made his way through the crowd toward me.

I was leaning on the bar and he just walked right up, half-pressing against me, to put his empty beer bottle on the counter. He smelled so good. "Evening," he said, his voice deep.

I smiled because that was kind of direct, and I was glad we were on the same page. "Evening," I replied. "Love your shirt."

His eyes never left mine; his lips pulled up on one side. "Thanks."

"Can I get you a drink?" I asked.

"Sure."

I signalled to the barkeep for another two. Two of what? I didn't care. I turned back to him. "I've not seen you here before."

He smirked. "I've not been here before."

Mmm. Playful, then.

"Can I be frank?"

"You can be whoever you want."

The server put two vodkas and lime on the bar, and I handed over a twenty before passing *The Clash* his drink. I didn't know his name. I didn't want to know his name. "Your friends are watching," I said.

He didn't turn around. "They're taking bets to see how long it takes."

"How long what takes?"

"For us to leave."

Okay then.

He stepped in a little closer. His eyes smouldered. "Did you still want to be frank?" His voice was like velvet.

"Depends," I replied.

"Depends on what?"

"On how much you have wagered on us leaving right now. I mean, how much will you win if we leave right now as opposed to twenty minutes from now? I'm all for enterprise bargaining and helping a guy out. I hope you backed yourself."

He chuckled, warm and throaty. "That's very considerate of you. And out of interest, when we do leave here, where do you envisage us going?" He glanced at his friends then, giving me a wonderful view of his jaw and neck before turning back to me. "Should I tell them to wait up for me?"

I sipped my drink, trying to hide my smile. "I live just two minutes from here, so the walk won't take long. But, that being said," I hedged, locking eyes with him, "I can't see us being done until morning."

His smile became a grin, he threw back his drink and again pushed me against the counter, closer this time, so he could put his empty glass down. With his strong body against mine, he grunted softly, and the sound sent a shiver through me. Warmth pooled low in my belly.

"I'm ready when you are," he murmured.

Fucking hell, I was so ready.

"Then let's go."

His friends laughed as we walked out, and I couldn't even be pissed about it. So what if he'd come out tonight to pick up. So had I. It was my one and only mission tonight, and it had taken all of five minutes. From locking gazes with him across the room to walking out.

Five minutes, tops.

I liked that there was no small talk. There was no 'come here often' bullshit. Hell, I still didn't even know his name.

This was just the means to an end. And this was going to be a very good end. I knew it already. He was confident, gorgeous, and well-built.

The size of those boots better not be a disappointment . . .

Okay, you know what? Don't judge me. I said from the very beginning that I wanted a dicking.

A very thorough dicking.

It was the entire reason I went out.

I was ready for it. And so help me God, I wanted it. So fucking bad.

I swiped my key to get us into my apartment building, thumped the elevator button with the anticipation kicking in. We hadn't spoken on the short walk over, and I was kinda glad. I didn't want to ruin it. So far it was all mystery and heat. Small talk would have ruined the game.

I let us into my apartment and threw my keys onto the counter.

"Nice place," he said. But he didn't even look around, and I was pretty sure he hadn't noticed the view of the harbour out the window. He hadn't taken his eyes off me.

I shucked out of my jacket and threw it over the back of the leather couch, and it was like I'd waved a red flag at a bull.

In three long strides, he crossed the floor and took my face in his hands and kissed me. He walked me backwards until I was pressed up against the back of the couch, his body against mine, his tongue in my mouth.

Hell. Fucking. Yes.

I let him kiss me, invade my mouth, press his hard cock against me. His boots were no exaggeration, let me tell you. My knees went weak with desire, with pleasure. I broke the kiss to breathe, to speak.

"Bedroom."

He smiled, and when I took his hand, he followed me down the hall. In my room, I toed out of my shoes and began undoing my shirt as I walked over to the bedside table. I threw a bottle of lube and some condoms on the bed, and he was standing there, staring at me. Dark eyes, kiss-swollen lips, sex on fucking legs.

I undid another button on my shirt. "I want you to fuck me," I said. "Thoroughly. For hours."

The heat in his eyes darkened, his lips parted, his chest rose and fell. He kicked off his boots and pulled off his shirt, revealing his well-muscled and tanned torso.

Christ.

I managed to get out of my shirt before his hands were on me, skimming across all the bare skin he could touch. His mouth found mine and he pulled me in, rough, and so help me God, there was nothing I liked more than being manhandled in bed.

I pulled at the button and zip of his jeans and shoved my hand in to grip his cock.

"Holy fuck," I breathed, stepping back so I could look down.

So not only was the size of his boots no lie whatsoever, but I was beginning to wonder if I'd bitten off more than I could chew. So to speak.

He was *big*.

He chuckled. "Still want it for hours?"

Motherfucker.

I managed to catch my breath. "God, yes."

He gripped my face, none too softly. "I will make it good for you." Then he crashed his mouth to mine, kissing me deep and hard until I melted against him.

He pushed my suit pants down and I took care of his jeans, and when we were finally naked, he walked me backwards until I hit my bed. He followed me onto the covers, kissing my neck, my ear, my mouth. He gripped my thigh and lifted my leg, then lowered his weight onto me.

Sweet mother of God.

His hands, his mouth, his body, his huge fucking cock . . . I was going to expire. I rolled my hips and tried to angle his bare cock closer to where I needed him.

He chuckled. "Impatient?"

"I need you to fuck me," I said. I didn't care how desperate I sounded. He was here for sex and I wanted it. Like I was going to die if he wasn't inside me . . .

Chuckling, he kneeled and flipped me over like I was an inflatable sex toy. *Hell yes.* By the time I untangled my arms and legs, he slid a slick thumb across my arsehole and pressed it into me.

I breathed into the bedcovers. "Fuck."

He leaned over me and whispered hot in my ear at the same time as he slipped in a second finger. "This what you want?"

I groaned. "Yessss."

He kissed my shoulders, the back of my neck, behind my ear while he fucked me with his fingers for a long time. Long enough for me to start rocking back, searching for more. He chuckled and pulled his fingers out of me, leaving me slumped on the bed, writhing for it.

Bastard.

I heard him rip open a condom and the snap of the lube bottle lid, and then he was back with more lube and more fingers. "Need more," I ground out.

Then he kneed my thighs apart and pressed the fat head of his cock against my hole. "Be careful what you wish for," he murmured right before he sank into me.

Fuck.

Fuuuuuuck.

I groaned and cried out, gripping the bedcovers, trying to breathe through the breach of him . . . but he held my hips, pinning me with his huge cock, until he was all the way in.

All the fucking way.

"Oh god," I cried.

He grunted in my ear. "You're so fucking tight."

"You're so fucking big."

His laugh rumbled in my ear and he bit down on my neck when he pulled out and pushed back in. He moaned, such a filthy sound, and before I knew it, I was moving with him. Rocking with him, lifting my hips and arching my back for him. Taking him over and over, and it felt so fucking good.

He took control of every move, of every thrust. He played my body like a harp, plucking at chords I didn't know I had, playing the sweetest song I'd ever heard.

His tempo changed, his urgency, and he was deeper and harder, and oh my god, he was groaning and grunting. I'd never heard anything so hot . . .

But then he stopped and repositioned me, drawing up onto his knees. He gripped my hips, impaling me again and again, before reaching around and pumping my dick. "I want you to come while I'm inside you," he rasped out.

Fuuuuuck.

I was so full of him, so owned by him in that moment, I came so hard I almost blacked out. I was on all fours, my knees barely on the mattress because he was lifting me onto him, driving into me hard and deep, and then my orgasm became his and he thrust into me, swollen and pulsing into the condom.

We collapsed onto the mattress, his weight on me, breathless and boneless. He chuckled again as he pulled out, groaning as he did, and then he was lying next to me, splayed out, grinning. We were covered in sweat and lube, and I couldn't bring myself to care.

After a few moments of us catching our breath, I was about to say something corny along the lines of 'that was amazing' when he ran a tender finger down my spine. "How much time do you need?" His voice was rough and deep.

But my brain was in some stupid sex haze and I couldn't follow. "Time for what?"

"Round two."

I laughed. "Christ. Can you do that again?"

"You said we wouldn't be done until morning," he murmured, smiling. Then he rolled me over onto my back and lifted my leg up to his chest. He kissed me, settling his weight on me again, and I could feel his cock was already hard again. Or maybe it was still hard, I didn't know. Didn't care.

But more condoms and lube later, my brain short-circuited somewhere between my second or third orgasm.

Because he *could* do it again. Twice. And sometime just before the sun came up, we showered and I put on my robe while he dressed back into his jeans and shirt. I was disappointed when he put his boots on.

"I probably should go," he said.

"Uh, yeah. I'm supposed to be at work in . . ." I looked for a clock of some kind, but not finding one—I thought I'd left my phone in the kitchen—I nodded to the early morning sky outside my bedroom window. "Soon."

He grinned, not even remotely sorry. "It's been fun." He stood up. "Actually, it's been pretty fucking awesome. We should do this again sometime."

"Next Friday night?" I shrugged. "We don't even have to bother with the bar. You could just come straight here."

He made a face as though he was considering it.

"No strings, no complications," I added. "Just more of the best sex I've ever had."

"The best?"

"You can turn up here and use my body like that any time you like."

"If you want me to turn up here and use your body like that, I'm more than happy to oblige." His eyes shone with humour. "You took my dick like a champ."

This wasn't a weird conversation to be having at all. "You give dick like a champ."

He laughed. "Friday night. Nine o'clock?"

"Yes, please."

He left with a smile. No goodbye, no thanks, no awkwardness, no regrets.

I still didn't even know his name.

CHAPTER TWO

BRYCE

"YOU DIDN'T WASTE ANY TIME," Terrence said, giving me a knowing smirk. "You were back in the country for what? Five hours?"

I laughed and handed him the coffee I'd bought for him. "I had a mighty need."

He pursed his lips. "You've got a mighty something. I've seen it, I know how mighty it is. And I take it that cute little blond guy liked it, because we didn't see you for the rest of the night."

I chuckled. "Oh, yeah. Several times."

Terrance laughed and sipped his coffee. "And the last two days were spent recovering? For you or him?"

"He was fine when I left him on Saturday morning. I spent the weekend trying to shake jetlag and having dinner with my dad."

"How's your dad, by the way?"

"Yeah, he's good. Same as always. Busy with work. You know how it is."

He nodded, because yes, he knew. I'd met Terrence in our first years of university and we'd been friends ever since.

Both his family business and my family business were in the hotel industry, and we were both expected to step into our obligations. Terrence was happy to do just that, and it suited him. The fancy city office, the responsibility, the paperwork, the money.

I wasn't quite so keen.

Which was why I'd spent the last two years in Singapore, Fiji, and New Zealand. Mostly Singapore though. I was unhappy and ready to walk away from everything, but my dad had offered me an overseas venture. It was a hotel venture, of course, one he'd hoped would allow me to see the bigger picture; that experiencing the world while setting up new structural management could be fun and exciting.

And it was. I guess. For a little while.

But it wasn't where my heart was.

I knew it wasn't for me.

So I found myself back in Sydney, trying to figure out what to do with my life. Well, I had some ideas, I just needed to work on them. It was good to be home, but a little daunting if I was being honest.

"Have you told him you don't want to work for him yet?"

I shook my head. "Not yet. But I can't put it off. He's expecting an answer."

Terrence frowned. "It's just chess, man. You need to anticipate his response and counter it with your next move. As soon as you tell him you don't want to work for him, he's going to ask you what you do want. You need to have an answer. Believe me, your dad and my dad aren't too different. So, what's your countermove?"

I sighed. "I have a business idea. And it could be good if it's done right. But I'm pretty sure I know what he'll say."

"If it's watertight, he can't argue. Give him figures,

numbers, projections. Show him how serious you are and he can't argue with that." Terrence smiled. "Want to tell me what it is?"

"Not yet. If I get something on paper, I might let you take a look at it."

"You mean, you might let me draft up your business plan for you?"

I laughed because he was no fool. "How's Mara?"

Terrence smiled, then rolled his eyes. "She's great."

"Damn, Terrence, you need to start thinking about putting a ring on that girl."

"Oh, shut up," he replied. "You sound like my mother. And my father. And my sisters. And my brother. And my aunty."

I laughed. Terrence's family insisted he find a nice Chinese girl to settle down with, and about five years ago, Terrence's cousin introduced Mara as a possible match. Much to Terrence's dismay, Mara was perfect for him in every way. "Is it because she's smarter than you? Prettier?"

Terrence leaned across his desk and motioned for me to do the same, as though he was going to whisper some lurid secret. Except he didn't. "Fuck off."

I laughed again and sat back in my seat. "Well, ask her when she's free for dinner and I'll take you both out. My shout."

"She mentioned something about being free this Friday."

"Oh. Well, if we're done by nine, I'm free."

He raised an eyebrow at me. "A date?"

"Nope. Not really. More of an appointment." I cringed. "An arrangement sounds nicer than appointment."

"With?"

"The blond guy from Friday night."

He studied me for a second, sipping his coffee. "Having seconds?"

"Oh no, I had seconds and thirds the Friday just gone. This would technically be fourths, fifths, and hopefully sixths."

He blinked. "Three times. You weren't kidding about that . . . You know, statistically speaking, you make the rest of us look bad."

I laughed. "Well, I would apologise, but I'm not sorry."

"So, is this a casual agreement or . . . ?"

"Super casual. In his words, 'no strings, no complications.'"

"You know how these things end, right? More complicated than Chinese arithmetic. And I can say that. I am Chinese. That shit is complicated."

I laughed and shook my head. "I don't think it will. He seemed pretty sure about that. He's got a very nice apartment on the wharf, a wardrobe full of expensive suits, so he's good at whatever he does, obviously. Sure of himself, anyway. And he seemed like the emotionally detached type to me."

Terrence smiled at that. "Sounds perfect for you."

I snorted. "Why do I get the feeling that was not a compliment?"

He laughed again. "So, does Mr Emotionally Detached have a name?"

I shrugged. "I'm sure he does."

Terrence snorted. "Oh, Bryce. I've missed you. Now get out of my office. I have work to do."

I got to the door. "Talk to Mara about dinner and let me know."

He waved me off and was already on the phone with some overseas client by the time I'd walked out. He was so driven by his work, and I envied that passion. I wasn't afraid of hard work. I was just afraid of putting years of my life into something I didn't love.

I didn't want to dedicate my life to my father's business. That was his passion, not mine. I was proud of all he'd done and everything he'd accomplished. But I wanted something that was mine. I wanted to build my own dreams, and it was time. It honestly felt that if I didn't do it now, I never would.

So, with Terrence's advice ringing in my ears, I went home, opened my laptop and started to put a business plan together. He was right. I couldn't just sit down with my dad and tell him I wasn't interested without having a fully fleshed-out, step-by-step plan. That was how my dad's brain worked.

And sure enough, that's exactly how it went.

Dad got home late, with containers of takeout in his hand. I'd been so busy on my laptop, I hadn't even realised the time. But I soon grabbed some plates and we sat at his kitchen island bench. "Thought I might have seen you in at the office today," he began.

I shook my head and swallowed down my mouthful of food. "No, I . . ." And I didn't want to lie to him. "Dad, I've been working on a business plan. I don't have much of it put together yet, just getting ideas on paper, and I wasn't going to say anything, but . . ." I put my fork down. "I really appreciate everything you've done. And I love your business and everything about what you've built . . . for you, Dad. Not for me. I've told you this before."

"Bryce, you can walk right into senior management of a multimillion-dollar corporation. Do you know how many people would kill for that opportunity?"

"That's just it, Dad. I don't want to walk right into anything. I want to build something that I've started. Something that's mine." I sighed. "Please don't think I'm being ungrateful. Because I really do appreciate every opportunity, and I know how hard you've worked. You deserve the success, but . . ."

God, why was this so hard?

"I don't want to hurt your feelings," I added. "And I don't want you to be mad or disappointed."

"Well, of course I'm going to be disappointed. I thought we'd be working together . . ."

Oh god.

"Dad."

"But I get it."

My eyes shot to his. *Wait, what?* "You do?"

He stared out at the view of the city lights. "I'd hoped you'd come back from overseas ready to step into my shoes."

"Your shoes? Are you kidding me?"

He cracked a smile. "Okay, well, maybe not for another twenty years. But one day. In the meantime, I thought you could run a division of holdings."

"And make redundant someone who deserves their job? Or walk into a made-up position. Dad, that's not me. I don't want to be handed a job or a title just because I'm your son. Working overseas was fine, but they all knew who I was. Bryce Schroeder, son of *the* James Schroeder of Schroeder Hotels. No one was ever going to disagree with anything I said."

"Well, you could apply for a job in the mailroom if you wanted."

"You don't even have a mailroom."

Dad smiled again and finally conceded a nod. "So you're doing a business plan, huh?"

I nodded. "I've barely got the bones of it put together so far, but yes."

"Want to give me the elevator pitch?"

"No."

"Why not?"

"Because I want you to see the big picture. I don't want you to tell me it won't work from a thirty-second spiel."

Dad considered this for a moment, then ate some more dinner. "And the funding for this business?"

"I'm working on start-up costs."

"If you want financial backing—"

"I don't," I replied, a little too quickly. My answer even surprised me, but it was the truth. "If I'm going to do this, Dad, I need to do it by myself."

Dad's expression was unreadable. Surprise? Humour? Pride?

"Fair enough." He nodded slowly. "So your business model?"

I barked out a laugh. "I'm basically using yours." He shot me a look. "What? I know it works. I've worked in it myself for years. Four years here, two years in three different countries."

He raised an eyebrow and almost smiled before he pushed a container of katsu chicken closer to me. "Eat some more dinner. And if you want me to look at your business plan before you approach investors or a business banker, let me know."

I smiled, so bloody relieved. "I will. Thanks."

"And if it's not good enough . . ."

And there it was.

I met his gaze. "It will be."

It had to be.

I SPENT the next four days pulling apart financials and projections and data analysis, and by Friday night, I was itching for nine o'clock.

Well, itching wasn't the right word.

I was aching for it.

I had no idea what to expect when I arrived at his place. I dressed kinda casual: jeans, boots, and a grunge T-shirt. I mean, it was expensive, but whatever. I was hoping not to have it on for long.

I wondered if he'd even answer the door.

Maybe he'd changed his mind. We had no way to contact each other, so me just turning up at nine o'clock was a shot in the dark.

But he buzzed me in and he answered his door with his shirt half unbuttoned, suit pants, his belt off, and a bonfire of heat in his eyes.

I grinned.

He stood aside.

I walked in, and he closed the door behind me. His apartment was just as nice as it was last week. The huge windows showing the lights twinkling on Darling Harbour. There was a bottle of vodka on the kitchen counter and two tumblers. He picked up the bottle. "Drink?"

"Sure."

He poured two and handed me one, looked me right in the eye as he took a large swallow. His blond hair was neatly styled, pushed up off his face. Very different to how I left him last week.

"Have you eaten?"

"I just had dinner." I had to stop myself from saying I met with some friends for dinner. He didn't know about Terrence or Mara, or any of my friends. Or anything about me. That's not what this was.

"I wasn't sure if you'd turn up," he said.

"I wasn't sure if you'd be here."

He smiled. "I'm glad you're here." He finished the rest of his vodka in one go. "I haven't been home long. Wasn't sure if I should just answer the door naked . . ."

I laughed at that. "I wouldn't have minded."

Staring right at me, he undid another button, then another, and let his shirt fall from his shoulders. He tossed it onto the couch. His body was creamy white, smooth, and lean. I wondered if he was a swimmer or a runner. He looked like he might be a swimmer . . .

Then he undid his pants and slowly unzipped the fly. "I've been looking forward to tonight," he admitted, his voice rough and low. "I have high expectations after last week."

I laughed, then finished my vodka, slid the glass onto the counter, and pulled off my shirt. "I better not disappoint."

His grin widened, his stare darkened, and he took a backward step toward his bedroom. "You better not."

I pulled off my boots, already getting hard in anticipation. This little game of foreplay, the suggestive words, the fire in his eyes was fucking hot.

I undid the button of my jeans and his mouth opened, wanting, needing. So I pounced on him, pulling him in for a bruising kiss. He grunted, opening his mouth for me, leaning flush against me.

I walked him backwards into his bedroom, all but carrying him, threw him onto the bed, and climbed on top of him. I licked up his stomach, bit his nipple, his collarbone, jaw, his lips. I gave him my tongue and he fucking loved it.

"I'm going to fuck you three times again," I murmured into his mouth.

He arched up into me; his erection twitched between us. His lithe body felt on fire. "Then get my fucking pants off," he rasped out. "And do what you want with me."

Sweet mother of God, those were some dangerous words.

He was teetering on that edge of control. That line between desperate and wanting to stay in control. So I dug my fingers into his hip and teased his lips with my tongue. "Oh, I plan to. I'm gonna plant my cock in your tight little body soon enough. But I'm gonna make you want it a little more yet."

CHAPTER THREE

MICHAEL

I'M VERY WELL aware that telling a virtual stranger to 'do what you want with me' was probably not a good idea. But he was so fucking sexy, and his body, his hands and his mouth, and that huge cock I could feel . . .

Apparently that was all it took for me to throw my dignity and self-preservation out the window.

But then he said the thing, the thing about planting his cock in me, and I was gone. My brain short-circuited and my balls took over.

The next thing I knew I was face down in my pillow with my arse in the air getting the best rim job of my life.

I've mentioned his tongue before, right?

And his fingers?

They bear mentioning again.

I was considering making a shrine to them when all of a sudden, they were gone and he was sliding his cock into me.

Slow, deep, perfect.

He gripped my hips. "Oh fuck."

I fisted my pillow and took him in. "Oh god."

He eased back, then pushed in again, giving me a

moment to adjust before beginning a steady pace, fucking me as he wanted.

As I wanted.

I came with him buried to the hilt inside me, and he followed straight after. I could feel him come. I could feel his cock pulse and fill the condom.

And that was just round one.

We showered and then spent a good amount of time making out on the couch. He was ticklish, which was funny. When I dragged my fingernails over his ribs, he squirmed and laughed, a magical throaty rumble, then grabbed my hands and pinned them above my head and kissed me until I gave in.

Then he took me back to my bed for round two.

And somewhere before the sun came up, he squeezed in round three.

I was lying on the bed, exhausted, every muscle spent, and very, very sated. He was having another quick shower and I was trying hard not to fall asleep.

"So," his voice woke me. "Next Friday?"

"Yes, please and thank you."

He laughed. "Though I probably should put in a disclaimer now to avoid future disappointment . . ."

I smiled at him. "And what's that?"

"Twice really is adequate. Some would say great, even. Three is a milestone seldom reached."

I laughed and held up three fingers. "You set this precedent, not me."

"Nine o'clock?"

"I'll be here."

"Naked when you open the door, I hope."

I groaned out a laugh as I rolled over. "If you insist."

"I do."

"Please don't consider me rude if I don't walk you out. But I seem to be having a little difficulty keeping my eyes open."

He laughed as he left the room. I heard the front door latch close, and I was asleep.

"MORNING," Carolyne said brightly as I walked into the office.

I gave her a smile. "Good morning."

She handed me some messages. "Staff meeting at eight thirty."

"Thank you," I replied as I made my way to my office. I worked for CREA, one of the biggest corporate real estate companies in Australia. We had a staff, nation-wide, of almost four hundred. There were over sixty in this branch alone. We dealt with corporate spaces, offices, retail, and industrial, amongst others. I specialised in retail, sales and leases, in the central business district of Sydney.

I studied markets and trends, tailoring solutions and pairing the right retailer with the right high-profile assets. I'd moved rather fast through the ranks because I was good at my job, which no doubt pissed a lot of the old-timers off. At twenty-eight years old, I had my own office overlooking the city and my sights set firmly on the Managing Director of Retail's desk.

The eight-thirty meeting was a rundown on targets and profitability, clients and accounts. Same old, same old. Until my boss declared the meeting over and gave me a nod. "Michael, can you stay back a second?"

Not really what anyone wants to hear on a Monday morning . . .

My boss was Natalie Wang. Sharp, smart, and could read the real estate market like it was a neon billboard.

We waited for the last person to leave the boardroom and I figured it was best to start the conversation. "What can I do for you?"

She smiled, then paused, chewed the inside of her lip for a moment. "I've heard rumours . . ."

Fuck.

"About?"

"That Mortimer Incorporated might be looking for new representation."

I stared at her. "Mortimer . . . Which asset? If you tell me King Street Wharf, I'll—"

"King Street Wharf."

"Fuck."

She smiled. "That's what I said."

"What do you want me to do?"

"I want you to get that contract."

My smile became a grin. Excitement buzzed in my veins. "Time frame?"

"Unknown." She pursed her lips. "It's just a rumour. I heard a little birdy say Mortimer was pissed that Carter & Co had raised fees across the board, outside and above the CPI, and one long-term tenant has already given notice. They've had some other issues for a while but that was the final straw."

Just to catch you up; Mortimer Inc owned a sizeable portfolio of prestigious real estate in Sydney's central business district, or CBD as we locals called it. Carter & Co was a real estate management company who held the Mortimer contract. Oh, and if Natalie heard a *rumour*, it was real.

"You don't hear rumours," I replied with a smile. "You hear facts before anyone else."

She almost laughed. "What's your schedule like?"

"I'm wrapping up the Holdings job today and was meeting with the Qin group this afternoon. I'd rather not hand those off . . ."

She shook her head. "No, I wouldn't ask you to. Finalise what you have going, hand off whatever paperwork you can to a junior, and let's start putting in some groundwork."

I gave her a nod. "On it."

Natalie rubbed her hands together. "Excellent. I'll touch base with you on it tomorrow."

I went back to my office, excited but wary. Sure, Natalie told me not to hand off my current contracts but also expected me to report on something tomorrow. When she said, 'Let's start putting in some groundwork,' she meant, 'I want you to give me a full report first thing.' Which was fine. It was what they paid me big money for.

And who was I kidding? I liked a challenge, and I liked to kick arse at work.

My personal life was a different ball game. I liked to be the one who was tossed around on a bed, handing over all the control, all the responsibility, and all the pressure to perform, to excel.

I could let the other guy take charge, and it felt good to let it all go.

And thinking about Mr Friday Night—I didn't know what else to call him—made me smile. Goddamn, the man had skills. And I would gladly hand over all the control, all the responsibility and pressure to him in the bedroom. Or in any other room he wanted me, to be honest.

I could get hard just thinking about the things he'd done to me, but I never relieved myself during the week. Oh no . . . I was very deliberately leaving that in his very capable hands. And honestly, Friday couldn't come around fast enough.

Work kept me busy. I worked late every night and my sister insisted on dinner on Thursday night, so I had to rush from the office directly to meet her at the restaurant by eight. "You work too hard," she greeted me with after clearly noting I was still in my work suit.

"Hello Susannah," I replied, taking my seat at the table. "You look lovely tonight." And she did. She wore a black dress with a small designer denim jacket and killer heels. Her blonde hair in waves past her shoulders, her skin flawless, though I'd expect nothing less from a beauty specialist at one of the city's best salons.

She rolled her eyes. "Sorry, Michael. You know what I mean though. You *do* work too hard. I hope they appreciate the hours you put in."

"They do. And I do." I sipped my water. "I actually like my job. Did Mum or Dad put you up to this?"

Susannah's smile told me they possibly had. "They're both well, by the way."

"I spoke to Mum on Monday." It was brief, but it wasn't a lie. I needed to change the topic. "How's that gorgeous man of yours?"

"Still gorgeous," she replied with a smile. She'd been seeing Jad for a while now. Two years, maybe. He treated her well and she was happy, so that's all I cared about.

We ordered our dinner and had a glass of wine. She chatted about work and Jad, and I told her what my circle of friends had been up to. Well, it was more of a triangle, given there were only three of us. But they, they were just as busy as me, and we usually caught up for a few drinks and a laugh at a bar on Darling Harbour when we were free. The last time I'd seen them was at the bar the night I met Mr Friday Night, and that was almost three weeks ago.

I needed to give them a call.

God, have I really been that busy?

Susannah seemed to read my mind. "All work makes Jack a dull boy," she hedged.

"I've been out." I clearly didn't sound convincing.

"Come out with us tomorrow night. We're going to the lights festival at Barangaroo."

Shit. Tomorrow was Friday . . .

"I can't tomorrow."

"If you're working late, I will stage an intervention."

I chuckled. "No, I, um, I have plans tomorrow night."

This, of course, had her interest piqued. "Oh? Do I know him?"

"I don't think so."

"Michael, spill the details. You're smiling like you just learned the secret ingredients to Coca-Cola."

I laughed at that. "There's nothing to tell."

"So it's new?"

"No, that's not it. I mean, it is new, but it's not what you're thinking."

"How do you know what I'm thinking?"

"Well, it's not anything remotely serious, let me put it like that."

"Ah." She nodded knowingly. Her smile was cheeky and she leaned in. "A booty call."

I made a face. "I hate that phrase."

"Well, what would you call it?"

"A . . . a pre-arranged meeting."

She snorted and took a sip of her wine. "A booty call."

I sighed. "He's agreeable to our mutually beneficial . . . understanding."

"And how long has this understanding been a thing for?"

"Two weeks. Tomorrow will be our third . . . mutually beneficial understanding."

"Michael, you're blushing."

"No I'm not."

"You totally are."

"I just wasn't expecting to have this conversation with you."

"So I take it it's very beneficial."

I met her scrutinising gaze. "Oh, yes."

She laughed. "Give me details."

"Absolutely not."

"Not those kind of details. I meant his name."

Oh.

"Um . . ."

"Oh my god. You don't know his name?"

Now it was me who laughed. "It just never came up in conversation."

"Michael," she leaned in and whisper-hissed at me. "Is he living some secret life? Does he live a double life? Oh my god, is he married? Michael, what if he's married?"

"He's not married," I said, though we both knew I had no clue if that were true or not.

"What if he has kids?"

"Can you please stop?" I put my fork down. "I don't know anything about his personal life. So if he's cheating, then that's on him. Not me."

She sighed. "Just . . . just be careful."

"Always am."

She took a bite of her salad and chewed thoughtfully. "So I take it he's good then. In bed, I mean. This is your third—"

"Susannah!" I could feel my cheeks heat and I let out a flustered breath. "But if you must know . . . he's better than good."

She laughed and thankfully let the conversation about my sex life go. Though when we were done and going home, she squeezed my arm and gave me a serious look. "Be careful. And for the love of God, Michael. At least get a first name."

I rolled my eyes and put her in the cab before walking half a block home.

I was happy not knowing his name. It didn't add to the mystery or play out like a movie in my head. Simply put, the less I knew, the less complicated it was. Our arrangement was purely sex. And what awesome sex it was.

I didn't need to know his name.

But there was a niggling part of me that wondered . . . like a pulled thread that could unravel the whole thing. Would knowing his name make it personal on some level? Or did it make no difference at all?

Goddammit.

Now I was thinking about it.

And the truth was, he knew where I lived. It wouldn't be too hard for him to find out my name . . . What if he knew my name already?

Okay, so what if he did?

I wasn't hiding anything. It wasn't like he could use our arrangement against me.

But maybe he wasn't so lucky. Maybe he wasn't out at work or at home. His friends at the bar certainly knew he was into guys, and they clearly had no issue with it. But maybe he wasn't in a position to be outed in some aspect of his life. Not everyone had the privilege of zero ramifications of their personal and professional lives colliding.

No. I wouldn't ask him his name.

I'd just have to make up a name for him instead.

I could just go with the obvious like Mr Ed for his horse dick. Or I could call him Friday at Nine. Or maybe The Clash for his T-shirt, or Ticklish, or Sexy as Hell, or Cutest Laugh.

Or maybe I could call him Late.

Because nine o'clock on Friday night came and went with no sign of him.

Five past nine, still no sign. Ten past nine and I decided to put my robe on because I felt foolish for wanting to be naked when I opened the door.

Like he'd asked me to be.

Fifteen past and I considered going out but quickly shot that down because I couldn't be arsed getting dressed. I poured myself a drink and resigned myself to not having three orgasms wrung out of me. I might just have to settle for some porn and a wank.

By twenty past nine, I'd had a second vodka and was trying not to be pissed off. Disappointed, yes. But anger was a futile emotion, or so I told myself. Why get angry and expend all that energy and emotional output when you could just not care? It was easier not to care.

I was glad I never knew his name.

But then at 9:26, my intercom buzzed.

I checked the security camera. It was him, and after very briefly entertaining the idea of pretending not to be home, I buzzed him through.

I waited by the door and pulled my robe around me tight. He knocked once and I opened the door. He was wearing tight jeans, a shirt with The Killers on it, and an apologetic smile. "You're late," I said flatly.

He looked me up and down before meeting my eyes. "And you're not naked."

"I was. At nine."

He smiled but it was tight and forced. "Sorry. I got . . . caught up."

Upon closer inspection, he looked tired and a little down. Which, for some strange reason, made me feel bad. I stood aside. "Come in." I closed the door behind him and followed him toward the kitchen counter, to where the bottle of vodka sat with my drink and one empty glass. "Drink?"

He hesitated. "Yeah. Sure."

I poured him a healthy nip and handed it over. "For you."

He managed a more genuine smile. "Thanks. And I am sorry I'm late. It's um, it's been a long week and I lost track of time."

"It's okay," I said, sipping my vodka. "I'm not really mad."

"I would have shot you a text or something," he said, looking out the wall of glass to the harbour. "But I don't have your number."

Oh shit.

"Do you want my number?"

"Well, it would have saved you putting on your robe."

I snorted. "Right."

"And then you still would have answered the door naked."

I laughed. "True."

God, were we going to exchange numbers?

"You can have my number on one condition," I said.

"And what's that?"

"That we text only. Unless it's an emergency or

whatever."

"An emergency like what?" He smiled behind his drink. "Like you not being naked when you answer the door?"

"I'm beginning to think the robe is an issue for you?"

He looked me up and down again. "I mean, it's very nice. Versace, right?"

I raised an eyebrow. "I'm impressed." But getting back to the number exchange . . . I picked up my phone. "What's your number?"

He smiled as he ran it off to me, and I entered it in and shot him a quick text. *Nice shirt.*

His phone beeped and he pulled it out of his pocket. He smiled when he read the message. He replied. *You're still wearing the robe.*

I chuckled. "Just so you know, I'm saving your name in my phone as SAF."

"Saf? What does that mean?"

"Sexy as fuck."

He sipped his vodka, smiling. "I'm saving yours as Still Wearing the Fucking Robe."

Chuckling, I pulled the waist belt, letting the silk robe fall open. I was very naked underneath.

He let out a breath and swallowed the last of his drink. "You're really fucking hot."

I smiled and took his empty glass. He still looked like he'd had the week from hell and I wanted to fix that. "Go and sit on the sofa. I'm going to grab the condoms and lube. Then I'm going to sink down on your monster cock and ride you till you come."

His nostrils flared and his breath hitched. But he began to thumb through his phone. "Gimme one sec. Just gonna change your name to Bossy."

I took his phone and put it screen-down on the counter,

leaned in real close. "Get your arse on the couch. When I come back out, you better be naked."

He chewed on his bottom lip and groaned out a breath. "I like it when you're bossy." Then with one finger, he opened my robe some more and looked at me like I was something to eat. "I like it when you let me do what I want with your body too. I can't decide which one I like more."

"Tonight, you can have both." I palmed his erection and spoke against his lips. "I want you naked."

I turned and left him with that, feeling kinda brazen and sexy. I got what I was after from my room, and sure enough, when I went back out, he was stepping out of his jeans. He threw them on the other sofa, pulled the throw blanket down and sat on it. He was hard, his cock was pointing upward, thick and so fucking hot.

Warmth spread through my belly and my balls, desire and lust burned through my veins. He pulled his shirt off and tossed it, then smiled at me in a way that made my knees weak.

"You're still wearing the robe."

I was barely wearing the robe. It hardly clung to my shoulders; the front was wide open. "I am."

I threw the condom beside him but took the lube and knelt on the floor between his legs. Sure, I could suck and lick his cock, but it also allowed me to slick my own arse. I poured lube onto my fingers, moving my hand behind me, and once he realised what I was doing, he growled.

"Fuck."

I leaned up and licked him from base to tip and he hissed when I tongued his slit. He moaned when I sucked on the head, pumping him with my free hand. My other hand was working my arse, slicking and stretching. Until he tapped me on the shoulder.

"You're a little too good at that."

I smiled as I pulled off. "Then put the condom on."

He did and I applied more lube. Like a lot more lube—to both him and myself. Then I climbed up, straddling him. His hands went to my hips, raking up my sides, sliding over the cool silk of my robe.

I tilted his head back roughly and crushed my lips to his, sweeping his mouth with my tongue and sucking on his. His cock slid along my arse crack, huge and hot, and I was aching with the need to feel it inside me.

So, breaking the kiss, I positioned him where I wanted him the most and slowly, so fucking slowly, let him in.

Fuck.

He sucked back a breath and his fingers dug into my hips, maybe to stop himself from pushing me onto him. "Oh god," he hissed. "You're so tight."

I took a handful of his hair and yanked his head back, partly a distraction for him and partly so I could kiss him again.

And I rocked a little as I took him, finally letting out a shameless groan when he was all the way in. After a few seconds, he tried to raise his hips, so I yanked on his hair again, harder this time.

"I am in control here," I murmured.

He squeezed his eyes shut. "Fuck."

I relaxed my hold on his hair and kissed him gently, tenderly. "Relax and let me do this for you."

And he did.

His whole body let go of the tension. He relaxed onto the couch and I began to move, back and forth, up and down.

And he let me lead. I set the pace, I took control, and he sat there and enjoyed the show.

Christ, he felt good.

He touched places inside me no man ever had. Heat and electricity sparked in my blood and my bones, pushing me closer and closer to the edge. And as I went faster and harder, needing more of that thrill, that high, he finally fisted my cock and brought me undone.

Pleasure ripped through me like a bomb. He didn't let me ride it out. Oh no. He gripped my hips and drove up into me, his whole body rigid as he came, pulsing inside me. His neck was corded, his jaw clenched, and his eyes rolled back as he let out a strangled cry.

I'd never seen anything so hot.

We both collapsed, panting. I was dizzy and spent, and I barely had the energy to lift myself off him.

As soon as I did, he pulled me back, scooped me up, and we lay on the couch in a mess of limbs, lube, and ragged breaths. He laughed, and when I pulled back, he showed me his hand. It was shaking. "Fucking hell," he mumbled, his voice deep and rumbly. "I'm gonna need an intermission before round two."

I chuckled, damned proud of myself. "Same. I'd suggest a shower, but I don't know if my legs'll work yet."

So we stayed there, lying together on the couch. He was so warm, and I reckon if I'd have closed my eyes for a second too long, I'd have fallen asleep. His heartbeat was lulling me . . .

But then his stomach rumbled. He put his hand to his belly, embarrassed. "Oh, sorry. I skipped dinner. I was busy with . . . a work thing, then realised the time and came straight over."

"Then you need to eat," I said, sitting up. "How about a shower, then some food, then round two."

"You don't need to feed me," he said, his cheeks flushed.

"It's just food," I replied gently. "You're allowed to eat."

He made a face. "But then it's not just sex, is it? It's sex and food."

Was that weird? Why did I think that was a weird thing to say? We had agreed that it was just sex, but I wasn't going to starve the man. "Food and sex are two of my favourite things," I said, trying to make light of it. "And if you don't keep up your energy, then you can't fuck me for hours later. You need sustenance."

He laughed at that. "Right, then."

"I called you SAF before. For 'sexy as fuck' but there's no reason it can't be for 'sex and food.' Either works for me." I stood up, feeling the muscles in my thighs and my arse were a bit sore. "And it's not like we're going out for dinner on a date or anything."

He stood up too. "You winced. Are you hurt?"

I smiled at his attentiveness. "My legs are telling me I should do more squats. Nothing a hot shower won't fix." I looked at my come smeared on his belly, then down at his dick . . . his softening dick with the condom still on. "Christ, that's hot. How can I want more after what we just did?" He pulled the condom off and his huge cock hung, glistening and heavy. "Aaaand you just got even hotter."

He laughed. "Bin?"

"Under the sink," I waved toward the kitchen as I walked to the hall. "I'll start the shower. And I'll need help washing my back, so don't keep me waiting."

I heard him chuckle as I got to my bedroom, and I threw my robe onto my bed and headed straight for the walk-in shower. By the time I'd turned the water on, he was right behind me. Hot water, soapy hands, and tender kisses, and all my aches and pains were washed away.

But then his stomach growled again, so I left him in the

shower to go and find the man some food. I had no idea what he liked, if he had any allergies, or whatever, so I grabbed a few plates and raided the fridge.

He came out wearing nothing but a towel, tied off low around his waist. His dark, wet hair was sticking up in all directions; his grin was lopsided and stupidly cute. He knew damn well how fucking cute he was, and he knew I liked what I saw. I'd seen him naked before, plenty of times. I'd seen him fully clothed, half-dressed. I'd seen his orgasm face, his ecstasy face, his laughing face. And he was sexy as fuck.

But in a towel, half-wet, with a smile that made my heart take notice . . .

"Whatcha got there?" he asked.

Apparently I was just staring at him like a simpleton. *He asked a question . . .* I looked down at the plates. "Well, I wasn't sure what you liked, or could or couldn't eat. So I kept it all separate in case you're allergic to something."

There was a plate of grapes, a plate of cheese, a plate of crackers, some strawberries. He went straight for the crackers and cheese, followed by a few grapes and then a strawberry. "Not allergic," he mumbled, but he was clearly hungry. He must have rushed over here—from where, I didn't know—when he realised he was going to be late.

I put a bottle of water in front of him and picked up a strawberry, biting into it. It was juicy and sweet, and then it was his turn to stare at me. Well, at my mouth. And when I took another bite, he leaned in and kissed me, tasting the strawberry juice on my lips.

"Mmm," he said, his eyes alight. "Sweet."

"I am, thank you." He was making short work of the cheese and crackers, so I went to the fridge. "I have leftover

Thai from last night; if you want it, it's yours. Or I can order you anything you want."

He washed down a cracker with some water. "No, this is great, thank you. I should have eaten before but I got sidetracked. Once I realised the time I ran over here."

"So, do you live even remotely close?" I picked at another strawberry. "I mean, you don't have to tell me where you live, obviously. I just wondered if it takes you two hours to get here . . ."

"Two hours? God, no." He smiled. "Do you think you're worth a two-hour commute once a week?"

"I know I am."

He laughed. "I'm inclined to agree. I would take a two-hour commute once a week to get here. If I had to. But I don't. Takes me ten minutes, tops."

I found myself smiling at him. He would commute for two hours to see me . . . that was unexpectedly sweet and I liked that. But ten minutes, be it walk or drive, put him in the city at least.

"Anyway," he furthered, "I don't mind. I know where you live, so it's only fair, right?"

"Agreed." Now we were getting somewhere. "But it's up to you. If we're doing the whole anonymous thing."

"The anonymous thing is fun, isn't it?"

"It is."

"Even though I'm curious."

"Same."

He smiled as he ate some more cheese. "I'm staying at a hotel in Circular Quay right now. I was away for two years."

"Prison?" I joked. Christ, I shouldn't have said that. What if it was? "God. Don't answer that."

He barked out a laugh. "No, not prison. Singapore. Other places, but mostly Singapore."

The natural question to follow that would be 'Oh, what were you doing there?' but keeping things anonymous made that difficult. "Such a beautiful place. Was it work or pleasure?"

He made a face as though he considered not answering. After a beat, he said, "Work."

"Lucky." I popped a grape in my mouth and chewed, trying to think of how to be discrete. "I'm trying to not ask personal questions. It's kind of hard."

He smiled and ate some more cheese. "I've been back for three weeks and I'm throwing myself into a work thing. It's a good distraction."

"Just three weeks . . . But this is our third weekend."

"I got back; my friends were going out. I went with them to catch up. Saw you." He sipped his water, still smiling. "It had been a little while for me."

"And that might explain the three times in one-night thing, but then you backed it up the next weekend."

"And I did hint at maybe twice might be the new norm," he said. "Three times is a lot of pressure."

"You might doubt your ability, but I don't."

He chuckled and aimed that smug smile right at me, making my heart stutter. "You always get what you want?"

"Mostly." I shrugged. "Not to say I don't work hard for it, because I do. I'm very good at what I do."

His gaze never left mine, so intense, so full of humour and daring. "And what is it that you do?"

"I . . . work hard."

He chuckled again, and picking up a strawberry, he put it to my lips. I took it into my mouth and he kissed me, tasting it for himself. He licked his lips, watching my mouth before looking into my eyes. "Do you love what you do?"

"I wouldn't do it otherwise."

"I like that answer. And you play the anonymity game well."

I smiled at that. "It's surprising, to be honest, given I've never played it before."

"Never?"

"Never had to."

He kind of flinched, just for a split second, like that might have hurt to hear. "Is it not fun for you?"

"It's a lot of fun for me. What about you?"

"Oh, I like it." His smile was back. "It keeps it uncomplicated."

"It does." I took a deep breath and steeled myself. "Though, can I ask you something?"

He studied me for a long-drawn-out second. "You can ask, but if I can answer without giving too much away might be the real question."

"Fair enough." I met his gaze. "Are you out? Do people in your life know you like to have sex with a guy?"

He took a moment to answer. "Yes. People know."

"Okay. Cool. Not that it would bother me. It's a deeply personal thing, and I just wondered if that was part of the reason for the anonymity."

"I'm going to assume people know you're gay or bi, or whatever," he said.

"Why would you assume that?"

"Because you exude confidence. I can't imagine you not being direct about anything."

Interesting. "Confidence?"

"Yep. On anyone else it'd be arrogance. But not on you."

I smiled at that. "Well, I can be arrogant too. And what was it? Bossy. Isn't that what you called me?"

"It is. It's in my phone, so it stays."

I raised my chin. "It's true. I am bossy. So I can't even be mad about it."

"You called me Sexy as Fuck."

"Because you are. And it's in my phone, so it stays." I waved my hand at his torso, at the towel, at his face. "Exhibit A, your honour."

His eyes lit up. "Oh, you're a lawyer?"

I laughed. "Nope."

"No?"

"Not even close. Just making a point." I put my hand on his chest, swiping my thumb across his nipple, watching the skin prickle in my wake. "So fucking sexy."

He pulled my robe open and hummed. "So, tell me, Bossy. What did you want for round two?"

"I'm going to lie on my bed, and you can fuck me any way you want."

He blinked, his eyes darkening, his breath hitched. "You sure do have a way with words."

"I know what I want, and I ask for it."

"You demand it."

"Same thing."

The corner of his mouth lifted and he bit down on his bottom lip. "Bossy."

I pulled at the knot of towel below his navel and let it fall to the floor. Christ, he was hung. "You know you could enter a three-legged race by yourself, right?"

He laughed and skimmed both hands up my chest, under my robe and pushed it off my shoulders. It slithered down my back to the floor, and he still wore that smug smile. "Your bed, face down, arse in the air. Now."

I hummed and my body sang in anticipation. I was just about to say that was both bossy and sexy as fuck, but he crushed his mouth to mine and took me to bed.

CHAPTER FOUR

BRYCE

"THANK YOU FOR MEETING WITH ME," I said as we took our seats at a table. I'd had dinner at his place last week, but this was more of a work lunch.

"You're buying me lunch," Terrence replied. "I wasn't going to say no to that. Plus, Tuesdays are the new Monday. I welcomed the break today."

"If Tuesday is the new Monday, then what's Monday?"

"They're both Mondays. It's been a week. Actually, it's been a month."

"From hell?"

"A month of Mondays."

"Ouch. I saw the ASX has taken a hit."

He groaned. "Yeah, ouch. Add in the fact that my dad is stressed about it. Like hearing your dad yell is bad enough, but when he's your boss too? No thanks." He shot me an apologetic look. "Sorry."

"No need to apologise. I get it, believe me."

"How is your old man?"

"Same. He's in Perth for a few days. And speaking of, I have this." I handed over my business plan. "It's not finalised. I wanted your input before I give it to my father. Pretty sure he's gonna tear it to shreds anyway, so I'm not sure why I'm bothering, to be honest."

Terrence flipped the first page, then the next, then the next. The waiter came for our order, and Terrence rattled off something without even looking at the menu. The waiter nodded, so I assumed it was fine, and I held up two fingers. "Make that two."

All the while Terrence kept reading.

And reading.

And flipping pages and reading.

He had a great eye for data analytics and statistics, and he didn't need a calculator for percentages and bottom lines. He could do maths in his head faster than I could enter them into a spreadsheet.

Our meals came and he was still reading. And I was nervous. "I didn't mean for it to take up your entire lunch break."

Without taking his eyes off the report, he shoved a dumpling in his mouth, then waved his chopsticks at me. "Shh. I'm reading."

I chuckled and I was almost finished with my meal when he closed the folder. He took another bite, and before the suspense could kill me, he smiled. "It's a very thorough report."

He sounded surprised. "Um, thanks?"

"Bryce, it's very thorough. And it's good. Like really good."

"I just want my father to know I'm serious."

"Fuck your father," he said. "Give him this report and he can't say shit. And anyway—" He ate his last dumpling. "—you don't need him. You've got a solid idea, thoroughly researched, and the figures are great.

What you need is an investor with some financial backing."

"I've got an appointment next week to see my business banker."

"And your first location? I take it you have scope for further development."

"I have a few places in mind. Just need to know where I stand financially first. Then I can move forward, I guess."

"It's exciting, Bryce. You should be proud."

"I'll feel better after my dad has his say. I mean, I'm moving forward with it regardless, but I need to get that out of the way first."

"You know what you need?"

"About two million dollars?"

He snorted. "That too. But seriously, you need a night out with the boys. No ditching us for the first guy who looks at you this time. I mean, a full night out with us. Drinks, laughs, more drinks, and questionable stall food at three in the morning."

"I didn't ditch you guys," I replied. "It had been a while for me, as everyone knew, thanks to you and your big mouth."

"You're welcome."

"So I had some *pressing concerns* that needed to be addressed. I didn't ditch you."

Terrence laughed. "You totally did, but that's okay. I get it. But no ditching us this time. Ditching is forbidden. This Friday night. Eight o'clock."

I winced. "Actually, Friday's aren't great for me . . ."

His eyes went wide. "Oh, that's right. The nameless guy. Seeing him again?"

"Well, yeah. We have a thing on Friday nights."

"So change it."

"I don't know . . ." Then I remembered I had his number now. I could change it if he was amenable. "I'll ask."

Terrence blinked. "You need his permission?"

I snorted out a laugh because Mr Bossy would probably think I did. "No, I'm just being considerate."

He seemed confused for a second, then stunned. "You like him."

"Well, yeah. I'm not gonna keep seeing some guy I don't like."

"No, I mean you *like* him."

"As in *like* like?" I scoffed. "I don't even know his name."

"How can you not know his name?"

"Easy. We don't talk about personal stuff."

"What do you talk about?" He made a face. "I mean, do you even talk?"

I laughed. "Yes, we talk. We just don't discuss names or occupations or anything like that. We are otherwise occupied."

"So he has no idea who you are."

"Nope. None."

"No idea who your dad is or that he—and technically you—own Schroeder Hotels."

"Nope. None."

"That was your idea, I take it. The secrecy thing."

"More his, but I don't mind one bit. Actually, I like the fact he doesn't know who I am."

Terrence let out a breath but he smiled. "So shall we take a bet as to how long it is before this no-complications thing gets complicated?"

I leaned in and motioned for him to do the same. When he was close enough, I whispered, "Fuck off."

He laughed and leaned back in his chair. "Drinks this Friday."

I took out my phone and found Bossy's number and sent him a quick text. *I have a thing this Friday night. Can we change to Saturday or Sunday?*

"Okay, I've asked," I said, putting my phone on the table.

"And if he says no?"

"Then I still meet with you guys on Friday night and he can find someone else."

My phone beeped with a message.

How's Saturday at eight?

God, I felt giddy. I sent a quick reply. *Perfect.*

Good. I'll order dinner.

Hm. Dinner. Dinner wasn't complicated, was it? It wasn't crossing our no-complications rule, was it? After all, I was the idiot who forgot to eat and he had to feed me. So no, it wasn't a complication. He was just a decent guy.

Sounds great.

"Ah, Bryce," Terrence said, startling me. "You're doing an awful lot of smiling at your phone for a guy you don't like."

I pressed my lips together in some attempt to not grin. I put my phone on the table, screen-down. "Drinks with you and the guys on Friday night is fine. And you're right. It's just what I need."

My phone beeped with another message but I didn't pick it up. As much as I wanted to. *God, I really wanted to.*

Terrence sighed and shook his head. "Just read the goddamned text."

I picked up my phone. *Robe or no robe?*

I laughed. *Robe.*

When I looked up at Terrence, he was staring at me.

"Bryce, my guy. Do me a favour. When you get home, just google the word complicated. Because there seems to be some miscommunication somewhere about what *no complications* means."

"It's not complicated."

"Yet."

I conceded a shrug. "It's fun. And the texting is new. As in, this is our first text conversation. He's just funny, that's all."

"And gorgeous and he doesn't know about your money. And he clearly likes your little arrangement."

Yes, yes, and yes.

I sighed. "He's also a bit arrogant. Well, no. I mean, he is. But it's not a bad arrogance. It's confidence. I don't even know what he does for a living, but I know he's good at it."

"You can't even say a bad thing about him without turning it into a compliment."

I chuckled. "I don't even know his name. Or what he does. Or where he's from, or if he's seeing someone else . . ."

God, that thought soured my belly.

Terrence's smile became a bit smug and all too-knowing. "Mm. That's what I thought."

"Shut up."

He stood up and handed me back my business report. "My suggestion is, if your father is in Perth, email him this report the day he comes home. He will have a four-hour flight to read it. But don't let him tell you it won't hold water. Because it will. You find the right location and the right financing and you could be onto something good."

I took the report, more relieved than I expected to be. "Thank you."

"And for the love of God, Bryce. Find out a first name."

"But we—"

"I hate to break it to you, but the no-complication train left the station already." He waved me off. "I gotta get back to work. You're paying?"

"Yes, I'm paying for lunch. Give Mara my love."

He smiled and dashed out the door. I went to the counter and handed over my credit card, thinking about what Terrence had said.

My dad was coming home tomorrow. I needed to put the finishing touches on this report tonight.

I was going to go home and make it as perfect as I could and very deliberately not think about getting Bossy's real name. Bossy suited him. I didn't need to know his actual name. It made no difference to me either way. Because I didn't need to know it. It served no purpose in knowing. There was no benefit, nothing gained, nothing lost.

Or so I told myself. And kept telling myself. Over and over. And over.

God. What if he was seeing someone else?

Fuck.

I SENT my dad the report the morning of his flight, knowing—hoping—he'd read it on the plane. At least it would give him four hours to go over it and, no doubt, rip it apart.

And by the time his plane was expected to arrive, I was just about beside myself. My chest felt all tight and my belly was in knots. I don't know why his opinion mattered so much. He was my dad, sure. And he loved me, I knew he did. He'd never had any issue with me when I told him I was bringing a guy home. He didn't even bat an eyelid.

But he was incredibly successful.

And to attempt my own business idea and fail in front of him would be the worst. Because no one wants to hear 'I told you so' from a parent. And he *would* say it, several times. And he might talk about it for years to come like how he still brings up the time I made him take the training wheels off my bike and he said I wasn't ready, but I promised him I was. So he did, and in trying to prove myself, I ran right into his Audi.

I was four.

This was like me asking him to take off my training wheels.

I heard the elevator ding and took a deep breath to steel my nerves. Then his footsteps and suitcase wheels on the tiles, and even though I was expecting him, I still jumped when he spoke. "Hey, Bryce. Didn't think you'd be home."

I'd just been here, wearing my shoes out pacing back and forth for hours. "Ah, yeah. Sure. How was your flight?"

"Long."

"And you got Perth all wrapped up?"

He nodded. "Yeah. They're a good team."

I nodded. God, this was awkward. Was he stalling to torture me?

"So, I read your business proposal," he began.

Oh, fuck. Here goes . . .

"And?"

He put his messenger bag down, took off his coat, and went to the fridge.

I took a deep breath. My brain and my heart were clawing for patience. Did I want to hear this? Maybe I wasn't ready to hear this.

Dad took out the lemon mineral water and poured himself a glass. "Want one?"

"No, Dad. I don't."

He sipped his drink.

Now disappointment and anger were vying for pole position.

"It was good, Bryce."

I shot him a look. "What?"

He smiled. "I said it was good. Did you want me to tell you it was terrible?"

"No, I didn't *want* you to. I *expected* you to."

He sipped his drink, all the time in the world. "You did your homework."

"Yeah, of course I did. I'm serious about it."

"How serious?"

"I have an appointment to see Jerry next week."

Jerry was our business banker. Correction. He was Dad's business banker. Now he was also mine.

Dad raised one eyebrow. "That serious."

"Yes."

He took a deep breath and ended with a nod. "Okay, well here's the thing."

And here it came.

"Your proposal was good."

"Yes?" There was definitely a but coming.

"But—"

There it was.

"—it still needs a lot of work."

I wasn't sure it did, and in that moment, it was hard to tell if he was being a tough-love father or a businessman plumping his own feathers.

"Such as?" I asked. "I'm willing to listen, Dad. I'm not naïve enough to think I have nothing to learn."

"You have a lot to learn, Bryce. And I'm not just saying that to beat you before you begin. You need to know what you're in for, and I'd be remiss as your father not to tell you that."

"I know I have a lot to learn," I replied, keeping my voice even and calm. "I know this will be a steep learning curve. But Dad, I want it to be. I want to learn everything I can."

He stared at me for a long, hard moment before a smile won out. "That's my boy."

WE LEFT the restaurant on Clarence and headed toward the Brewery. We'd had a great dinner, and catching up with the guys—Terrence, Massa, Luke, and Noah—was just what I needed. Sure, I'd caught up with them briefly the night I got back from Singapore, but what Terrence had said was right.

I did ditch them.

When I saw a certain Bossy Blond across the bar looking hot as hell and giving me the eye, my dick was suddenly giving the orders.

But not tonight.

Tonight we laughed and talked. We ate and drank, and we caught up on everything. I'd missed them. I'd missed this level of mateship and familiarity that I had not had the last few years overseas. I'd known these guys for years. We'd gone to college together. Sure, I was better friends with Terrence, but I'd call the others good friends too. And I'd needed reminding of that.

I filled them in on all the ground I'd covered so far in my new business venture. I'd sourced possible suppliers and was happy with the quality and price. My finance meeting was next. Then I could source an appropriate location and begin the fit-out. I'd priced all that too.

"Give me a ten-second sales pitch," Massa said. He was a business marketing major, so this was his thing.

"Uh . . . ten seconds?"

"Now you've got eight."

"Fuck."

"Seven."

"A Singaporean-style coffee house. Think Starbucks, but better. And Singaporean. Kopi and bubble tea, Asian desserts, merchandise, mugs and tumblers, coffee beans and syrups."

They all stopped walking. Terrence grinned and Massa, Luke, and Noah were all kinda stunned. "Bryce," Massa said. "That sounds . . . that's actually a really good idea."

I laughed. "Thanks. I loved the kopi places in Singapore. Loved the whole aesthetic. I think the market is looking for the next coffee experience."

"Well, listen to you," Luke said. "Being all smooth with the marketing buzzwords."

"Sounds awesome," Noah added. Then he looked at Terrence and Massa, then back at me, and he made a face. "Are we mentioning your dad's take on this?"

I snorted. "I'd rather not. Nah, he's okay with it. Well, he's pissed and disappointed, and I'm pretty sure he hates the fact that he liked my business proposal. Oh, and apparently I have a lot to learn, and I am one hundred percent certain he thinks I'll fail. But . . ." I put my hand up. "He liked the idea."

Terrence put his arm around my shoulders and we began walking again. "I told you. It's a good plan. Your projections are strong; it's sustainable and forward-thinking."

"You just like the idea because you know I'll be selling pandan cakes."

He laughed. "That shit is like crack."

We basically laughed all the way to the Brewery. It was a bar that served their own brewed beers and spirits. It was always busy on a Friday night but it had a relaxed feel. There was usually some kind of sport on the TVs, the music was good. It was just chill. And the perfect place for the five of us to find a table, have a few more drinks, and laugh until they kicked us out at closing time.

And I was probably four beers into that plan when there was some cheering at the other end of the bar. I turned to see what the fuss was about when I saw a very familiar tuft of blond hair in the crowd.

He was in the centre of the cheering, dressed in a suit, jacket, no tie. His tailored shirt was pale blue, his suit pants were navy and extremely well-fitting. He was laughing at something, holding up his glass, and a round of 'cheers' went up and they drank.

It was a mix of men and women, all dressed in suits and expensive office-wear. It looked like a work thing, and I hoped to God it was, because if it was a social thing and a guy put his arm around him in front of me—or kissed him—I wasn't sure how I'd feel.

Devastated came to mind.

Fuck.

"What's fuck?" Noah asked.

"Huh?"

"You said fuck," Massa answered. "Looking over to them . . ." They all looked over.

"Oh, fuck," Terrence said. "It's Nameless Blondie."

"Who?" Luke asked. He was pretty smashed.

"Nameless Blondie," Terrence repeated. "The guy

Bryce ditched us for the night he got back. The same guy he's been seeing every weekend since then, aaaaaand the same guy he doesn't know if he has a name. Well, we can assume he *has* a name, but Bryce here doesn't know it. Their little arrangement doesn't include much talking, apparently."

I shot him a look. "Are you done?"

Terrence laughed. "Nope."

"Oh, that reminds me," Noah said to Massa, holding his hand out. "You owe me fifty bucks. You said he'd crash and burn."

Terrence put his hand out too. "Bryce here did not crash and burn. Cough up."

Massa shoved my shoulder. "You cost me a fortune, fucker."

Ugh. "I will pay each of you a thousand dollars to never talk about it again."

They, of course, all cheered and high-fived, yet I couldn't stop staring at where Bossy, or Nameless Blondie, was now laughing with a woman. My stomach was tied in knots, my heart felt sick, and my hands were clammy.

"Bryce, you okay?" Terrence asked. When I looked back at him and the others, I could see they weren't laughing now. They were looking at me, concerned.

My mouth was dry. "Uh, yeah. I'm, um, I'm just gonna go say hi." I stood up. "I'm not ditching you. I'll just be a few minutes. I'll grab us another round."

So I went to the bar, closer to . . . him.

I wondered if I should text him. Would that be weird? That would probably be weird. And what if he read my message and cringed, and I saw it? God, this was a bad idea. I should leave. Maybe we could go to a different bar. The guys wouldn't mind if I wanted to change bars.

"What can I get for you?" the barman asked, startling me.

"Oh. Um." I tried to swallow. Should we leave? Or should I just pretend I didn't see *him* at all? Yeah, that sounds like a better plan. Maybe he'll see me and he can be the one who decides to say hi. I smiled at the barman. "Yeah, five pale ales, thanks."

I put my card on the bar, and of course my eyes betrayed me and looked in *his* direction again.

Only to find him looking at me.

His smile was instantaneous; bright and honest. He wouldn't look at me if his boyfriend was with him, would he? Or maybe his boyfriend didn't care?

Fucking hell.

He weaved through his friends and came over to me at the bar. "Hey."

"Hey."

"I didn't know you'd be here," I said, lamely.

"We didn't expect to be here," he replied. He glanced back to his group. "We had a win at work today. It was late, and it's Friday so we thought drinks were in order."

I was so freaking relieved he was here for a work thing. "Good. Good. Yeah, I, um, I'm just here with my mates."

I nodded to the table, and sure enough, Terrence, Massa, Luke, and Noah were all watching. Which wasn't embarrassing at all . . .

I cleared my throat. "We were supposed to catch up a few weekends ago but I ended up leaving early with this cute blond guy. Sexy as hell, but a bit bossy."

His eyes lit up when he smiled. "He sounds great. You know, some people think being bossy is a bad thing, but knowing what you want and asking for it can't be wrong. I would take it as a compliment."

I laughed. "Oh, I'm pretty sure he does. But I've been told I'm not allowed to ditch my friends tonight though. So I had to change some plans for tomorrow night instead."

"I'm glad you did," he replied. That smug smile pulled at his lips, and so God help me, I wanted to kiss him right there.

The barman put my card back on the bar next to the beers I hadn't even seen him pour. "So, eight o'clock still good?"

He nodded. "Or seven. Or six. I don't mind."

I chuckled. "Or lunchtime."

He grinned, and he was just about to say something when the woman I'd seen him with earlier came over, clearly tipsy, and put her arm around his shoulder. "Michael, Michael, we need you over here."

His eyes shot straight to mine.

Michael.

Michael . . .

I didn't even try to hide my smile.

I had his first name.

"I'll be right over," he said, sending her off. Then he met my gaze, his cheeks tinted pink. "I don't know who she was talking about."

I leaned right in close and whispered in his ear. "Mmmmmichael."

His breath hitched and I pulled back and had to bite my lip so I didn't smile too big. "Tomorrow." I picked up the tray of beers. "Oh, and it was a yes to the robe. Nothing else."

He glowered at me and I laughed as I walked back to our table. Terrence, Massa, Noah, and Luke were still watching me. I chuckled as I sat down, but they were all stoic . . . or perhaps stunned was a better word. "What?"

"Should we start looking at wedding venues, or . . . ?" Massa asked.

I rolled my eyes. "Oh, fuck off and drink your beer."

He and Luke and Noah could take the piss out of me and rib me all they liked, but it was Terrence's knowing smile that bothered me the most. "Just say it," I prompted.

"You're in over your head already," he replied.

I motioned for him to lean in across the table. He did, and he was smiling because he knew what was coming. "Fuck off."

"So, Mr Nameless," Terrence said.

I smiled as I sipped my beer. "Is nameless no more."

Terrence's eyes went wide. "You know it?"

"I do."

"Well?"

"Oh no. Absolutely not. I'm not telling you guys anything."

"If it's any consolation," Noah said casually. "He was looking at you like you were looking at him."

"How was I looking at him?"

"Like we should be sussing out wedding venues," Massa replied.

I rolled my eyes because I was not looking at him like that. I wasn't. That was the biggest crock of shit I'd ever heard.

I sipped my beer and ignored them. Until what Noah said came full circle in my head. "Was . . . how was he looking at me?"

The four of them laughed. I told them all to fuck off again, which just seemed to prove their point, so then I offered them two grand each to please shut the fuck up.

CHAPTER FIVE

MICHAEL

FUCK FUCK FUCKITY FUCK. He knew my name.

When Natalie just waltzed on over and said my name three times right in front of him, I could have just died.

And of course he heard it, and of course his smug fucking smile told me he just loved knowing it.

And don't get me started on the way he murmured my name into my ear.

It sounded like sex. It was pure want and lust.

How could one word derail me like that?

One fucking word and my body wanted to lean into him, closer, pressed in tight, and let those very talented hands do whatever they wanted. One word was all it took.

It was obscene.

So he'd won the name game. He knew my name—my first name, at least—and I still had no clue about his.

He may as well have whispered 'checkmate' into my ear instead of my name.

Christ.

And now he was about to turn up at my place. Six o'clock instead of eight, because apparently waiting eight days instead of seven was far too long. For both of us. Not just me, thank you very much. When I'd suggested an earlier time in the bar last night, he'd jumped at it.

I was starting to think he was as into this arrangement as I was.

And I had to admit, seeing him at the bar last night did something to me, wearing those tight black jeans and boots, but his T-shirt with the black metallic black stripe across the sleeve and the back—I think I remembered it from an Armani collection. Or maybe it was Amiri . . . Any-fucking-way. It was hot as hell.

He wanted me in my robe when I opened the door. And I considered maybe not doing that to try and take back some semblance of power after the name thing, but who was I kidding? He clearly liked me in my robe, and he clearly liked the feel of the silk under his hands, and I very much liked that too.

At 5:53 my intercom buzzed.

He was early this time.

I opened my door and he stood there in a goddamn Purple Rain T-shirt, those black jeans that were made just for him, and a different pair of black boots. He was clearly a fan of Alexander McQueen.

"Love the boots," I said.

"Love the robe."

I stood aside and he smirked as he walked in. But he didn't go far. Just enough to step inside, and when I closed the door, he pushed me against it, and with a gentle finger-tip, he lifted my chin. My breath caught, his face just an inch from mine, his brown eyes as dark as night.

"Eight days is too long," he whispered before claiming my mouth with his own.

He was not timid, nor was he tender.

He was rough and ready, pushing me against the door with his body, raking his hands everywhere he could reach. He was already hard, and I was on fire with want and need.

He hoisted me up onto his hips, I quickly wrapped my legs around him, and he carried me to the couch where he all but threw me on to it. He was quick to climb on top of me, his hips searched for friction, and I finally pulled my mouth from his. "Not here. I need you inside me."

He shivered and I slid out from underneath him, took his hand, and led him to my room. Only when I got to my bed, he turned me around, and leaving my feet on the floor, pushed me face-first onto the mattress. He lifted up the robe, the smooth silk sliding over the heated skin of my arse.

"Oh fuck," he breathed.

"Yes, please." Just like this, right now, just fucking take me. "Like this."

I blindly tried to reach for the condoms and lube but he took my hand and, pressing me into the mattress, held my wrist above my head. He whispered behind my ear. "Don't move."

Fuck yes.

His cock was a huge bulge in his jeans and I tried to lift my arse, tried to get more of it, and he chuckled as he pulled back. "Eight days is too long for you too, huh?"

"Stop talking, and fuck me."

He froze, and I wondered if I went too far.

But then I heard his zipper and then he was on top of me again, his delicious weight on my back and hips, his cock slid between my arse cheeks, and he breathed into the back of my neck. "Be careful of what you wish for."

I tried lifting my hips, but he had me pinned. Goddammit. "You're still talking."

He chuckled and bit my neck, hard. It was a jolt of pain

against the pleasure and then his weight on my back was gone, but his legs were still between mine. I heard the foil of the condom wrapper and the lid of the lube snap, then slick fingers were on me and in me.

It was rough and fast and still not enough. I wanted more. I should have been grateful that he didn't just drive his huge cock into me without any kind of prepping, but so help me, I wanted it.

"More," I bit out, trying to lift my arse onto his fingers.

Then his warmth was gone, there was more lube, more cold slickness, then finally, *finally* what I wanted.

He pushed inside me, and I regretted my urgency immediately. He was so big and so hard, I gripped onto the bed covers and moaned. "Fuck."

He leaned over me then, his breaths ragged, his body heat scorching, his cock still pushing into me. "Is this what you wanted?"

It was almost too much, yet I still wanted it. There was a hollow ache deep inside me that only he could fill. And when I relaxed, when I let him in, when I let him do the work, it was exactly what I wanted.

"Yes."

His fingers dug into my hips, his lips kissed my shoulders, the nape of my neck, behind my ear . . . and he started to move and flex and fuck.

It was so, so very good.

"God, I'm gonna come so soon," he hissed.

So I lifted my arse for him and tightened my grip on the bed covers, basically telling him to go hard. He didn't disappoint.

He drove into me, harder and faster, until he stilled and his cock pulsed into the condom. He let out an almighty groan, his fingernails biting into my skin, and there was nothing I loved more than being manhandled and used like that. Being at the mercy of a powerful man and turning him on so much satisfied something inside me.

He collapsed on top of me, his forehead pressed against the back of my neck, his breaths ragged and his cock was still twitching. "Christ."

I chuckled, moaning at how good he made me feel. He pulled out slowly, then flipped me over. He was still completely dressed, except his jeans were undone and his cock was hanging out. It was so fucking hot.

He looked three parts dazed, but he pulled my robe completely open, took my erection into his mouth, and finished me off in record time.

Afterwards, when the room was still spinning, he collapsed onto the bed next to me. "Eight days is too fucking long," he repeated. I turned my head to look at him, he met my gaze, and we both laughed.

We lay there for a bit, collecting our breaths, chuckling and smiling at the ceiling, at each other. I sat up, feeling that pleasant ache in all the right places, and tapped my hand on his flat belly. "Let's do food. I'm starving."

We cleaned up in my bathroom. I righted my robe and could do little with my hair, given he'd run his lube-covered fingers through the back of it. He discarded the condom and tucked himself back in, washed his hands, and then he tried to fix my hair.

It was sweet and surprisingly intimate. "I think it's a lost cause," I murmured after a while.

His gaze went from the top of my head to my eyes and he smiled. "We might have to shower later."

My god, he was so freaking cute.

I nodded, trying not to think about how much I was

willing to go over and above the just-sex rule. For as little as I knew about him, it was so easy to be with him.

Maybe it was easy to be with him because I knew so little about him. Maybe the no-complication rule made it tangle-free. Maybe my heart rate kicked up a notch when I saw him—when I thought of him—because this whole arrangement was exciting and because I knew the sex was going to be off the charts. Maybe my heart liked the way he laughed or how he kissed or how he would casually touch me. Maybe the butterflies that swarmed my belly were all about anticipation.

Maybe I was fooling myself.

Shut up, shut up, shut up.

"You okay?" he asked.

We were still standing in my bathroom, facing ourselves in the mirror. I must have zoned out because I had no idea what he'd said before now.

"Yeah, I'm fine," I said quickly, looking at his reflection and not at him standing right beside me. "Great, actually. Now, about dinner . . ."

He stared at my reflection as well. "I just asked you about that."

"Oh, sorry. I was thinking about . . . something else." I tightened my robe. "Did you want Thai food? Pizza? Lebanese? Which is your favourite?"

"I eat anything."

"Good. Lebanese it is." Then I changed my mind. "Actually, pizza sounds really good. There's a place not far from here that does a Greek pizza with marinated lamb and haloumi, and they serve tzatziki on the side. It's amazing."

He stared at my reflection for a long few seconds like he was trying to make sense of something, and his smile made my heart do that thing . . . that traitorous thing where it beat too fast and loud. "That sounds great," he murmured.

I let out a quiet, unsteady breath. "Good. And they deliver. And they're fast." I went to my walk-in wardrobe and pulled on a pair of briefs.

He pouted. "Underwear?"

I waved at him, head to foot. "Says he who is fully dressed."

He laughed. "Yeah, we didn't get very far, did we? Perhaps you shouldn't answer the door wearing that robe."

"So it's my fault?"

"One hundred percent."

I chuckled. "I'm not even remotely sorry."

He laughed too, then toed out of his boots and pulled his socks off. "Does that make you feel better?"

"Yes." I met his gaze. "You have sexy feet."

"Sexy feet? No, feet are gross."

I held my foot out, pointing my toes. "My feet are not gross."

He grinned, walked over to me, and planted a kiss square on my lips. "No, they are not. And I think I like your hair all messed up."

I raised one eyebrow. "You like knowing you messed it up."

He grinned without shame. "I am not even going to deny that."

I rolled my eyes. "Dinner?"

He nodded and followed me out to the kitchen. I took my phone, quickly using the app to order the pizza, and slid my phone back onto the counter. "Did you want a drink?" I asked. "Water? Juice?"

"Oh, I thought you meant vodka."

"Did you want one? I have some in the freezer."

He shook his head. "No, I had enough to drink last night."

"Same." And there it was. The first mention of last night. Of running into each other outside of our agreement. Of him hearing my name . . .

His sly smile told me his thoughts had taken him to the same place mine had. "About that," he began.

I held his gaze, my chin raised, waiting . . . I knew it was coming . . .

"You had a good week at work," he said, trying not to smile. "Given you were out celebrating."

He was toying with me, like a cat with a mouse. "I did." We'd secured the Mortimer contract. And when I say we, I meant me. Not that I was going to explain that right now. He knew enough about me, when I knew nothing about him. "It was a very good week." I took another mouthful of water while he watched me, still smiling. "And you were out with your friends."

He nodded. "Yep." He left it at that for a long few seconds, because he didn't have to elaborate. Even though we both knew he knew more about me than I did about him. He clearly liked knowing more about me. This little game we were playing had him as the clear winner. But then he added, "I hadn't seen my friends much since I got back. It was good to catch up with them."

That was basically what he'd said to me last night, so it wasn't anything new. But it was better than a closed, one-word answer.

He grinned, that shit-eating grin that I wanted to kiss right off his stupidly gorgeous face. "It really bothers you that I know your name, doesn't it?"

I glared at him. Possibly even growled. "No."

"Liar." He put his finger to my chin and kissed me, soft,

sweet, lingering. He whispered against my lips. "Mmmmichael."

I let my head fall back and I groaned. "I'm changing your name in my phone from Sexy as Fuck to Annoying as Fuck."

He laughed. "That's up to you. But just so you know, I'm keeping your name as Bossy in my phone."

"Good."

"I like the name Michael though," he added wistfully. "It suits you."

I glared at him. I couldn't even be mad when he was being so damn cute and playful. "I'm glad you approve."

He stared at me for a long moment, like he was trying to decide something. "Want to know my name?"

"Yes," I said, waaaaaay too quickly. "I mean, no. No, I don't."

Of course he laughed again. "I think you do."

"I think I don't."

"It's a one-time offer," he added.

Fuck.

God, I wanted to. Every part of me was screaming to say yes. I wanted to know his name so bad. Just to be on equal footing. Because he knew mine. But then what? What was next? Our last names? Our jobs? Our families?

I sighed. "No." Then I cringed and groaned. "Fucking hell, yes. But no, don't tell me."

He laughed again and collected me in a bear hug. He rocked me from side to side, kissing my neck and shoulder as he chuckled, and it was strangely a comfortably intimate thing to do. Fuck buddies usually just fucked and left, right? They didn't stick around, they didn't laugh, they didn't embrace or kiss or make jokes. Did they? I had no first-hand experience in this kind of long-term arrangement. I'd had one-nighters, sure. But nothing like this. And I had no idea what was expected or what the ground rules were.

And god, he smelled so good it was hard to think straight. And he was broad and big and strong, and his back felt so good under my hands. And his front fit against me like he was made just for me.

It was all starting to mess with my head.

I worked up the courage to speak. "Can I ask you something though?"

He pulled back, his hand still on my hip, his face unguarded like he had no problems in the world. "Sure."

"Are you seeing anyone else?"

That wasn't how I wanted to ask that, but that's how it came out and it was too late to take it back. I considered amending it, or adding some kind of qualifier, but decided against that too.

He stared at me for a few thunderous beats of my heart, and then the corner of his lip quirked upward. He opened his mouth to answer . . .

And the intercom buzzed.

Fuck.

"That'll be dinner," I said, walking over to press the intercom. I used the moment away just to breathe.

While he—and I could only call him he because I didn't have a name—opened my fridge like he owned it. "What would you like to drink?"

Right then. "A mineral water would be great, thanks."

He put the bottle on the kitchen counter and then he began opening overhead cupboards looking for drinking glasses. He found them, put two tumblers on the counter, and poured us a drink each.

I let the delivery guy in, took the bag, and completely ignored the way he eyed me in my robe. Well, I ignored him, but *he* certainly didn't. He, being the SAF fuck-buddy, Purple Rain T-shirt wearing guy in my kitchen. The delivery guy clearly appreciated me and *he* clearly didn't appreciate me being checked out.

"Thank you so much," I purred, taking the pizza and the food bag. I closed the door and smiled at the disgruntled Purple Rain guy, now holding two drinks. I gave him a high-voltage grin. "I think this robe is a magnet."

He chewed the inside of his lip. "Mmm."

"I really love that Prince shirt, but I have to say, jealousy looks *way* better on you."

He gnashed his teeth and laughed. "You are trouble."

We sat on the couch together, not close but not exactly far apart, and ate the pizza. It was amazing, and he obviously enjoyed it. I, on the other hand, enjoyed the way I caught him looking at me. But then his brow furrowed and he sipped his drink, something clearly on his mind.

"I'm not, by the way," he said. "Seeing anyone else."

Oh, shit.

"Good," I replied, trying to play it cool though my heart was thumping against my ribs.

He watched me as I finished my slice of pizza. "And you?"

I was half tempted to play his little game from earlier and string him along a bit, but this was a serious question. I shook my head. "Seeing someone? No, I'm not." But then, because I couldn't help myself, I lifted my glass to my lips and smiled. "But I *am* kinda seeing this guy, just one night a week. He wears these really cool vintage band shirts. Super casual, no strings, best sex I've ever had. Sex three times in one night, no problem. Don't ask me what his name is though. I don't have a clue."

His smile became a grin. "Best sex you've ever had?"

"Hm," I mused. "But he set the bar pretty high. Not sure how he's gonna keep it going, to be honest."

"Three times in one night, huh? He sounds amazing."

"Well, I don't know if I'd go that far. He's a bit of a smart-arse, and he thinks he's funny."

He laughed. "He sounds hilarious. Though about that 'three times in one night' thing. Perhaps you should tell him that twice is fine."

Now it was me who laughed. "Nah, I'll keep the three times, thanks."

"You drive a hard bargain."

"Thanks."

"Poor guy's probably got performance anxiety."

"Oh, he has *nothing* to worry about. To be honest, just between you and me, I'd settle for once. But I'm not going to tell him that."

He chuckled. "Just once?"

"Believe me, he's that good. But I won't take once when I can have it three times."

"He's *that* good?"

I nodded. "Oh yeah."

"Sounds like you both enjoy the stress relief."

There was an edge to his voice when he said that, like he was telling me something about himself without actually saying it. "Yes for me, and I assume yes for him. Though I don't know what he does for a job or even if he has one. Pretty sure he said he'd spent time overseas and hasn't been back long, but he's working on something . . ."

His eyes met mine and he gave the slightest of nods. "Sounds like he's trying to make his own way."

Interesting choice of words . . . "Yeah, I don't know what field he's in, but I think he's pretty smart so I'm sure he'll work it out."

He gave me a thankful smile. "Smart, funny, and good in bed?"

"No, I said he's smart, he *thinks* he's funny, and he's amazing in bed."

He chuckled. "Well, he sounds like a great guy any way you look at it. But you know, he's not the only one who can go three times in one night. Are you not in that equation?"

"I am."

"So I'd reckon you'd have to be just as good, if not better. I bet you'd have a long list of guys waiting in line . . . I mean, I saw how that pizza delivery guy was looking at you. You must get that all the time."

I scoffed. "I wouldn't say the line is long. And I saw just how you didn't like how that pizza delivery guy was checking me out. Someone seemed a little jealous."

"I was not jealous."

"I don't mind—"

"I wasn't jealous. I just didn't think it was appropriate that he ogle you so blatantly in your house, like some creepy weirdo."

"Mm, I like jealous you. It's kinda hot."

He rolled his eyes. "I wasn't jealous."

I raised an eyebrow. "So you won't mind if I call the pizza shop and order another delivery. I could invite him in and let him fuck me over the back of the sofa. I mean, if you only want sex once a night, maybe that guy can go twice—"

He pounced on me, pushing me onto my back and lifting my knee up as he settled his weight between my legs. Smiling, he kissed me. "I'll give you your three times, you bossy shit."

I laughed and draped my arms around his neck, bringing him in for another kiss. "One down, two to go."

"Do you always get what you want?"

"Only when he's willing."

And holy hell, was he willing and did I ever get what I wanted.

I FELL ASLEEP AROUND three in the morning, so wrung out I couldn't move, couldn't keep my eyes open. I fully intended to tell him maybe twice was enough. I was going to be sore. But he collapsed beside me, a sweaty, smiling mess, and I closed my eyes just for a second, only to catch my breath.

I woke up just before eight, sunlight streaming into my room. I stretched out, smiling at the ache in my muscles and in my arse, and I rolled over . . .

To find him sound asleep next to me.

Well, shit.

And so, God help me, in the morning light, naked in my sheets, he was the most beautiful thing I'd ever seen. He had morning scruff, long eyelashes, his lips parted just so . . .

My heart thumped, strong and steady, telling me what I already knew. Sure, it was still uncomplicated. It was just sex, and our arrangement was great. But there were also some fun conversations, laughs, food, and intense chemistry I'd not felt with anyone.

The truth was, if the offer of more was ever on the table, I'd take it. Complications be damned.

I'd not woken up with a guy in my bed for a long, long time.

I liked it.

I wished I could stay there all day, but I had some errands to run before lunch. I slipped out of bed, careful not to wake him. I showered quickly and dressed in jeans and a plain navy T-shirt. That was me, a sensible dresser. Stylish, yes. Expensive, yes. But I'd never be cool enough to wear something like the Purple Rain T-shirt that was strewn over the couch.

I smiled as I made fresh coffee and toast, and I hoped the smell would wake a certain sleeping beauty. Or maybe it was me 'accidentally' banging a plate on the counter or a cup in the sink . . .

Sure enough, I heard a toilet flush and a very sleep rumpled gorgeous *him* emerged. He was wearing nothing but a towel around his waist and a sheepish smile. "Guess I fell asleep. Sorry."

I slid a coffee over toward him. "Don't apologise. We wore ourselves out."

"Yeah, it's that three-times rule, I think." He smiled as he sipped his coffee. "Oh, this is good, thanks."

"Yeah, I think my arse might agree that twice might be enough."

He lowered his coffee, his gaze trained on mine. "Are you . . . did I hurt you? Shit, Michael, I—"

I put my hand up and shook my head, my heart thrilling at him saying my name. "I'm fine. Better than fine, actually. You didn't hurt me. I seem to remember me begging you to fuck me harder last night. And I'm one hundred percent certain you did exactly as I asked."

His concern gave way to a smile. "I remember that too."

The toast popped up and I handed it to him on a plate with the butter and a knife. "What would you like on it?"

"Just plain butter is fine, thanks," he said. He buttered his toast and demolished the first two pieces, so I popped in some more. "I, um, I don't know where my clothes are."

"Well, your shirt's over there," I said, pointing to the far couch. "And I think your jeans got thrown . . ." I walked over and sure enough, they were behind the couch. I picked them up. "Here."

He laughed. "I don't remember throwing them there." The toast popped up and he climbed off the stool at the breakfast bar and hurriedly went about buttering them. "You have to butter them while they're hot. There's a small window of toast with melted butter perfection."

I snorted. "Is that right?"

Him standing in my kitchen wearing nothing but a towel, getting his own breakfast, and smiling like that was enough to catch my breath. He was so freaking cute . . .

A muffled buzzing noise sounded, and I tilted my head. "Can you hear that?"

He froze, listening. "Shit. That's my phone."

His phone?

I looked around the room. Where the hell was it? I followed the sound, closer to the couch we'd made out on, but then the buzzing stopped. "Dammit." I pulled a few cushions up to no avail when it buzzed again. I dropped to the ground and found it pushed under the couch. "How the hell did it get under there?"

It was still buzzing and I made a point of not looking at it as I held it out to him, but when he turned it over, the name Dad was on the screen.

"Shit."

"I'll just give you some privacy," I said, walking down the hall and into my bedroom. I could tell from the look on his face he wasn't looking forward to that conversation. The smile, the relaxed body language were instantly gone.

I went into my bathroom and could hear the mumble of his voice, not the words exactly. It sounded a little heated, but mostly frustrated and resigned. After I'd fixed my hair a few times and brushed my teeth, I stripped my bed, shoved my sheets into the washing machine and set it going. When I listened, there was no more talking, so I went back out. He was leaning against the kitchen counter, coffee in hand. He looked . . . sad.

"Everything okay?"

His gaze shot to mine as though I'd startled him. "Oh, yeah. Just . . . he . . ." He sighed. "My dad . . ."

I waited for him to continue, wondering if he would or not.

He made a face. "He's a good guy, he just expects a lot. And that's not always a bad thing. He's . . . very success-ful . . . at what he does." He sighed. "Apparently he had plans with me this morning that I didn't know about. Plans he didn't tell me about. He just assumed . . . Anyway, things are a bit tense between us at the moment because of . . . my career choice. But it's fine. We'll be fine. When he gets over himself. He won't be home when I get there anyway. He's away this week. So I have plenty of alone time."

HE JUST SAID *HOME* . . . but I thought he lived in a hotel. I tried not to connect the dots because that would complicate things and that's not what this was. But I had to say something . . . I put my hand on his arm. "Hey, if you don't want to go home, if you can't, you can stay here. All day if you want."

He studied my eyes for a long moment before he shook his head. "Nah, it's fine. Thank you. But he'll cool down. It's just . . .complicated."

I rubbed his arm. "Well, my offer stands. You can stay here. I have to duck out for a few hours, but I don't mind.

You'd have the place to yourself to decompress and avoid him."

He pinched my chin, his smile creeping back into place. "Thank you. You're really sweet. But honestly, it's fine. Thank you."

That twinge of sadness was back that just killed me. So then, because my brain was stuck in first gear while my mouth was gliding along in fifth, I said, "I'm free on Wednesday night. If you're bored, or lonely, or horny."

"Wednesday night, huh?"

That gleam in his eye told me he wasn't opposed. "After eight."

"Mm, I have a busy week this week," he allowed. "But I could be looking for some stress relief by Wednesday night."

I laughed. "In all fairness, I think we established that eight days was too long. So four is much safer. And I will allow for just one round on Wednesday night and two on Friday night. If you still want to come over on Friday, that is."

His eyes widened and he fought a smile. "Oh. You will *allow* that? How considerate."

I shrugged. "I thought so."

He took a second to consider it. "Is this a new arrangement moving forward? Or just a this-week-only thing?"

Well, originally it was just a one-off thing, but now he'd mentioned a more permanent thing. "How about we see how it works? I mean, are we going back to Friday nights or does Saturday work better for you?"

"Friday night, normally. Or Saturday night. My social calendar isn't exactly thumping right now. Most of my friends are in relationships, and I have my business . . . plans. So that's keeping me pretty busy. So basically, I'm free most nights . . . is the point I was trying to make."

His little ramble just made him more adorable. It didn't help that he was still only wearing a towel.

"Okay then. So," I prompted. "How about we leave it as Friday nights, or possibly Saturdays if we have something on, and maybe Wednesdays if we have a certain itch that needs scratching."

"But just so I'm clear, because I'd hate to disappoint you. The weekly quota is three rounds of sex. So Wednesday will count as one." He counted on his fingers. "Weekends is two."

Laughing, I leaned in and kissed him. "I wasn't kidding when I said I'd be happy with one."

"But you'd be really happy with three."

I palmed his half-hard dick. "Three rounds of this? Yes, please."

He grunted low in his throat. "Exactly how sore are you?"

I bit my lip.

His eyes were dark as he looked me up and down. "And it would technically be round four in twenty-four hours and I hate to think what you might expect of me next time—"

His words died right there when I pulled at his towel, dropped it to the floor, and knelt on it in front of him. I wasted no time in finishing him off, and when he was done —and when I was sure he could see and walk—I led him to my bathroom.

"What about you?" he asked, aiming to undo my jeans.

"Oh no, that was just for you. But you can think of all the ways to make it up to me on Wednesday. Right now, I have to go. Use my shower, whatever you need." Looking in the top drawer, I found a new toothbrush, still in its box. "For you. Leave it here, in case you fall asleep again."

He took it like I'd handed him a wedding ring. "Oh. Thanks."

God, it was just a toothbrush. A practical hygiene tool. No big deal. Right?

"Well, my sister will kill me if I'm late. So I have to go," I said. "Please just pull the front door shut behind you."

He nodded woodenly. "Um . . . thanks. For not being weird about me staying the night. And for breakfast. And for what you just did to me in your kitchen."

"Oh, that was my pleasure," I murmured.

He took my chin in his hand and swiped his thumb across my bottom lip. His gaze followed his thumb, then drew up to my eyes, like he was mesmerised. "You are . . ."

I swallowed hard. "I am what?"

He shook his head and dropped his hand. "I will be here on Wednesday, eight o'clock."

Christ. This was getting absurd. As if my heart being a traitor wasn't bad enough, now my lungs wouldn't work and my feet were stuck to the floor. "Good," I managed to say. "Don't be late."

He laughed, and I left him to it. I needed some distance, and a day with my family was as close to a bucket of cold water as I could yet.

I pulled up out the front of Susannah's place and she came out before I even had the engine off. I was expecting her to roast me for being ten minutes late but she didn't. "Is Jad not coming?" I asked.

"God no. I actually like him, Michael. Why would I subject him to lunch with our parents?"

I laughed at that. "Fair enough."

She eyed me for a second. "What's different?"

"What do you mean?"

She scanned my face, my hair, my eyes. "Something's

different."

I ignored the blush on my cheeks. "No it's not."

"Oh my god. Is it Mr Nameless? Does he have a name yet?"

Fuck.

"Well, I'm sure he does have a name . . ."

"But you don't know it. Still."

"No, I do not." I wasn't telling her that he knew my first name. God. I'd be bleeding out my ears before we got out of the suburb if I told her that.

"And how's the uncomplicated aspect going?"

I sighed and dug the heels of my hands into my eye sockets. "It's . . . complicated."

She didn't say anything, and when I looked at her, she reached over and patted my leg.

Before she could say, 'I told you so,' I blurted out, "He's just perfect. He's sweet and funny and hot as fucking hell. So yes, uncomplicated is going just about as well as you'd expect. Because now I think we're seeing each other twice a week, and he spent the night, and we ordered dinner, and I'm having serious problems trying to keep things *un*complicated when he just went right ahead and landed, with both feet, in complicated territory." I took a deep breath. "And that's both feet in Alexander McQueen boots, mind you."

Susannah smiled. "I'm happy for you."

"You're happy that my life is falling apart and everything's a disaster?"

She laughed. "It's not falling apart and it's not a disaster, Michael. Sounds to me like you're falling in love."

I opened my mouth to argue—outraged, defiant, horrified—but I couldn't find the words. Well, nothing intelligent anyway.

"Fuck."

CHAPTER SIX

BRYCE

I KICKED my boots off as I walked into my dad's apartment, knowing he wouldn't be home to rib me about leaving my shit on the floor. I planted my arse on the couch and put my socked feet on the coffee table and sighed.

I felt good.

No, not just good. I was happy.

And that wasn't something I expected to feel. And when I pictured that happiness, Michael's face swirled around in my head. His laughter, his smell, his touch. How he moaned, how he came, how he gave himself into pleasure. How he murmured in his sleep. How he was the most beautiful man I'd ever seen.

Yes, the sex was amazing. I only had to think about him and my dick took notice. Even after three orgasms over the last day, it still wasn't enough. But not just the sex. I wanted to be with him just to be with him. To make him smile, to hear him laugh, to touch his smooth, pale skin, and to taste those pink lips.

I liked him.

Really liked him.

Maybe it was more than that, but I could put that down to the excitement of it all. It was new and exhilarating. We had chemistry. Sizzling chemistry. We had fun when everything in our lives was serious and all work, work, work.

I couldn't say it was any more than an infatuation because I could list what I knew about him on one hand. Let's see . . . what did I know?

I knew his first name was Michael. I knew where he lived. I knew he liked Thai and Lebanese food and pizza. He kept expensive vodka in his freezer. His fridge was full of fruit and salads, cheeses, juice, and about four types of water. He liked to swim. His shower gel smelled like summer rain . . .

Jesus Christ.

Did I really just compare him to summer rain?

I've never thought about anyone as summer *anything* before. What the hell?

Okay, so maybe he was under my skin more than I wanted to admit.

Like waaaaay under.

Goddammit. I wanted to be mad about it. I wanted to be pissed off that this uncomplicated arrangement was starting to look not uncomplicated. And I *should* be mad about it. I needed to focus one hundred percent of my time on getting my business operational. I needed to prove to my father—and to myself—that I could do this. So yeah, I should be rightly pissed that I'd let myself be distracted.

But all I could do was smile.

Fuck it all to hell.

Focus, Bryce. Focus.

And this was my problem. I had to remind myself to focus. Thank God Dad wasn't here to see this. I could already hear the lecture coming from him, that splitting my time between personal matters and professional meant I wasn't giving one hundred percent to my business.

And he should know.

Him being the mega-successful businessman didn't *cost* him his marriage to my mother. It was a currency he knowingly, *willingly* exchanged. He wanted to be the best. And he couldn't give one hundred percent when a wife required a few moments of his precious time.

My father would be horrified if he could see me now. He'd also tell me to quit my foolish dreams of opening coffee houses and that I'd be expected at his office at eight on Monday morning.

And I couldn't allow that. I wouldn't.

I had one shot at doing this. I couldn't mess it up. I couldn't afford anything more with Michael right now. Meeting for uncomplicated sex was fine. Wishing for something more was just a luxury I couldn't afford right now.

So with that in mind, I took out my phone and called Terrence. "Morning."

"Ah, he yet lives!"

I snorted. "Was there a bet to the contrary I missed out on?"

"There should be."

"Nice."

"Well, you keep meeting Mr Mysterious. When and if you disappear and I file the missing person's report, I'll be forced to explain to the police how stupid you were to repeatedly meet up with a guy you don't know."

I laughed. "Thanks. And Mr Mysterious does have a first name now. Not that I'm telling you what it is, but I do know it."

"Oh, exchanging names now? Things are getting serious."

"Not exchanging, exactly. I know his, but he still doesn't know mine."

Now it was Terrence who laughed. "Nice one."

"What can I do for you this fine Sunday morning? Mara and I are taking her parents to lunch, so I need to get moving."

"Oh sure. Sorry. I'm viewing some locations for the store this week," I said quickly. "I'm waiting to finalise appointments, but I was hoping you could join me."

"Bryce, I'm busy—"

"I know. But I'd really appreciate a second opinion. And if they try and spin bullshit with numbers and percentages on the spot . . ."

"You want someone with you who can actually count."

"Yes." I laughed. I was pretty quick with maths, but no one was as fast as Terrence, and I knew my mind would be trying to take in every single aspect of every location, and I didn't want to miss anything.

I heard Terrence say something to Mara, then he spoke back into the phone. "Text me the details when you have them. And you can buy me lunch."

I chuckled. "Deal. Tell Mara I said hi."

"If I don't get off the phone and help her carry bags to the car, she'll kill us both."

I heard Mara say something to him, then her voice was closer. "Hello, Bryce."

"Don't take any shit from him, Mara," I yelled.

"She can't hear you now," Terrence said. "But I do have to go. And you met with your finance banker?"

"Yes, last week." Which I'd told him about on Friday night but he'd clearly had a few too many drinks.

"Send me whatever he sent you. I'll go over his figures before we meet with anyone."

I sighed. "Okay. Thanks, mate. And enjoy lunch with your in-laws."

He swore, and I disconnected the call and sent the documents to him, knowing he'd have it memorised by dinner time. I was confident with my business banker. I was pretty sure he'd expected to meet me, son of James Schroeder, and thought he'd be babysitting me or placating a child's whim. But I went in with a plan—a good plan—and I listened to his advice, so by the time we were done, he was on board and one more step in my dream was complete.

Now I just had to find a suitable location for my first store.

I'd already shortlisted my top five choices. I had a favourite but I wasn't going to derail myself by not having options. The thing was, with prime shopfronts in the CBD, they moved fast. Most of them never even made listings; they were snapped up before they could even be advertised.

I'd made appointments to see these listings and was waiting on confirmations which I expected first thing tomorrow morning. So I spent half my Sunday reading over business insurance policies and the other half going grocery shopping and doing laundry. Doing the mundane stuff was actually a nice change. It gave me a chance to clear my head and not think about anything for a while.

By dinner time, Dad's apartment was dark and quiet, and I enjoyed that too. I had some mindless show on Netflix playing, but with no other business thing to go over for the fifth time, my mind wandered to Michael.

I smiled as I pulled out my phone, just about to text him, when I stopped myself. *No more contact than necessary*, I told myself. Uncomplicated sex with no strings attached didn't include a bunch of cute texts or even a phone call just to chat because I missed his voice and wanted to hear him laugh . . .

Wait, what?

I missed his voice?

What the fuck was that about? I didn't miss his voice. Or his laugh. Or his blue eyes, or pink lips, or . . .

Fucking hell.

He was just sex. That's all, no more, no less. There was absolutely nothing special about him or our arrangement. I could have gone home with anyone that night we first met and rigged up some kind of sex-only deal with anyone. It didn't have to be him.

Hell, I could do that right now. I had Grindr on my phone.

I told Michael I wasn't seeing anyone. And that was true. Seeing someone implied regular dating or some kind of commitment. And Grindr hook-ups weren't seeing anyone. Just pure sex, no strings, no complications. So I could absolutely check out Grindr and swipe any guy who looked like fun.

It wasn't cheating. It wasn't wrong. I was not in any kind of committed relationship with Michael. We had both expressly said it was just sex, no commitment.

So, to prove to myself that I could, I hit the app and scrolled. And scrolled, and scrolled some more. I looked twice at a few guys but kept scrolling. They were even kinda close by. I could be dicking some guy within thirty minutes. Hell, I could dick three guys before sun-up.

But none of them were right. They weren't what I was looking for, and my dick didn't even care that I could be dicking random strangers all night. There was no interest. At all. Not a twitch, not an inkling.

Nothing.

Hell, I could even hit a club and fuck some random guy in a bathroom stall.

I looked down at my crotch from where I lay on the couch, eyeing my very-not-interested dick. It just lay there, all snug and flaccid in my jeans, not one iota of interest.

But when I thought of Michael and those lips and his tight little arse, his hands, his laugh, and the line of his throat and how he moans . . . and my cock pulsed at that.

"Fucking traitor."

Great. Now I'm talking to my dick.

I could just get up and go out to some gay bar. I could do that right now. But it wasn't just my dick that wasn't interested in that idea. My heart and head weren't into it either.

I held my phone, reconsidering sending Michael a text, just to say hi or to tell him it was his fault that my dick was no longer interested in some random hook-up with some stranger. And then I had a thought . . .

What if he was meeting some random stranger for a random dicking?

My heart did some weird squeezing thing and I felt hot and cold all over at the thought.

Oh, fuck this.

So I threw my phone onto the couch across the room, found some other mindless shit on Netflix to watch, turned the volume up loud to drown out my internal monologue, and spent the rest of my night *not* thinking about Michael.

Much.

MY APPOINTMENTS TO view some prospective site locations were scheduled for Wednesday and Thursday, which suited me fine because I spent all day Monday going over the store design specs.

We were just gathering ideas and finalising general concepts, so when the location was chosen, these concepts could be adapted to suit. I'd spent a lot of time in kopi houses in Singapore and took many photos to use as a portfolio of ideas and themes. The design company was a young Sydney based team whom I entrusted with my plan to be eco-friendly and forward-thinking, and after spending the day with them, I was invigorated and energised.

I spent Monday night looking over their concepts and crunching some numbers on sustainable bamboo flooring and fixtures, water- and energy-saving kitchen appliances, and they gave me a lot of information on government rebates for going green.

I spent all day Tuesday with the digital marketing team. Which was, admittedly, led by Noah who was very good at what he did. We laid the groundwork for a website and phone app for ordering, digitalised receipts and reward programs. I was no fool, but this was way out of my area of expertise and Noah could do it with his eyes closed.

Tuesday night I got home late and ordered dinner in. Dad's apartment was dark and quiet, not to mention big and very empty. Don't get me wrong, I loved the me-time and probably wouldn't have coped too well with Dad asking me fifty questions and grilling me on all aspects of my imminent failure. I was very used to being alone. I had no issue with being alone.

But my mind began to wander back to a familiar smile and deep blue eyes. And now I had a reason to text him . . .

Hey Bossy, still on for tomorrow night?

It was only polite of me to ask and confirm beforehand, right? He wouldn't think it was weird or clingy if I texted to confirm. And what if he said no? What if something came up and the new Wednesday arrangement no longer worked for him?

Well, if he did, I'd make myself swipe right on Grindr or go to a bar to find some rand-o, just because I could. That's what I'd do.

Then the text bubble appeared. He was typing, and my heart was in my throat.

Please say yes. Please say yes. I didn't really want to have sex with anyone else—

Hey SAF. Wednesday is a 'yes please' from me.

I damned well laughed at my phone. Thank God. And that whole sense of relief, that heart-thumping relief was way more than I was ready to unpack just yet.

Then he sent another message. *What will you want for dinner?*

I thumbed out a quick reply. *It's my turn to buy. Do you like Italian food?*

Love it.

Are you allergic to anything?

Tardiness.

I laughed. *I did notice the adverse reaction to my being late before.*

Yep. The antidote is a body massage and two rounds of sex.

I laughed again. *I would be deliberately late to receive that punishment. Try again.* I knew it was wrong as soon as I hit Send but his reply didn't disappoint.

How about this: If you want my body to do with whatever you please tomorrow night, you won't be late.

I was grinning like an idiot. *Message received and understood.*

Is eight o'clock still okay?

Perfect.

Good. Looking forward to it.

God, Michael. Me too. *Same.*

Don't be late.

Oh, I'll be early. And his body will be mine to do with whatever I please. And fuck, my dick was very interested in this development. *Wouldn't dream of it.*

You're thinking about what you want to do to my body right now, aren't you?

I barked out a laugh despite the way my dick was now getting hard. *Hell yes I am. Any requests?*

You already know how I like it.

Yes, I do. Fuck. He loved every inch of me buried to the hilt, he loved being face down, arse up, and he loved it when I banged him into the mattress . . . And now I was hard. *Christ now I need to jerk off.*

Or you could leave it for tonight and do me twice tomorrow night.

Or I could go jerk off now AND do you twice tomorrow night. You know I'm capable of doing both.

Bastard. Now I need a cold shower.

I chuckled. *My shower will be hot and soapy, and I'll be thinking of you.*

I hate you. Make it 7:30 tomorrow night. And don't be fucking late.

I laughed at that. *You're so Bossy.*

I am, and you like it.

I really fucking do.

I hit Send before I really thought about my reply. '*I really fucking do.*' What did that even mean? That I really liked his bossiness? Or that I really liked him?

It certainly put an end to our conversation anyway. He was probably trying to figure out what the hell I meant just as much as I was. I contemplated adding something but figured the hole I'd just dug myself was big enough, so I switched my phone off and put it out of my mind.

But my still-aching dick wasn't going away on its own, so I made good on that hot and soapy shower, thinking about him, and I came so damn hard I had to lean against the tiles so I didn't fall over. I climbed into bed, smiley and sated, and fell asleep thinking of blond hair, pink lips, and those feisty blue eyes.

―――――――

"YOU WHAT?" Terrence stopped walking and I had to pull him to the side of the footpath so the people walking behind didn't run into us.

"I think I kind of told him I liked him," I repeated. "Kind of. Not directly, but I did."

Terrence's expression went from confused to annoyed. "My god, Bryce. I mean, it's great that you're seeing someone and things are progressing for you. But you're about to embark on a serious business venture. You need to get your head in the game."

I growled out a sigh. "You sound like my old man. That's exactly what he'd say."

Terrence clapped my shoulder and smiled apologetically. "Sorry. But . . ."

I groaned this time. "But you could both be right." I scrubbed my hand over my face. "I know. The timing sucks. But he's . . . he's different."

Terrence shook his head, back to annoyed. He nodded up the busy street. "Come on, they're waiting."

They were Antony and Valene, a real estate duo with some huge company, showing me the three places today.

The first place was a hard and fast no from me. I didn't need Terrence's input at all on that one. Venue number two was more promising. Better location and floor size, new electrics, awesome natural lighting, with great foot traffic.

"This is not bad," I said to Antony and Valene, standing in the middle of the empty floor space. "It could work."

Valene spouted off some stats and figures and I hoped Terrence was listening. And that thought right there stopped me. I was checking out potential business locations and my mind was stuck on Mr Bossy Michael and what we were going to do tonight.

Or more to the point, what I was going to do to him tonight.

I really did need to get my head in the fucking game.

The third site we checked out was okay too. It could work if it had to, but the second site was better.

And at least it was a productive day. I was very upfront with Valene and Antony, saying I had two more sites to check out the next day, but the second venue we'd seen today was a contender. I was given all the information they could give me on it and I told them I'd call them in twenty-four hours.

I was home by four, read everything I could about the venue and the lease, sent the specs to my design team as a possible site, showered, and was ready to leave by half-past six.

I picked up Italian takeaway, as promised, and was at Michael's building at 7:24. He said 7:30 and to not be late, and I was definitely not being late tonight.

He buzzed me through and I had butterflies in the elevator ride up to his floor. I was just about giddy walking to his door, and when he opened it and stood there like sex on a plate, I had to make myself not grin.

"No robe today," I said, though I was hardly disappointed. He was wearing what looked like gym clothes, his hair was wet and combed back, and as I walked past him, I could smell chlorine. "Mm, been swimming?"

He closed the door and leaned against it, all smug and gorgeous. "I was considering having a shower."

"Or I could lick it off you."

"Yes, you could . . ." He inhaled deeply and eyed the takeaway bag. "But I'm famished. The last thing I had to eat or drink today was a coffee at ten this morning. You said Italian food, right?"

I told my dick it'd have to wait. The man needed to eat first. I held up the bag. "Yep. We better get you fed. Can't have you passing out on me."

He smiled, and as he walked past me, he gave me the gentlest of touches on the arm. "Thank you." It sent a thrill through me. His touch, his smile. I'd envisioned me taking him straight to the bedroom, bending him over the side of the bed, and taking him hard and fast. But somehow that kind of gentle touch was better.

I unpacked the bag on the kitchen counter, he grabbed plates and cutlery, and he quickly dished out some food. I don't think he even cared what it was. God, he was really hungry. "This is a lasagne that uses zucchini and eggplant instead of pasta," I said. "I thought I should get one thing that's easy on the carbs."

He ate two quick mouthfuls and groaned. "My god, it's divine."

I ignored the sounds he made as he devoured half his plate. Instead, I opened the second container. "This one's a chicken, ricotta, and spinach ravioli. They make it in-store and it's amazing."

He stabbed a forkful and devoured that, moaning like a porn star.

I swallowed my mouthful and ignored my still-aching dick. "Busy day then?" I asked. "If you didn't have time to eat."

He nodded and sipped his water. "Flat out. I got in at seven, managed to swim a few laps because I missed yesterday."

"You probably shouldn't swim when you haven't eaten," I offered lightly. "You could have passed out in the pool."

He smiled and licked his lips. "You said you were bringing Italian food. I didn't want to spoil it. It's amazing, by the way." He ate some more ravioli and hummed. "God, that's good."

I put my fork down, stepped in close, and slid my hand to his cheek. I tilted his face so his eyes met mine. "You keep moaning like that, and I'll fuck you right here."

His pupils blew out; his chest rose and fell. "I wasn't moaning," he whispered.

I thumbed his bottom lip, his lips parted with a gasp, and I crushed my mouth to his for a bruising kiss. His mouth was hot and welcoming, his cool fingers raked through my hair, and I pressed him against the kitchen counter.

Feeling how turned on he was almost buckled my knees. "Have you had enough to eat?" I asked, kissing down his neck. The taste of salt and chlorine on his heated skin was like heaven.

He slid his hands up and under my shirt, skimming down my back to pull me closer. He ground against me. "For the time being. Now I'm hungry for something else."

I pulled his shirt over his head and kissed his pale shoulder, goosebumps rising in the wake of my hot mouth. "I've thought about this all damn day," I admitted. "Trying to concentrate at work, and all I could think about was being inside you."

He groaned, leaned into me, pulled my face back, and claimed my mouth with his. He kissed me until we were breathless, our erections pressed together. His eyes were dark, his lips swollen. "So take me to bed and do whatever you want to me."

I grinned like the devil. "You shouldn't say that to me." I lifted him onto my hips and he was quick to wrap his legs around me, and he laughed as I carried him to his room. I had every intention of throwing him onto the bed but he clung to me, so I knelt on the mattress and gently laid him down.

He asked me to do whatever I wanted to him, so I did. What I wanted was to hear him groan and gasp when I was buried inside him. I wanted to wring every ounce of pleasure out of him, to hear him beg and plead for more, to hear him cry out as he came, and to hear him moan when my own orgasm took hold of me.

That was what I wanted. So that's what I did.

"Christ almighty," he breathed.

We'd collapsed onto his bed, both of us sweaty and panting, boneless and smiling. "You're welcome."

He laughed. "You know, there could possibly be such a thing as being too good at sex."

I chuckled, and rolling onto my side, I pulled him in close, tucked him into the crook of my neck, and closed my eyes. This kind of post-coital cuddling was more intimate than we'd probably done before, and I could tell by the way he froze that he thought so too.

"You said I could do what I want," I murmured. "This is what I want."

He relaxed then and snuggled in, and after a few minutes, his breathing evened out and we dozed.

This is what I wanted.

His slender form fit perfectly with mine, his arm draped around me like luxurious fabric. He felt like silk . . .

Christ, this was everything I wanted.

He stirred a little while later and I peeled him off me, only far enough so I could hold his face and kiss him. Soft and tender, teasing with my tongue, sucking on his bottom lip. He traced patterns on my back, humming against my lips, his leg hitched up over my hip.

It just felt really fucking good.

Eventually he put his hand to my cheek, his eyes warm and lovely, his smile much the same. "How about we shower, then take what's left of dinner to the couch and watch some Netflix?"

I couldn't help but smile and nod. Because, all the incredible sex aside, *that*—what he just said—was exactly what I wanted.

———

"YOU KNOW the best thing about Netflix?" I asked. We were sitting on his couch, freshly showered. He'd given me a pair of running shorts to wear, which fit me like Lycra. I thought they were a tad tight, but the way he eyed the outline of my junk and licked his lips, I was keeping them on.

He had a plate of pasta and had just shoved in a forkful when I asked my question. "Wh-thah?" he mumbled through a mouthful of food.

I laughed. "Charming."

He managed to swallow and tried to playfully kick me. "Shut up. What's the best thing about Netflix?"

I pressed the Netflix button on the remote. "That your 'because you watched' section will tell me more about you than what you ever could."

He laughed but didn't seem to care too much. There was a mix of action and comedy movies and TV shows like *Suits* and *Sense8*. I probably could have guessed those, and I was pleased there were no horrible surprises, like if he had a penchant for Adam Sandler movies.

"What does your watched list look like?" he asked.

"Not Adam Sandler movies," I said.

He stopped, his fork halfway to his mouth. "Thank God."

I chuckled at that and decided to offer him a truth about me. "I love Japanese yaoi and Asian movies. Love Korean TV dramas and Chinese movies. Thailand and Taiwan have a lot of good stuff. It's kinda corny but I love it."

He smiled as he chewed, then swallowed. "Find something for us to watch."

I grinned at him and began to scroll through the thumbnails on the screen. "You're gonna love it." I settled on a TV series that I'd watched several times and settled back to enjoy it all: the food, the company, the show.

He did a double take at the screen. "Who is that?"

I laughed. "He's hot as hell, right?"

He ate some more and then began to pick at mine. "You're still hungry?" I asked. Michael was trim and lean, there wasn't much to him at all. Where the hell did he put all that food?

"Yes, don't judge me. I didn't eat all day. Then I did twenty-five laps, and swimming makes me hungry." He pointed his fork at me. "Then you fucked me to within an inch of my life. And I have a high metabolism."

I chuckled. "We should wear Fitbits next time so we can see just how many calories we burn." I handed him my plate, which he took, and kept eating. It made me smile.

I watched the show for a bit, and Michael slid the plate onto the coffee table and settled against me as the little spoon. I kissed the back of his head and he sighed. "You spent time in Singapore, right?" he asked.

"Yep. I was based there for a while."

"And you loved it?"

"Yep. The people, the food."

"Why'd you come back?"

"My visa said I had to," I replied. "And my dad's here. His business."

He nodded, never taking his eyes off the TV. "And the business you're setting up now, is that like his business?"

"Nope. Not at all."

He was quiet again for a bit, and I wondered what he was asking for. Asking questions out of interest without asking for direct information isn't easy.

"How did your lunch thing go with your sister?" I asked instead.

He turned his head and shuffled a bit so he could see my face. "You know more about me than I do about you. Like, a lot more. And that's not fair."

I chuckled again, because he was right. "Well, I don't have a sister."

"A brother?"

I shook my head. "Nope."

"Just you and your dad?"

I'd never mentioned my mother so that was a fair

assumption. I nodded. "Yep. And his business. Don't forget that. It's the most important thing in his life."

Michael stared up at me, his expression sad. "I'm sorry. That must be awful."

I sighed. "I'm used to it. It's the way it's always been, ever since I was little."

He sat up, looking right at me, and put his hand to my cheek. "That can't have been easy."

I took his hand and kissed his palm. "Honestly, I've never known any different. And he's not a bad person. He's actually a good guy who found himself as a single parent. Admittedly, he just paid for a lot of help. I had nannies and drivers and tutors, that kind of thing. But he's just driven to succeed." I shrugged. "I mean, aren't we all?"

His eyes searched mine and he conceded a nod. "I guess, yeah. But still . . ."

"What are your folks like?"

"They're nosey, love to pry, and they need to know all the details of my entire life."

I chuckled. "So, they're the opposite of mine."

"Sounds like it." He smiled. "My folks live in Newport, and they cannot understand my love of living in the city centre."

"But they'd have to be proud, right?" I shrugged one shoulder. "I mean, clearly you've done well for yourself."

He smiled, and his blond hair flopped down onto his forehead. He brushed it back up with his long, slender fingers. "Oh, sure. To them I'm a 'high-flyer' which is ridiculous, but I'd hate to burst their bubble."

I wasn't going to ask this, but then I thought, fuck it. It was now or never. "So, your parents know you like guys?"

He nodded and gave me a small smile. "Yeah. Since I was fourteen. What about you?"

"Yeah, my dad didn't even blink. Just gave me the awkward 'be safe, use protection' speech that was as horrifying as it was humiliating, considering I'd just brought a guy home and my dad wasn't supposed to be there."

Michael put a hand over his mouth, his eyes wide. "No . . ."

I laughed. "Yep. First and last nugget of fatherly advice he ever bestowed on me."

"Oh my god. I would have died."

"It was funny. Well, it's funny now. It wasn't back then."

Smiling, he leaned in and kissed me again, then turned back around and pulled me down to be the big spoon. He watched the TV for all of three seconds. "Oh, who is that gorgeous man?"

"He's the new detective," I explained. "He's the good cop. The other guy is the lone-wolf cop, and well, we all know he's not really an arsehole, he's just misunderstood and he has his reasons, and the good cop has to mend his broken heart."

"This is a gay cop show?"

"Ah yeah, didn't I say that?"

"No." Michael pulled my arm under his head to use as a pillow and he was quiet as he watched for a while. "This is going to be my new favourite show, isn't it?"

I chuckled and kissed the back of his head. "Yep."

We watched another episode, but after Michael yawned a second time, he turned the TV off, and taking my hand, he led me to his room. We stripped naked, climbed into bed, and we began to make out, kissing and touching, lying on our sides.

But it never led to sex. It was just sensual and lovely without going to that next level. And then kissing became nuzzling, and nuzzling became snuggling, and the next thing I knew, it was morning.

———————

"SHIT, I'm going to be late," he said, trying to dry himself with his towel. We'd just showered together and jerked each other off. I had promised him two orgasms, and I refused to not deliver on a promise.

I stood at his bathroom vanity, a towel around my waist, a toothbrush in my mouth—my toothbrush, I might add. Well, it was a new toothbrush he'd opened for me the other week, but it was now technically mine. "I'd like to say I'm sorry, but I'm not."

He slapped me on the arse as he rushed into his walk-in wardrobe. "I'm not sorry either, but I will be sorry if my boss gets in before me."

I pulled on my jeans and found my T-shirt in the living room, and just as I was putting it on, he walked out in a smart navy suit, crisp white shirt, and brown shoes. His hair was done to perfection and he looked damn good, and he smelled even better. "Christ, I'd like to take you out of that suit. Maybe instead of opening the door in a robe or swimming gear, you can wear that."

He stopped, looked me up and down. "Love the Duran Duran shirt," he said. "Though I can't decide if I prefer the Purple Rain shirt or The Clash one. But either way, those band shirts help you live up to your name."

What? "My name?"

"Yeah, Sexy as Fuck. We've established that's your forever-name now."

I laughed. "Do you want to know my real name?" I asked. "I'll tell you if you want."

He seemed to consider this for a moment. Then he shrugged as if he couldn't have cared less. "No thanks."

"Ouch." I pretended to be hurt. Or maybe I wasn't pretending. Maybe now I wanted him to know.

He laughed and pocketed his phone and wallet. "You ready to leave?"

I slipped into my boots and stood up. "Yep." I grabbed my phone, wallet, and keys. "Sure you don't want to know my name?"

He grinned as he held the door for me. "Nah, I'm good. See, you know way more about me than I know about you. So me choosing to not know your name is the only power play I have left."

"Power play?" I hit the elevator button. Power play . . . Was this still a game? He clearly thought it was, but somewhere along the lines, I'd stopped keeping score.

Christ, I was in trouble.

He smiled at my reflection as we stepped into the elevator with the mirrored back wall. "I really do like that shirt," he said.

I looked to the real him, not his reflection. "And I really do like that suit."

"Want me to wear it tomorrow night when you come over?"

Tomorrow night? Oh shit, tomorrow was Friday. "Hell yes, I do. And you might want to keep some lube near the sofa so I can just bend you over the back of it as soon as I walk in."

His lips parted and his nostrils flared; then he had to readjust himself. "Fuck," he breathed. "I can't go to work with a hard-on. You shouldn't say shit like that to me."

The elevator doors opened and we stepped out. This was where we would part ways: he'd go in one direction, I'd go the other. So I turned and grinned at him. "That, my dear *Michael*"—I emphasised his name, because I could—"is what I call a power play." I laughed at his expression, gave him a salute. "Have a good day, Michael."

I walked a few metres before I turned to find him still standing there. "I hate you," he called out.

I laughed again. "No you don't."

He snarled at me and turned, walking in the opposite direction. I waited for him to turn and look at me, and for the longest while, I didn't think he was going to. But he did. He turned to look at me. He did the thing where if they look over their shoulder or turn around, it means something, right?

Well, he fucking turned.

And I stood there on the footpath, facing his direction instead of mine, looking directly at him. I raised my hand in a small wave, and he groaned at getting caught. I laughed and he smiled and shook his head before going on his way.

But he turned to look at me. He turned, and that meant something right?

The fact I was standing there like a lamppost waiting for him to turn around didn't have to mean anything though. I wondered if I should text him some smart-arse comment when my phone rang. I grinned as I fished it out of my pocket, thinking it would be him.

But it wasn't. It was Terrence.

I answered his call. "Hey, what's up?"

"Just checking what time you need me today."

Ah, head in the game, Bryce. "First is at ten, second is directly after. It's with the same firm, so there's no messing around in between," I explained as I began to walk home. "You should be back at work by half eleven at the latest."

"Okay."

"I really do appreciate it. I know you're busy."

"You owe me dinner."

I laughed. "Deal."

"Are we meeting at the real estate office or at the site?"

"At the site. The lady's name is Natalie and she's part of the CREA group."

"CREA? Even I've heard of them."

"Yeah, they're kind of a big deal. She's going to meet us there to save time."

"Good. Text me the address. I'll meet you there."

"Will do."

"And the first venue is the one you want, right?"

"Yep. It's my favourite."

He was quiet a moment. "Where are you?"

"Just walking home."

"You're doing the walk of shame? On a Thursday?"

I laughed. "Believe me, there is no shame on this walk."

Terrence snorted. "Stop boasting, and text me the address." He sighed. "How is Mr Nameless anyway?"

"Oh, he's kinda great, actually."

"But he still doesn't know your name."

"No, he doesn't. But in my defence, I offered to tell him and he declined."

Terrence laughed. "Oh my god. The great Bryson Schroeder got shot down."

"I didn't get shot down. It's all part of the game." God, was it a game anymore?

"Game?" He laughed again. "Bryce, I don't need to tell you this, but it's not a game when only one of you is playing."

CHAPTER SEVEN

MICHAEL

I RUSHED into the office with my phone to my ear, and a smiling Carolyne handed me my messages. I mouthed thank you to her as Natalie gave me a rundown of my day's agenda.

She would be on-site most of the day with some potentially big clients, and I had a list of shit to do as long as my arm. I made it to my desk, still listening to Natalie while reading messages and waiting for my computer to boot up.

I'd worried that I'd be late and Natalie would be looking over my shoulder all day. I hadn't expected SAF to stay the night again. I hadn't expected him to shower with me or to be so damned cute in the mornings. And sexy. My god. Sexy as Fuck was the best name I could give to him.

Not that I'm complaining. Because last night had been amazing. And I'm not even talking about the mind-blowing sex. I'm talking about after that. When we ate on the couch and watched TV, cuddling and making out in bed before falling asleep in each other's arms, I was one hundred percent certain that was outside the parameters of 'just sex' and 'no complications.' I knew it was sprinting headlong into 'over-complicated' but I couldn't bring myself to pull back.

So God help me, I was loving it.

But Natalie wasn't going to be back in the office until lunchtime and that meant I could breeze through my to-do list without distraction. Don't get me wrong, she's a great manager and I loved working with her and for her. But I got more done on my own without her breathing down my neck or feeling her watch my every move.

I'd crossed off the first five things off my list and was on track to have it all done by lunchtime when my phone rang again. It was Natalie again. I smiled as I answered. "Yes, the Lister contract has been done, the renovations on the Queen Street job are ahead of schedule, I'm meeting with Castlereagh tomorrow at nine, and there's been a litigation hold up with the Market Street purchase but it should be sorted out by close of business tomorrow."

"Well, I'm glad you're over-competent," she replied. It was hard to detect if that was sarcasm because she sounded on edge.

"What's up?"

"I'm stuck in traffic in the goddamned tunnel. There's an accident up ahead and I'm not going to make my ten o'clock."

I checked the time. It was nine forty-two. "Shit."

"I need you to take it. He's a big-name client and I can't have us reschedule. The job file is on my desk." She paused for one second. "I can't hear you walking. Why are you not walking to my office? Michael, you need to move."

I was up and out of my chair, running to her office. There were several job files on her desk. "Name?" I asked.

"His name is Bryson Schroeder," she said. "He's seeing

two properties. First is York Street at ten. Then you'll take him to the second on Kent."

I checked my watch. Shit. I had sixteen minutes to get to York Street. I took the file, signed for the keys, and raced to the elevators. "A little more notice would have been good."

"Phone reception is sketchy in here," she said, and she was starting to break up again. "I've been trying, sorry."

"Tell me what I need to know about this guy," I urged.

"He's a Schroeder," she replied, like that explained everything. "Of the Schroeder Hotels."

Oh, holy shit. Schroeder Hotels were the Australian equivalent of the Hiltons.

Now I saw why she called him a big-name client.

"Is this for a hotel development?" I asked, because we didn't deal with hotels. Our real estate firm had whole other divisions that did that. Natalie and I managed CBD corporate retail.

"No, a new business. He's scoping a few sites and I want him for his name alone."

I didn't have time to stop and peruse the folder. "What else do I need to know?"

"There'll be two of them. He said he's bringing an associate. He's the son, I think, of the Schroeder name. He's our gen, not old school, but he's very serious—" The phone crackled and her voice dropped in and out.

"Look, Natalie, you're breaking up. I'll move faster if I'm not talking on the phone. Text me anything I need to know."

I disconnected the call and picked up the pace, all but running toward York Street. I was going to get there a sweaty mess, but at least I'd be there. I was familiar with the site. It was a corner building which fronted York Street and a smaller laneway. It was prime real estate with great foot traffic. The last tenant had been there for over a decade, very freshly vacated, and the site would be snapped up real quick.

I made it to York Street and raced down one block to the laneway and had the side entrance door open at 9:57. I stepped inside what looked like a service delivery room and took a moment to catch my breath. Christ. I took out my phone and sent Natalie a quick text.

I'm here. You can pay my gym membership for that running effort.

I noticed, then, a guy standing by the door who looked a little familiar. He was a tall Chinese guy, maybe twenty-five, incredibly good looking, dressed in this spring season's Versace suit pants, if I could guess correctly, and he was obviously searching for someone.

I went to the glass front door and unlocked it. "Good morning," I said brightly. "Mr Schroeder?"

He kind of smiled but turned his head and called out, "Bryce? Over here."

So the Versace guy was the associate. I stood aside to welcome him in and waited for Mr Schroeder to appear. I'd get a better look at his face if it wasn't in the sunlight. "I do apologise on behalf of Natalie Yang. She's stuck in traffic in the tunnel, I believe. My name is Michael—"

My words died right there, because the Mr Schroeder who walked in stopped me in my tracks.

SAF stood there, staring at me. My SAF, the Sexy as Fuck, no-complications fuck-buddy who left my place this morning. But he looked different. Gone were the band T-shirts, skinny jeans, and trendy boots. Now he wore dark charcoal pants, Italian wool . . . Brioni, I was certain. His shirt was white, starched, and tailored just for his body.

I'd never seen anything so gorgeous.

He stared at me, and his surprise was replaced with a slow smile. "Michael? I'm sorry, you trailed off there. I didn't catch your last name."

I barked out a laugh, because honestly, what else could I do?

The guy he was with looked between us, then recognition dawned. "Oh . . . Oh, this is your nameless guy?" He stared at me with no attempt at hiding his grin. "Oh, this is perfect."

SAF cleared his throat and nodded toward his friend. "Terrence Huang, this is Michael . . ." He deliberately trailed off.

I shot him a quick dirty glare before turning to Terrence. "Nice to meet you, Terrence. My name is Michael Piersen." Then I looked right at SAF. "Piersen. With an e. P-i-e-r-s-e-n. And you must be Bryson Schroeder."

He stared for a long, heart-stopping moment. "Correct." He held out his hand, which I shook without thinking. "It's very nice to meet you, Michael Piersen. With an e."

"Likewise, Bryson Schroeder," I replied, and we both seemed to notice at the same time that we still had hold of each other's hand.

"Well, I'm glad this isn't awkward at all," Terrence said brightly.

Right. Right. Business first. *Christ, Michael.* I took a step back. "Yes, sorry. As I said before, Natalie sends her apologies. There was an accident in the Harbour Tunnel and she's stuck in gridlocked traffic. Which is most unfortunate. She was disappointed not to be here."

"It's not that unfortunate," SAF replied casually. "I mean, then you wouldn't be here."

I withheld the laugh of incredulity I wanted to let out and focused on the manila folder I was holding instead. I read straight from the listing information. "This site is eighty-six square metres, with existing gas and water connections with grease trap and kitchen exhaust, if you're looking at food and beverage. Approximately twenty metres squared of space is available in the basement, comprising large cool room and secure dry storage. Lease terms are negotiable, one year or three. Rent per annum is fixed at 99,600."

"Eleven hundred and fifty-eight per square metre, Bryce," Terrence said. "Plus fit-out at 1,600 per square metre, and you're going to need 250k upfront. That's 20,800 a month before you start, and if you want to maintain a percent margin of—"

I let them talk about figures and percentages and profit margins. Clearly Terrence was a genius at maths and Bryson wasn't far behind him. I'd have needed a calculator and ten minutes to work that out.

Bryson . . .

His name was Bryson.

It suited him, if names could suit a person.

God, I couldn't believe of all the people in this city that I had to run to meet for a last-minute appointment, it had to be him.

Of all the people.

And Schroeder. He was Schroeder fucking Hotels. When he said he was staying at a hotel in Circular Quay, I just assumed it was temporary, between staying at his dad's and returning from two years overseas.

I had no way of knowing he was living there because his family *owned* it.

Fucking hell.

He'd talked about his dad being successful and a little overbearing at times, with high expectations and standards. It was no wonder, given he was a luxury hotel magnate.

Fucking hell, again.

"Uh, excuse me, Michael?" His voice snapped me from the spiral of my thoughts.

I turned and smiled. "Yes?" God, I hadn't heard a word they'd said.

"You're . . . distracted," Bryson said, smirking like he knew why.

I met his gaze and held it. "Sorry. What can I help you with?" I tried for some modicum of professionalism, though we all knew that ship had sailed the second he'd walked in.

His smug fucking smile just about did me in. "I just asked if we could take a look at the basement storage?"

"Yes, of course. This way," I said, taking them through to the back where the stairs were. I stood at the top of the stairs, giving him space to go down. I assumed he wasn't trying to get me down there by himself—as much as I wished he might.

Bryson got halfway down the steps when he noticed Terrence wasn't following. "Terrence? You coming?"

Terrence looked at me. "No. I'm good, thanks."

Bryson stared at him, firing flaming daggers with his eyes. There was definitely an unspoken conversation between them, but Bryson eventually turned and went down to the basement by himself. It wasn't a big space. He certainly didn't need a babysitter.

I could feel Terrence's gaze burning into me. I glanced his way and he raised an eyebrow. "So . . . you and Bryce?"

I'm sure I blushed scarlet fucking red. "In a professional capacity, Mr Schroeder—"

"Now he's Mr Schroeder?"

Christ. I was getting the third degree by his friend. Who very obviously knew all about me. "I didn't even know his name until twenty minutes ago."

Terrence shook his head. "He's not his name. That's not all he is. He's more than that."

"I know that," I replied a little frostily. Because I did know that. I'd spent weeks getting to know him, little morsels of information here and there, without ever knowing what preconceptions his name would bring. Maybe that's why he didn't want me to know who he was. When I spoke next time, it was more of a whisper. "I know who he is."

Terrence nodded because he knew I got it. Bryson didn't want me to know he was a Schroeder. He wanted me to know who *he* was, not his name.

He was funny and smart, generous and attentive. He was compassionate. He loved movies and TV shows with subtitles, and vintage T-shirts. He loved all kinds of foods, and he carried around the weight of expectations of a rich and famous father. And he was really, really good in bed.

"Don't let this change anything," Terrence murmured just as Bryson came back up the stairs.

"Are you two done talking about me?"

"No," Terrence replied casually. "If you could give us a few more minutes."

Bryson smiled as he trudged up the last few stairs. "Not a chance."

"This place has potential. Great location," I said, my professionalism in tatters. "Can I ask what kind of business you need a space for?"

Bryson looked at me, his eyes filled with a mix of daring and caution. "You can ask, but—"

My phone buzzed in my hand, interrupting him. Natalie's name appeared on the screen. Goddammit. "This is Natalie. I'll have to take this; please excuse me a moment." I stepped away to the front of the store and I saw Bryson shove Terrence and Terrence laughed. This was all going so badly. With a sigh, I answered the call. "Natalie."

"I'm still stuck. Haven't moved at all. How is it going with the client?"

"It's going great. We're still at York Street. I think he likes it, but we'll head to Kent Street now."

"Can I speak to Mr Schroeder?"

I frowned. "Uh, I'm not sure that's necessary?"

She was quiet for a second. "Michael."

Fucking hell.

I walked back over to Bryson and held my phone out. "Sorry to interrupt. Natalie Yang would like a quick word."

Bryson smiled as he took my phone and he looked right at me as he spoke. "Natalie, it's Bryson Schroeder speaking. ... Oh that's fine, these things can't be helped. ... Yes, thank you." His smile widened and his gaze bored into me. "Is that right? ... Excellent. ... Yes, we'll be in touch."

He handed me back my phone and I hit End Call whether Natalie was done talking to me or not. She could damn well text.

"I'm sorry about that," I said.

"No need to apologise," Bryson said with that stupid smug smile I wanted to kiss off his face. "She assured me that you're the best corporate retail property agent in Sydney. And she said I'm in *very* good hands."

I took a deep breath and exhaled slowly. "Is there any other information you need on this location? Or should we head to Kent Street now?"

Bryson grinned but he looked around the empty store. "I like this one. Except the stairs to the basement storage are an issue for accessibility and liability. So that's something I'll have to negotiate. I'll need all the specs to give to my fit-out people for quotes."

"Yes, of course. I can have my office email them to you now, if you'd like? I'm sure Natalie has your email address."

"Yes, she does," he replied. She also probably has all his contact details, his address, and full business proposal . . .

And while I shot a quick text to my assistant, Bryson and Terrence were engaged in some silent eyeball conversation which ended abruptly when Terrence noticed me watching them.

"So," he said, checking his watch. "I just remembered I have a thing. At work. I really should get back there, or my dad will be yelling."

"No you don't," Bryson said.

Terrence ignored him and held his hand out for me to shake. "It was really nice to meet you. And now we have a name, so that's nice."

"Nice to meet you too," I said, though it sounded more like a question.

"Terrence," Bryson cautioned. "You don't have to—"

"Yes, it's a meeting, see?" He held up his phone. The screen was blank. He walked backwards to the door. "And you know what my dad is like. Bryce, I will call you. You owe me dinner. And lunch. And I want details. Okay, bye!"

And he was gone.

I ran my hand through my hair and sighed. "He absolutely didn't have a meeting, did he?"

"No. But for the record, I didn't know he was going to bail."

"I could tell," I replied. "By the panic in your eyes."

He laughed. "That wasn't panic. That was my 'Terrence, I'm going to kill you' look."

"Oh, right."

"Yeah, we perfected that in college. I have it down to a fine art now."

I met his gaze, and all the tension melted away. I shook my head and laughed. "What are the odds that I'd get called in at the last minute to show some guy a property and it turns out to be you, huh?"

"Well, if we're going with just the population of Sydney, I'm going to go with about one in four million. If we opt for 'anyone in the world,' it'd be closer to one in about eight billion."

"Correct."

"But now we know each other's names," he said. There was something unreadable in his eyes. Was it defence? Was it fear? Vulnerability? It wounded me that he would fear a negative reaction because now I knew who he really was.

"So, is it Bryson or Bryce? Or can I just keep calling you SAF?"

He grinned. "My friends call me Bryce."

I bit the inside of my lip so I didn't smile too big. He considered me one of his friends. And not the friend-zone kind either, but more than an acquaintance. But that did bring up the professional aspect of this exchange. "I, uh, god, I really should apologise," I said.

"What for?"

"For how unprofessional I've been with you. Today, I mean. Your friend Terrence probably thinks I'm the least professional property agent he's ever encountered, but seeing you walk in here knocked me off my game. Natalie would be horrified if she were here and saw me try and speak."

"Well, I won't tell Natalie if you don't." His smile was slow and genuine. "I'm just kidding. You were fine. And don't mind Terrence. He's a great guy. He absolutely bailed out of here so we could talk. You know, about skirting around the professional slash personal boundaries in private."

I laughed quietly. "Gee, I don't know . . . I thought the whole awkward inability to string a sentence together thing was working really well for me. I'm normally a little switched on. I wasn't expecting it to be you."

Bryce met my gaze. "Disappointed?"

"What? No, of course not. Why would I be disappointed? I think 'shocked' would be the operative word here."

He smiled that sweet, almost shy-like smile before he looked around the storefront. "For what it's worth, I wasn't expecting the person we were meeting for these inspections to be you either."

"Are you disappointed?"

He barked out a laugh that sounded way too casual. "Absolutely not."

I had trouble looking away. I also had trouble gathering my thoughts and trying to lead this meeting. "Should we go to the second storefront?" I asked. "It's on Kent. It's not a far walk."

"Yes, we should do that."

"But you like this site? It could have potential?"

"Mm," he said. "I do. I think I like the location. I could make it work."

He didn't sound convinced. Not that I knew what he needed the site for. "Okay then, I'll lock this one up and we can get going."

Bryce nodded and waited for me to make sure everything was locked, and soon enough, we were walking down the footpath toward Kent Street. "Did you really run here?" he asked.

"I did. Natalie gave me fifteen minutes to get here."

"Lucky you're fit then," he said, giving me a smirk and a raised eyebrow. "I mean, your endurance is noteworthy."

Oh my god.

I shot him a glare and pretended to snarl at him, but I was thankful I was still holding the manila folder so I didn't do something stupid like shove him into traffic or try to hold his hand.

I changed the subject. "I must say, the suit is nice and all, but I think I prefer the Purple Rain shirt."

He grinned. "You already know how I feel about you in your suit."

I laughed. He wanted me to wear it when I opened the door on Friday night. "Right. The robe has lost its appeal. I forgot."

"Oh no, the appeal of the robe still exists. But those pants and your—"

I stopped walking. "Okay. I think I need to stop you right there."

Laughing, he took my arm and pulled me out of the way of the hurrying pedestrians. He didn't apologise for talking about my arse and what he wanted to do to it while bending me over my couch, as he'd described this morning. "You're right. This is business."

"But you're not sorry."

"No, I'm not." Those brown eyes glimmered with humour in the sunlight. "But I will behave. This new business is serious, and it's important to me. It's just when I'm around you, I forget . . ." He took his hand from my arm and ran his fingers through his hair, and whatever he was about to say was gone.

"I was going to say that I needed to stop you right there because thinking about what you said to me this morning, about how you wanted to undo my suit pants as soon as I opened the door, makes it hard—" Ugh, wrong word. "Makes it difficult to think about work."

He smiled at that. "Agreed. It most certainly does make it . . . hard."

I sighed. "Are you twelve?"

"Around you, yes. It would seem so."

I didn't want to find that endearing. I didn't want to like the fact that he could let his guard down around me. But a smile won out. "Come on, Kent Street's this way."

We found the storefront, I unlocked the door, and I knew from the second Bryce stepped inside, it wasn't what he wanted. The layout would need more work than the previous place. It was cheaper rent but the location wasn't ideal.

Bryce stepped out measurements, he tried to envisage how it would all work. "The counter would have to run this way for the refrigeration," he said, panning his hands along the side wall. "And that looks like a load-bearing wall so it can't be moved, unless we're talking major recessed beams . . ." He groaned. "I saw the plans and photos and thought maybe it could work."

"It's not right for you," I replied. "Not that I know exactly what you want the space for. And you don't have to tell me. That's fair. But I know almost every available retail site in the city centre. If I knew the purpose, maybe I could actually help."

Bryce looked right at me and paused, as though he was weighing up whether he should trust me. "I haven't told many people," he said. "Basically, my father, the mates I was out with the other night, and my banker."

"Fair enough."

"It's not that I don't want to tell you." He made a face. "I just don't want you to think it's stupid. I don't want anyone to tell me it's stupid."

"I would never tell you it's stupid?"

"Unless it's legitimately stupid."

I laughed. "Unless it's morally or ethically questionable. Maybe not even then. No idea is stupid. It just needs to be done properly and marketed right."

He smiled as if my words excited him. "Exactly! That's what I said!"

"If someone tells you it can't be done, what they're saying is *they* couldn't do it. If they're not good enough or not brave enough to make it happen is something only they can answer." I shrugged. Given that he was moving ahead with the venture told me his banker was on board, and Terrence was here with him today, so his mates were okay with it. And from the three groups of people he said he'd told, that only left his father.

Man, that sucks. Maybe what I'd said was a bit harsh, so I added, "People close to you shouldn't tell you not to do something. They should still be supportive and say, 'Let's look at how best to market this,' instead. Or open discussions on how to best tackle the problems."

Bryce stared at me, then took three long strides toward me, grabbed my face in his hands, and kissed me soundly on the lips.

"Thank you for saying that. Everything you just said is exactly how I feel."

I wasn't even remotely sorry that he'd kissed me while we were both working. We were very much alone, and no one could see inside the store. And how could I be sorry when what I'd said had plucked an emotional chord in him?

"Sorry, I shouldn't have kissed you. I just . . ."

My face felt as if it were on fire. "Don't be sorry."

He put his hand to his forehead, shook his head a little, and smiled. "I don't know what it is about you . . ."

I laughed. "What?"

He met my gaze again, his stare intense. "Do you know what kopi is?"

CHAPTER EIGHT

BRYCE

"KOPI," he repeated. "That's coffee, right?"

I grinned, relieved. I never had any intention of telling him about my plans, but once I'd started, I had to wonder why I'd ever considered keeping it from him.

He was supportive and excited, and he was, surprisingly, very insightful.

Why was I even shocked though?

He surprised me at every turn.

The more I told him about my concept, the more excited he got and the more excited I got. He could visualise everything I told him. He asked questions—*so many questions*—but his interest was genuine and well thought out. He wasn't just nodding and smiling. He wanted to know things like products and location ideas.

"But this place is a bust."

"Yeah, it's no good. Not for what you need."

"I think the York Street site was good. There was one I looked at yesterday too, it was on Pitt Street. It wasn't bad."

Michael shot me a look, and I wondered if he'd be

pissed that I'd seen other properties. But nope. Like I said, surprising.

"King Street would be good if you can get it," he said. "Pitt Street and York are both great locations." But then his eyebrows knitted together. "Can I ask you something?"

"Sure."

"You seem set on a business district or finance district location, and high-end retail."

I nodded. "Yes."

"And that's great."

"But?"

He smiled. "But . . . I could have a location that would suit you perfectly."

Hmm. "Where is it?"

"King Street Wharf, Darling Harbour."

I stared at him. Actually, I think my eyeballs almost fell out of my head. "Darling Harbour?"

He nodded. "Yes."

"What kind of outlay are we talking? Natalie never mentioned it."

"Because it's not official yet. The ink's not dry on the contracts. And Natalie will probably kick my arse for telling you. But Bryce, I think it could be perfect for you."

My heart banged against my ribs. "Say that again."

He tilted his head. "Which part? The Natalie kicking my arse part? Or the ink not being dry?"

I chuckled and stepped in close. I lifted his chin and got lost in those sapphire eyes. "You know which part."

His pupils dilated and his breath caught. He breathed the word I wanted to hear. "Bryce."

I kissed him again, harder and deeper this time, tasting my name on his tongue. And so God help me, it was divine.

A buzzing phone interrupted us, which was probably

just as well. It was Michael's phone, and he took a step back from me, flushed cheeks and dazed, and answered the call. "Michael Piersen speaking."

I couldn't hear the words exactly, but the caller sounded female, and my money was on Natalie.

"We're almost done here anyway," Michael said. "No, I have a one o'clock with Hardy and Co. ... Okay good, I'll see you there."

He clicked off the call and pocketed his phone. "The accident in the tunnel has been cleared. Natalie's finally moving again."

I checked my watch; it was almost twelve. I'd already kept him longer than I should have. "Shame we can't grab lunch," I said lightly. "But you have a one o'clock today."

"I have a one o'clock, a two o'clock, a three o'clock."

"Busy man."

"Always."

"Are you free for dinner?"

He smiled. "Tonight? Are we now doing Thursdays as well?"

"I'm not going to lie to you, Michael. I thought we could grab dinner on the King Street Wharf and you could show me the vacant store you were telling me about."

He laughed. "I can show you the outside. But the interior is off-limits until the aforementioned ink dries."

"Seven o'clock."

"Ooh, early dinner. Usually reserved for people with children or by the elderly folk who like to be home by eight."

"Or reserved by a guy who wants to eat early so he can then scope out a new venue, and then," I added brightly, "perhaps more sex."

"More sex? Does this impede on the three-times quota?"

He made me smile. "You drive a hard bargain."

"I'm having some serious concerns for my ar—a certain part of my anatomy. Given the bargain you drive is not small, by any means."

I barked out a laugh. "Well, I'm all for giving that certain part of your anatomy a break, but I seem to recall someone begging for it."

"Begging is a strong choice of verb. It implies the desperation of a homeless person in a Charles Dickens' book."

Chuckling, I cupped my hands and held them to him. "Please, sir. Can I have some more?"

He laughed, and the sound, the look on his face, did strange things to my heart. He shoved my shoulder. "Let's get out of here."

Michael locked up the store and we stopped out on the footpath. "So," I hedged. "I was serious about dinner. I know that'll be two nights in a row and then tomorrow is our normal Friday night thing. So if you wanted to do one and not the other, I'll understand."

"How about I see what I can do about getting us access before we make plans. Like I said, I don't even know if I can get us into the place. It's a new listing for us and I think they're still working on stripping out the last storefront."

"Natalie said you were the best," I replied. "I'm sure the best commercial property agent in the city has a few strings he can pull."

He narrowed his eyes at me, and after a few long seconds' stand-off, he growled and pulled out his phone. "I will make a phone call. You will be nice to me and you'll never again spout any of that 'best commercial property agent in the city' bullshit ever again."

He didn't give me a chance to reply, though I did grin at

him as he called someone and put the phone to his ear. "Yes, hi Carolyne, it's Michael."

He asked a string of questions, spoke to someone else, had someone relay a message, and disconnected the call. He looked right at me. "We have twenty minutes. Not a minute more."

"Now?"

"Yes, now."

No sooner had he tapped the Uber app that a car arrived. Michael opened the door for me, I grinned as I got in, and he rolled his eyes. "See?" I said. "You do have strings that you can pull."

He did that growly thing again. "I can't believe I'm doing this. And I want you to know that I'm not doing this for you because we have . . . a thing. I treat all clients the same."

"But you just said you can't believe you're doing this." I nudged his knee with mine. "Which is conflicting. So why are you doing this for me?"

He glared at me. "Shut up."

I grinned. "And I sincerely hope you don't treat all your clients the way you treat me." He raised an eyebrow, so I clarified. "You don't wear that robe for them, do you?"

"That robe," he said, glancing at the driver. He shot me a look, then whispered, "That robe and whom I wear it for is none of your business."

I pouted, because well, yeah, while it was none of my business, I wanted it to be. We had a casual agreement, nothing permanent and certainly nothing exclusive. "Did you just use the word 'whom' at me? Wow, I think I'm turned on."

"You're insufferable." He sighed. "And no. I haven't worn that robe for anyone else. See, I have this mutual agreement with some guy who likes me to wear it for him. It was supposed to be one day a week and *un*complicated."

I couldn't help but smile. "How's that working out?"

"It's a disaster. He now comes over twice a week. I'll be seeing him three times this week. He's taking me out for dinner tonight, and he's paying." He gave me a pointed glare on the last part. "And today, our professional lives just met like a car crash. Oh, and my boss is going to be pissed, but I can't seem to bring myself to care. So yeah. It's the opposite of uncomplicated."

"A disaster. Now that sounds like fun. Even though you've used words like car crash, disaster, and complicated. Or maybe it's fun because you used those words?"

He chuckled warmly. "Did I mention he's cocky and self-assured?"

"No, but I think you called him Sexy as Fuck a few times."

He laughed again as the car pulled up at the curb, so we thanked the driver and got out. Michael was already walking and I had to jog a little to catch up. "We have twelve minutes," he declared.

We walked down a short accessway to the promenade of King Street Wharf. Darling Harbour was a hub of tourists and locals on any given day. Thousands of people came through here every hour for food or photos, boat tours, or shopping.

"Why were you so set on a CBD location?" Michael asked, still walking at pace.

"I didn't think somewhere like this was an option. I don't know, to be honest. I was aiming at the inner city, office workers, shoppers. I wanted my first store to be an inner-city location because it made sense. I was aiming at the finance district because it's what I know. I know that market, those people, how they behave, and how they spend."

He nodded. "Okay. Makes sense."

"I considered the Queen Victoria Building," I added. "For about two seconds."

Michael made a face. "Different market." He stopped walking. "But I know someone who could get you a look in if it's something you wanted to pursue. It's not my firm, but I know other agents."

"You'd pass me off?"

"In a heartbeat. If it was the right thing to do for the success of your business, yes, I would. I'm not here to set you up in the wrong location just to take a commission. That's not what I do. The right or wrong location is the difference between great and mediocre. And I don't do mediocre."

His words squeezed around my heart. I nodded, unprepared for how hard that hit me. He wanted me to succeed even if it cost him the listing. "Thank you." I checked my watch. "I think we're down to about nine minutes. Should we keep going?"

"We're here," he said. I turned to the storefront outside of which we'd stopped. It was at the prime centre of the wharf. This wasn't just prime retail space; this was a world-class position. The glass walls were covered up with panelling branded with a construction company's logo. Michael pushed on the front door and a guy in work gear came over. "Silvan, Michael Piersen," he said, shaking the guy's hand. "My office called and said we'd be here. Two minutes tops and we'll be out of your hair."

It was interesting to watch Michael do what he does. Talking now, he was all business, sharp and focused, like he owned the city. Not like the flustered guy he'd been at the first location. I liked that he'd been so rattled by my presence. Surely that meant something, right? Surely that implied he had some kind of feelings for me. Good or bad, I wasn't sure. But he felt something enough to be derailed. I mean, if I meant nothing to him, if he couldn't have cared less, then he wouldn't have missed a beat.

I meant something to him.

And that made me happier than it had any right to.

Concentrate, Bryce.

Great. Now who was the rattled one?

Silvan gave us a bright smile. "Perfect for a two-minute coffee break, yes?" He called out to one of his workers who was just about to put an angle grinder to old wall signage. "Two minutes, smoko time!"

Another guy appeared, covered in paint or plaster, or both, and the three of them vanished out into the back room.

Michael turned to me. "You've got two minutes."

There was a kitchen out the back, a storeroom, perfect natural lighting. Well, there would be when it wasn't boarded up. There was more than enough room, and the dimensions for my layout were perfect.

Michael rattled off some specs. "One hundred and thirty square metres. Expected rent will be eleven hundred per square metre, so it's more than York Street. Obviously."

"Obviously."

"Meets all code requirements for accessibility and it has a five-star energy rating. And Barangaroo has just opened up a few hundred apartments and more retail space. It's going to get busier."

I stared at the front of the store, imagining the view on the other side of the boarded glass wall. The people walking past, more tourists than businesspeople, probably. People on holiday, shopping, walking on a lunchbreak. Boats on the water, ferries, water-taxis, cruises, and yachts.

Was this the aesthetic I was going for?

"Bryce?"

I turned to Michael, no idea if I'd missed anything he'd said.

"I want it," I said. "You were right. This is perfect. It's not what I pictured at first, and I can't believe I never contemplated it. I feel stupid for not considering it. I was adamant on an inner-city vibe. Well, at least I thought I was. But this feels right."

He smiled but there was an edge to it that I didn't like, as though he was trying really hard not to say something. We said thanks and goodbye to Silvan and his team, and they locked the door behind us.

The view from the front of the store was incredible. The harbour, the people, the energy. Now that I'd seen this place and realised it was a possibility, I wanted nowhere else.

Michael began walking back to Lime Street. "I need to keep going. I have a one o'clock I can't be late for."

"But you haven't had lunch yet," I said, feeling stupid as soon as the words were out of my mouth. "Remember what happened when you skipped lunch the other day?"

He smirked but there was definitely something wrong.

"Michael, what aren't you telling me?"

He stopped walking, and he met my eyes. He went to say something, but in the end he groaned, frustrated. "I shouldn't have shown you that place."

"What?" What the fuck? "Why not?"

"Because I can't guarantee you'll get it. While I'd like to say it's a possibility, it's highly likely it'll go to someone else."

"If I can't have it, why the hell did you show it to me?"

"Because I knew it'd be perfect. I want you to have the perfect place. And it was a good idea until you looked at me like you did back there . . ." He ran his hand through his hair. "Fuck!"

What? "How did I look at you back there?"

"You smiled . . . you smiled at me like . . ." He shook his head. "And now you'll blame me if you don't get it. Which will be fair. It will be my fault, and I don't want you to blame me. I don't want to see that smile die in front of me because I couldn't get you this place."

How I smiled at him?

"Michael . . ."

"Sorry. I just wasn't expecting—" He broke off, then tried again. "I will do everything I can to make sure you get this place. But don't bank on it yet. I wish I could say it was yours right now, Bryce. God, this isn't supposed to be so hard."

"I won't blame you," I said. "I know how these things work. But I have every confidence in you."

He growled. "Bryce. I'm being serious."

"And so am I. You're the best retail agent in Sydney, right?"

He gave me a death glare. Those blue eyes were like glass.

"Michael," I replied gently. "Pull those strings you can pull, and do what you're clearly very good at doing."

"Just don't hate me if it all goes to shit."

"Hate you?"

"The way you smiled at me back there told me how disappointed you'll be."

I shook my head. How could I tell him the way I smiled at him had nothing to do with the goddamn store? "It's not that," I said lamely. God, this was getting more and more complicated. "You're going to be late for your one o'clock and you still haven't eaten. Can we talk about this later?"

He swallowed hard and conceded a nod. "I'll call you if I have news."

"We're still having dinner tonight, right?"

Christ. Did that sound desperate? It definitely sounded desperate. Fuck.

Hello, complicated. Nice to meet you. My name is Bryson Schroeder, and I'm in way over my head.

I cleared my throat. "I mean, we don't have to go out to do a site inspection now because we've done it. But you missed lunch and that's my fault, so it's only right that I buy you dinner."

He studied my face, and for a godawful moment, I thought he was going to say no.

"Text me."

I nodded, chewing on my lip so I didn't grin like an idiot. He turned and disappeared into the crowd.

I quickly thumbed out a message to his number. *I'll pick you up at 7:30pm out the front of your place. Wear that suit.*

His reply was almost immediate. *Because there's a dress code? Or because you want to take it off me?*

I laughed. *Both.*

Now I just had to figure out where I wanted to take him. Somewhere special but not too special. I might be very well aware that I was in over my head, but I didn't need to broadcast it.

Bloody hell. Terrence was going to have a field day with me.

I turned around and took a photo of the shop, even with the front all boarded up. Then I took a photo of the view of the harbour.

I wanted it. This was it. This was the location. I could feel it.

But then the firing squad called me. His name flashed across my screen. "Terrence. I was just thinking about you."

"I have five minutes. Tell me everything."

CHAPTER NINE

_____

MICHAEL

I RACED into the office to swap job files, knowing Natalie would pounce on me as soon as I walked through the door. She met me in the hallway. "Where have you been?"

"With Mr Schroeder," I replied. "Natalie, I have a one o'clock in Pitt Street."

"How did it go?" she pressed, following me into my office.

"It went well. Kent Street is a no. York Street is a possibility."

She was confused. "A possibility? You said it went well."

"I took him to see the Mortimer property on the wharf."

She froze. "You what?"

I picked up the next job file and met her gaze. "I took him to the King Street Wharf property."

I could see her mind turning and her blood pressure rising. It appeared she'd lost the ability to speak for a moment. "Wh-why would you do that?"

"You said you wanted him as a client. That was the only instruction you gave me before I had fifteen minutes to run halfway across the city to meet him." That probably wasn't fair, but it wasn't a lie. "So we talked about his business and what he wanted and, as is my job to do so, I assessed his needs to our most suited property listings."

"It's not even a done deal, Michael," she cried. "What if—"

"I will make it a done deal. I will see it through." I held up the file like some kind of stupid shield as I walked around my desk toward where she stood in the middle of my office. "I have a client to meet. Natalie, we can talk about this later." I spotted Carolyne hovering outside the door, and she was quick to walk with me as I paced back to the elevators. "Pull everything you have on the King Street Wharf property and draft up a lease proposal for a Mr Bryson Schroeder."

She nodded, and as I stepped into the elevator, I added, "And please order me a sandwich or a salad or even a tub of yoghurt for when I get back."

She smiled and nodded as the doors closed. I checked my watch. I now had eleven minutes to get to Pitt Street.

I WALKED out of my apartment complex at 7:31pm to find a very sleek black Porsche 911 waiting. I paused, because it had never occurred to me to ask Bryce what kind of car he had, when the driver leaned over and opened the passenger door.

Of course he drove a Porsche.

I slid into the seat and noticed his charcoal pants and perfectly fitted white shirt. He grinned at me. "You're one minute late."

"If you'd arrived two minutes ago, you'd have seen me get home."

"You're just finishing?"

"I literally walked in, washed my face, brushed my teeth, put on deodorant, and walked back out. Lucky you requested me not to change my clothes because I didn't have time."

"I really do like that suit on you. But if you want to stay in . . ."

"No, what I want is a mountain of food."

He grinned. "That's what I like to hear."

"Nice car, by the way."

"Thanks. I've been waiting for this model for a while." He slipped it into gear and the engine purred as he pulled out onto the road. "I wanted electric, so I had to wait."

"Electric?"

He drove through the city streets like a pro. "I try to make greener choices when I can. I'm a bit of an environmentalist, if you can believe that."

I smiled at him as he drove. "I can believe that."

He afforded me a quick glance before he concentrated on the road. "It's not easy. Especially with the travelling I've done over the last two years. But I do try. It's part of my mission statement for my business to leave as small a carbon footprint as I can. It's more expensive, of course, but it's the right thing to do."

I really liked that about him. It spoke of principles, and with most guys like him I knew —rich, affluent, worldly— everything was usually disposable. No matter what it was, just throw it away and get a new one when you were sick of looking at it.

I liked that he was different.

It was then I noticed we were heading out of the city. "So where are we going?"

"Ah," he said with a grin. "I had myself a situation trying to think of where to take you."

"A situation?"

He chuckled. "Yep. I could have booked us in at Aria's or Bentley's. Just make a phone call, drop my name . . . you know." He shrugged. Jesus. Those were just two of the most expensive fine-dining restaurants in the city. "But I wanted somewhere a little more me."

"And that was your situation?"

"Well, yeah." He shifted in his seat. "Did I take you somewhere fancy to impress you? Or did I take you somewhere that showed you who I was?"

Oh.

A thrill raced through me. He wanted to impress me. He wanted me to know who he was. My hands were suddenly clammy and I found it hard to speak. "You taking me somewhere to show me the real you is the best way to impress me."

He took his eyes off the traffic so he could grin at me. He seemed relieved, as though it was a possibility that he was as nervous as me.

In no time at all, we were in Newtown, and he pulled into a parking spot. "Well, this is it."

I looked out my window. There were a few restaurants and cafés and I was interested to see which one he chose. Only he didn't walk into any of them. He headed for a dark alley, and I started to worry . . . until he laughed and took my hand. "You'll love it, I promise."

To be honest, I didn't care anymore because . . . he was holding my hand.

He led me to a gate in a brick wall, opened it like he

owned it. The gate opened to a set of stairs that went down below street level to another wooden door. He pressed a button, flashed me a bright smile, and when the door opened, it revealed a restaurant.

It was dark and neon-lit, with red lanterns hanging from the low ceiling. Obscure Asian murals graced the walls. It reminded me of an underground war-time resistance bar, only set in the 22nd century. Old but futuristic. Somehow. I wasn't sure how else to describe it. There were people at tables, eating and talking, laughing. Some kind of jazz played in the background.

We were shown to a private booth—had he requested that?—and it was then I noticed that Bryce was speaking to the waiter . . . in Japanese?

Because, of course, he spoke Japanese.

We were seated and he smiled across from me. "What do you think?"

"It's amazing. It has a Blade Runner feel."

He grinned at that. "Great analogy. The food here is the best I've had anywhere. It's like a Japanese burger joint. Which sounds weird."

"But there's a reason why you chose this over a place like Aria's or Bentley's."

"Exactly."

"And you speak Japanese?"

"A little. Enough to get by." His lips twisted in a cute pout. "And Malay, and a little Chinese, and Korean but probably only enough to say 'hello' and 'where are the bathrooms?'."

I chuckled. "Well, that's a lot more than me." I studied him for a second. "You miss Singapore?"

He gave a nod. "I do. It's an amazing city. I made some friends there, and the food is out of this world."

"And the coffee . . ." I added with a grin.

He laughed. "Oh yes. Kopi is an entire experience."

"It is." Then I thought of something. "So does your business have a name?"

"Ah." He blushed and sat back in his seat. "It does. I think. But it might sound stupid. I don't know yet. I've had a logo done but I'm having second thoughts . . ."

"Why?"

He shrugged. "It might be . . . immature. I dunno."

"What is it?" I was more than curious now.

"Kopi Kat." He tapped his fingertip on the table and chewed on his lip. "The cat is just an outline of a few lines. It's quite stylish but . . ." He thumbed his phone screen and showed me a picture of his logo. It was gorgeous.

"Oh, I love that. I think it's a standout."

"Really? You're not just saying that?"

"No, not at all. It's easily identifiable, sleek, and the product merchandising options are limitless." I smiled at him. "I see hundreds of logos a day. This is good."

His grin was real and I could feel the relief roll off him. "Thank you."

The waiter returned and Bryce took the liberty of ordering. We'd eaten together enough times for me to trust his judgement. I was famished and it probably wouldn't have mattered what he ordered, I would gladly eat it.

"So, was your boss pissed at you?"

"Yep. But I was so busy this afternoon we couldn't really duke it out. I left a message for the owners at the wharf property that I had a tenant ready to move forward."

"You did?"

"Yes. And I'm sure Natalie will have something to say about that tomorrow."

"I don't want you to get into trouble," he said gently. "That was never my intention."

"It's nothing," I assured him. "She's just pissed that I found you what you were after. It's a dog-eat-dog industry. She understands that. And she'll see that when she's over the butthurt. Our priority is the customer's satisfaction."

"Well," he said suggestively. He leaned in and whispered, "We both know you keep me very satisfied."

I rolled my eyes at that.

"Can I ask you something?" he added, serious again. "What would happen if she found out about us?"

I let out a breath. "I don't know."

His eyes widened a little. "Should we be out together in public?"

I chuckled. "We knew each other before today, and she asked me to take your appointment. It wasn't my idea. It's not like I lined this up."

He chewed on the inside of his lip. "I don't want you to get in trouble."

"If it's an issue, I'll hand your file back to Natalie. I probably should anyway. Once I hear back from the owners and you've signed the agreements, she can have you."

He snorted. "Thanks."

"She's very good."

He nodded. "But she wouldn't have offered to show me the wharf store. She wouldn't have asked me all the questions about my business. She wouldn't have . . . cared, I guess, for the want of a better word."

I sipped my water, ignoring the heat in my cheeks. "Can I ask you a question?"

There was the tiniest flinch in his eyes. "Sure."

"How old are you?"

He smirked, and he took a long moment to answer. "I'm twenty-six."

That surprised me. He seemed older. "How long have you and Terrence been friends for?"

"Since we were eighteen. We met in business college and we just clicked. He's the smartest guy I know. He's funny as hell. And he . . ." Bryce frowned. "He works for his father's business, so we have a lot in common."

Hmm. Another mention of his father, and again it was not a good vibe. I wasn't going to bring it up though. I didn't want to sour the mood.

"He's clearly very fond of you," I said. "Terrence, I mean."

"God, do I even want to know what he said to you when I left you two alone? He wouldn't tell me when I asked."

I chuckled. "It wasn't the 'you hurt him and I'll hurt you' speech exactly, but he was fairly direct. And full respect to him, honestly. He was just looking out for you."

He groaned. "Well, he likes you. Whatever you said to him, he said you were okay. And he's never said that about anyone I've been seeing."

Oh wow. So now we were seeing each other?

Well, I guess we were. To some degree. It was just weird to hear him say it. My belly tightened and I couldn't deny the thrill that rushed along my veins, and I was relieved when our meals arrived.

Bryce wasn't kidding when he said the food was amazing, and I ate way more than I should have.

"How did you hear about this place?" I asked, putting my cutlery on the plate. I literally couldn't eat another bite.

"Massa, a friend of mine. How he heard about it is anyone's guess."

"Well, thank him for me. That meal was amazing."

He laughed. "I'm not telling him. He'll ask if I blind-folded you to get here. It must remain a secret."

I laughed at that. "The *Fight Club* of restaurants."

Bryce chuckled. "Is that what me bringing you here says about me? I should have chosen Aria's."

"Hell no. You wanted to bring me to a place that told me who you are. This place is all you."

"I'm *Blade Runner*?" He pretended to be offended. "Guess it could be worse."

"That movie was epic, by the way. But this place is very you."

He leaned back in his seat and met my gaze. "How so?"

Oh god. How to phrase this? "Well, you want to fly under the radar, no fanfare, no pretences. You're fine dining without the signage and pretentious advertising. Under-stated, a little eclectic, but genuine."

He let out a small laugh and a bloom of blush crept down his neck. That was new.

Maybe that was too serious. Maybe what I'd said gave too much away. So I leaned in and whispered, "And like the meal sizes, you're also bigger than I thought I could handle, but I managed to fit it all in." I leaned back and rubbed my belly, though we both knew I wasn't talking about my stomach or food.

He barked out a laugh. "You do handle it very well."

I chuckled. "Why, thank you."

He stared at me for a long moment with a happy smile. "So, what's the Michael Piersen story?" he asked. "Given you made a point of spelling Piersen, is that Dutch?"

"My grandparents came from the Netherlands," I explained. "People usually spell it wrong. And the Michael Piersen story is quite boring, to be honest. I went to Knox Grammar and started at CREA the summer I graduated. They paid for me to get qualified, and here I am."

"So, entry-level, and you worked your way up."

"I worked my arse off."

He nodded. "Considering your apartment is over-looking Darling Harbour, I can see that."

"What about you?"

"I went to Sydney Grammar," he replied.

"Oh, sorry to hear that."

He laughed because Knox and Sydney Grammar were two of the most prestigious boys' high schools and were competitive in almost every field.

"Wonder what would have happened if we'd met on a rugby field in high school," he mused.

"Well, first of all, you'd need to assume I ever played rugby."

"Oh, I know you didn't."

"How so?"

"One, your nose is perfectly straight. And two, I'd have remembered you."

I chuckled. "Do you really think I could have ever played a full-contact sport like rugby? I'd have been snapped in half. You'd have met me in the library or the pool, swimming laps. And that's only if you were looking at older guys, because I'm two years older than you."

He raised an eyebrow. "Is that right?"

"I'm twenty-eight."

He grinned. "And you have a sister?"

Okay, so now the personal questions were flying. "Yes. Susannah. She's twenty-five."

"And you're close?"

"Yep. We meet once or twice a week."

"I wish I had a sister," he admitted.

"You know, I'm pretty sure the only people who say that are those who never had a sister growing up." I smirked at him. "Just kidding. I was probably more high maintenance than she ever was."

"You? High maintenance? I can't see that at all."

"Your ability to pull off sarcasm needs some work."

He laughed again, then turned his glass of water in a half-circle, his smile fading away. "A sibling would have been good. Being an only child is being the lonely child." He met my eyes then. "That sounds really morose, sorry."

"Don't apologise. And hey, if you want, I can loan you my sister. Then she can spend hours on end telling you of all the mistakes you've made, and not me."

That earned me a smile. "Hmm, maybe she could spill all the dirty details about you and all those mistakes you've made. Were any of them good enough to make twice?"

"There would be clauses regarding that. And subclauses and subsections regarding all secrets, dirty or otherwise. And no, very rarely was any mistake made twice. Though there was this one guy . . . The second time was a mistake, but the third time was definitely a choice."

He laughed. "I hope I don't fall into that category."

"Oh no. No mistakes were made. Unless we count today where we found out each other's names. If that was something you were trying to keep under wraps."

"Nope. I was going to tell you this morning. I asked you if you wanted to know my name and you said no."

"I was trying to give you the impression I didn't care."

His smile softened and his eyes were warm. "You were quite flustered when you showed us the York Street property."

"Quite flustered? I was a shambles, and I couldn't think straight. I really must apologise for that."

"Oh no, don't be sorry. I liked it."

"You liked that I spoke like an idiot?"

He grinned. "No. I like that I made you speechless."

I sighed, ignoring how hard I blushed. Maybe he couldn't tell from the red lantern above us . . . But then his gaze went to my cheeks and my neck and back up to my eyes, and I knew he saw it. "Is that a rash?"

"Fuck you," I whispered, making him burst out laughing.

"Are you ready to go?" he asked.

"No, I'd like to stay and be humiliated some more. I'm having a lot of fun."

He chuckled and reached over to squeeze my hand. No, not squeeze. He clasped my hand, giving it a bit of a squeeze, but then he threaded his fingers with mine and kept it there. He was holding my hand . . . "I'm glad I brought you here," he said quietly.

"I am too," I managed to say, barely above a rough whisper. I remembered how he stood on the street and watched me walk to work this morning. *God, was that today?* "It's been a pretty good day."

His smiling eyes met mine. "It has."

He signalled for a waiter, paid the tab, and we left. Not before I got an exquisite view of his arse and that fucking bulge in the front of those dark grey suit pants. He, of course, caught me checking him out. "See something you like?"

"I was just thinking that the suit designers and fitters at Brioni should get a pay rise and possibly a commendation of merit for their aesthetic efforts to gay men all over the world."

He laughed again. "I'll tell them that at my next fitting."

He held the door for me but I stopped at the bottom of

the stairs. "There's a very good chance the body in the suit pants is the reason they fit so well," I said. "So Brioni can't take all the credit."

But then, of course, I had to walk up the stairs in front of him, giving him the perfect view of my backside. "I could say the same about your arse in that suit, but you already know I like it on you."

I waited for him in the alley. "Yes, your eyes almost fell out of your head this morning. And you wanted me to wear this now when I open the door on Friday nights."

He grinned. "Hell yes. But then I'll miss the robe. It really is a conundrum. Maybe you could wear the suit on Wednesdays and the robe on Fridays. Or vice versa."

We walked toward his car. "Or," I replied, "I can wear whatever the hell I want. It's only going to end up on the floor anyway."

Bryce laughed. "That's very true. And in all honesty, I don't care what you wear. I don't care what anyone wears."

"Oh, I know. I seem to remember you taking me out of my gym clothes with just as much enthusiasm. And you wear vintage band T-shirts."

He opened the passenger door for me. "Don't knock my band shirts."

I smiled as I slid into my seat. "Thank you."

He closed the door gently and walked around the front of the car to his side. When he sat behind the steering wheel, I added, "I'm not knocking your band shirts. I secretly love them. The night we first met, it was your shirt I noticed first."

"You did?"

"For sure. In a bar full of expensive suits and egos, you walked in wearing a faded T-shirt with The Clash on it. You gave no fucks what anyone thought. Actually, my first thought when I saw you was that you didn't fit in in that bar. But now I realise I had that very wrong."

"Oh no. You were right. I don't fit in with that crowd."

I shook my head. "No, what I assumed was wrong," I clarified. "My first thought was that you didn't belong there, surrounded by ten-thousand-dollar suits, because you weren't rich enough. And that's where I was wrong. You don't fit in with that crowd because you're better than them."

"You think money means—"

"No," I reached over and took his hand. "I'm not explaining this right. It's not the money. Not to you. But it is to them. That's all it is to them. They think respect and self-worth are directly proportionate to their net value. But you're not like that. You walked into that bar wearing jeans and a T-shirt with more integrity than they could dream of. Because you know your self-worth, and you know that fake bullshit is cheap." I sighed, hoping I'd explained myself. "That was my first impression of you. Confident, classy, and sexy as fuck. In a vintage The Clash shirt."

"I get what you're saying. Thank you for explaining."

"Did I explain it right? What I mean is that you're not superficial like most of those guys. And I should clarify that yes, I can pick expensive clothes and shoes a mile off, but that's more to do with my love of fashion and my job. I can usually tell what kind of client I'm dealing with by what they wear. Sorry if that sounds shallow. It's not always completely accurate, but it tends to cut away a lot of wasted time."

"Not at all," he replied. "I get that." He played with my hand, running his thumb over my knuckles and fingers. "Want to know what my first impression of you was?"

"Um, probably not. But yes."

He smiled. "I took one look at you and thought you were fucking gorgeous. You were looking at me and didn't look away. It was quite the invitation."

"Then you walked over and pushed me against the bar. I was a goner."

"A goner, huh?"

In more ways than one. "Yep. It was sexy as fuck." Then I remembered something. "Did you ever get your hundred bucks from your friends?"

"No, the bastards." He smirked. "Guess I should get you home."

He let go of my hand, so I kept it on his thigh, which earned me a cheeky smile. He started the engine and pulled out into traffic.

"Thank you for tonight," I said. "I've had a really good time."

"Same." He pursed his lips as he drove, like he wanted to say something but wasn't quite sure how. I gave him time to find the words. "I know we began this hooking-up thing for uncomplicated sex."

Oh boy. Here we go . . . I had a sinking feeling I didn't want to hear what he was about to say.

"But I think we've gone past that now," he added.

"Uh, yeah. Probably. You know my name now, so," I said, trying to keep it light. Trying to keep the axe from falling.

"And you're the property manager I'll be renting my place of business through," he added.

Oh shit. "Yes, of course. Makes it kind of complicated."

"Kind of."

I withheld the mother of sighs. "If you'd rather not see me, you can just say it. I understand the 'keeping it professional' thing. In fact—"

"What? No." He shook his head. "That's not what I was about to say." He frowned. "Unless you don't want that."

"I can separate work and play. I have no issue with that."

He smiled, relieved, then slid his hand over mine on his thigh. "Good. Same. I don't want it to make things weird."

"I can pass the file off to Natalie," I said.

"Well, about that," he said, shifting in his seat. "I was thinking maybe we should?"

I shot him a look. "You do?"

"Well, yes. Then there's no blurred lines or conflicts of interest. But only if you want to," he added quickly. "I just thought . . . maybe . . ." He let out a laugh that became a sigh. "I want to keep seeing you. And if the professional thing is going to mess with the personal thing, I'd rather it didn't. If we had a choice, I'd rather choose the personal."

Oh my god.

"I want to keep seeing you too," I whispered, my heart in my throat. I put my free hand to my chest. "I thought you were going to tell me you didn't want to see me anymore."

He grinned. "I thought you were going to say that."

I laughed, so very relieved. "Thank you for speaking up. For saying that."

He squeezed my hand. "Thank you for not shooting me down." As he drove back into the city, he handled the streets with ease, and in no time at all, he'd pulled up out the front of my apartment. "I can't believe I'm going to say this," he began. "But I'm not going to come up."

"Oh."

"It's just that I spent last night there, we had a date tonight, and I have every intention of seeing you tomorrow night. Is eight o'clock still okay? I can bring dinner with me and we can watch a movie or something. Unless you wanted to go out?"

We had a date tonight . . .

I fought a smile, my belly giddy at his words. "Takeout and a movie sounds great, actually."

"Seven thirty?"

I nodded. "Even better."

We both sat there, smiling at each other for what felt like forever. I unbuckled my seatbelt and it seemed to startle him. "Um. Dates end with a kiss, right?" he asked. God, was he nervous?

"I think that's appropriate etiquette," I replied, leaning over the console. He slid his hand along my jaw and brought our lips together. It was warm and soft, with parted lips and a taste of tongue, sweet and tantalising . . . until he pulled me closer and kissed me deeper with the sweetest moan.

He still held my face, and when he broke the kiss, he looked almost pained to do so. He thumbed my bottom lip. His eyes were onyx. "Tomorrow night?"

I nodded. "Yes, please." I had to remind myself to actually make an effort to get out of his car. I grabbed the handle. "Thank you for tonight."

"You're welcome, Michael Piersen."

I got out of his car and he waited until I was inside the lobby before he drove off. His sleek red brake lights disappeared around the corner, and I had to lean against the wall. I was breathless and lightheaded and full of butterflies, and my heart was banging against my ribs.

I just had a date with Bryson Schroeder.

I mean, sure. We'd done all kinds of things in the bedroom, but this was an actual date. And he wanted to drop the anon-uncomplicated games. He wanted to see me. He wanted to date me. Officially, for real.

I hit the elevator button, and when the doors opened, I almost didn't recognise the guy in the mirror. His smile was borderline stupid, and he laughed and shook his head.

I walked into my apartment and threw my wallet and keys on the kitchen counter and still hadn't stopped smiling. My phone beeped with a message. It was Bryce.

Just so you know, I already regret not coming up.

I thumbed out a quick reply. *Are you home already?* I mean I knew it wasn't far, but still.

Sitting in my car.

I laughed, giddy like a schoolboy. It was already ten o'clock and he was right. He spent last night here; he'd be spending tomorrow night here. We had dinner together tonight. That was enough. So I replied, aiming for sensible. *I had the best night, thank you. And I'm already looking forward to tomorrow night.*

Me too.

I smiled at the screen for a bit. *Goodnight, Bryce.*

Night, Michael.

BRYCE'S LEASE agreement was on top of my in-tray. There were a few sections left blank for now, finer details we'd need to elaborate on, but I did smile when I read his name.

I had a lot of emails, but I searched for one in particular and couldn't click on it fast enough.

Mr Piersen,

Mortimer Incorporated are pleased to hear

you've found a lessee already. Please forward all necessary paperwork . . .

I shot Bryce a quick text. *Good news on King Street Wharf! Call me when you have a minute.*

I don't know why, but I expected an immediate response. He usually replied straight away, and he'd been waiting on this news. But two minutes passed, then five, then ten, then twenty. I assumed he was busy and I put a dent in my emails and was on my second coffee when Natalie walked in.

She still had her phone to her ear but was wrapping up a conversation that apparently she had to do in my office. I kept typing until she disconnected the call. "Morning," she said, the way she did when she expected a full run down to follow.

"Morning. Good news on the Schroeder job. Mortimer accepted the proposal and wants the paperwork. I'm just waiting on Mr Schroeder to return my call. I'm assuming his legal team will want to see any contracts before it's official. Oh, and the Ling project on Pitt Street is moving forward, which is also good news. Roser Enterprises wants another three-year lease extension but at a reduced CPI. I'm meeting with them at eleven."

And then, of course, my phone rang.

The name SAF scrolled across the screen and I picked it up before Natalie could see it. "Michael Piersen speaking."

"Well, you sound all formal. Is that your professional phone voice?" Then he paused. "Oh, someone's in with you right now, aren't they?"

"That's correct, Mr Schroeder."

"Is it Natalie?"

"Yes, yes, that's fine."

He chuckled. "It doesn't sound fine."

"I have some draft contracts that I require some more information to complete. Is now a good time?"

"That depends. If I said no, would you have lunch with me so we could discuss it?"

"That won't be necessary," I replied, trying not to smile. "I can have my assistant send it to you."

"Hm, assistant. I really need to get me one of those."

"Or two."

Natalie was growing suspicious, and thankfully Bryce decided to be serious. "All jokes aside, Michael, that's excellent news about the store. I'm actually really freaking excited. I've spoken to my banker this morning regarding the changes, and to my design team. I'll need all the paperwork you can give me."

"I'm happy to hear that. We'll email you everything we have this morning, and I'll be in touch."

"So we can't meet for lunch?"

God.

He added, "It's just that after these contracts are signed, I'll be dealing with Natalie, right? So this could be our last chance for a working-lunch, so to speak." Then, because the sultry timbre of his voice wasn't enough, he added, "Please?"

I cleared my throat, because that was better than groaning or sighing or calling him an arsehole in front of Natalie. "Sure, I can arrange a second inspection of the site for you. I'll double-check the renovation team is okay with another interruption, but I can meet you there at twelve thirty? If you confirm any details in the email this morning, I can bring some paperwork to make it more official."

"So I'm meeting you at my store at half-past twelve?"

"Yes, that's correct."

"You didn't take much convincing . . ."

"Goodbye, Mr Schroeder."

I ended the call, still trying not to smile. I met Natalie's curious gaze. "Everything okay?" she asked.

"Yeah, it's fine. He just wanted one more site inspection before he finalises his design fit-out. Should have signatures for you by the end of the day."

"Signatures for me?" she pressed, her head tilted.

"Yes. I've explained to Mr Schroeder that it was your listing. I'm happy to instigate the agreements on your behalf, but the job's yours."

Meaning so was the commission . . .

Her brows furrowed. "Why are you handing it back? You've done the groundwork . . ."

She was suspicious and I didn't blame her. I would be too. "I don't have time," I replied, which wasn't exactly a lie. "My schedule is full, especially with the new Cynex listings. I only stepped in because you were caught in traffic, and I told Mr Schroeder this from the very start."

Natalie studied me for a second, scrutinising, and she was as adept at reading people as I was. So I added, "If you'd rather I see it through to the end—"

"No, it's fine," she replied.

"I'll take him to the property after my eleven o'clock and finalise any details, and when he comes in to sign off on it, I can introduce you."

Thankfully Miah, Natalie's assistant, poked her head through the door. "Ah, Natalie, the developer for the Castlereagh job is on line two for you."

Natalie gave me a nod and followed Miah up the hall. I let out an almighty sigh of relief and Carolyne appeared and gave me a knowing smile. She slid two phone call message notes on my desk. "I've emailed you the job file for Schroeder."

"Thank you," I replied, opening the email in question. I asked her to forward all paperwork to Mr Schroeder, and then my phone rang with another client, and then another, and after stomping out spot fires all morning, it was time for my meeting at eleven. And that meeting was more spot fires and more of a mediation session, which wasn't too uncommon.

But soon enough, I was on my way to meet Bryce.

This would be the fourth time in three days, and we still had plans for tonight. But the closer I got to his store, the more nervous I was getting. Yes, nervous . . . anticipation, excitement, and a rush of familiar warmth pooled low in my belly.

He was fast becoming a habit I wasn't sure I wanted to quit.

I rounded the corner to find him standing there, a folder in his hand, his phone to his ear. He was talking and nodding, but when he saw me, his smile was immediate and just for me.

"Okay, I have to go. He's here. Yep, see you soon."

His eyes never left mine as he pocketed his phone, and that smile aimed right at me turned my knees to jelly. He was wearing dark jeans and a Grateful Dead T-shirt that was frayed around the neck and had a hole in it. It was so wild to me that he was worth literally millions of dollars and still wore vintage clothes. If it weren't for the fact his boots were worth about a cool grand, I'd have thought he looked like a broke uni student.

"Mr Piersen," he said, holding his hand out for me to shake. "It's so good to see you again."

"Mr Schroeder," I replied. "Full of charm and sarcasm this afternoon."

He squeezed my hand. "I'm not being sarcastic. Is that suit new? I haven't seen it before."

I rolled my eyes and went to the door, unlocking it, top and bottom, with the key. "The reno guys are done," I said. "So it's just us today."

I held the door open for him, then followed him in. When I locked the door behind us, he pushed me up against the boarded-up front glass windows. "Are there security cameras in here?" he breathed.

"Not operational during demolition," I whispered, and he crushed his mouth to mine.

The kiss was deep and dirty and hotter than hell. "Sorry, but you're so fucking sexy," he murmured. "And that suit . . ."

"What is it with you and suits?"

"It's you in the suit. I've never wanted anyone else like I want you." He kissed me again, deeper and harder, and holy hell, I would have let him fuck me right here. No condom, no lube, no matter. I just wanted him, needed him, ached for it . . .

Then he pulled away.

Christ almighty.

"Fuck," he gasped, taking a step back. He took a few deep breaths, a slow smile spreading across his smug and handsome face. "Glad you suggested here and not your office or we'd be putting on a very public show right now."

I barked out a laugh. "Suggesting we meet here wasn't for the purposes of privacy. Believe it or not. I have papers for you." Then I had to palm my now-aching dick. "Goddammit."

He smirked and bit his bottom lip. "I'll take care of that for you tonight."

"You fucking better." I held up three fingers. "Three times. I'm not accepting anything less at this time."

He made a mock-pained face. "You drive a hard bargain."

"I'd just like to point out that my demand for three times doesn't have to be three orgasms for you. It means three for me."

He laughed, long and loud. "Don't think for one second you're getting more than me."

I rolled my eyes but I couldn't help but smile. I held up the folder I was somehow still holding. "We should get down to business."

"Yes, we should." He took a deep breath. "It's not my fault that I lose all sense and reason when you're around."

"You're saying it's my fault?" I raised one eyebrow. "So by that reasoning, my lack of professionalism and ability to think straight are your fault?"

He grinned. "Believe me, there's nothing straight about how you think."

"That's not even remotely funny."

"Then why are you smiling?"

"Because you're ridiculously cute."

He grinned. "Oh, really."

"Shut up."

Just then his phone rang. He answered quickly and made a face. "Uhhh, just one sec." He disconnected the call, then he pointed to the door. "That might have been my design team. Who are right outside."

"Now?"

"Yes. Is that okay? I meant to ask, but then you were

wearing that suit, and my brain short-circuited. Which is not my fault. I believe we just had this discussion."

I checked my watch. "This is not supposed to be a long appointment. I'm on my lunch break."

He held up two fingers. "Two minutes. Promise."

Since when did a two-minute meeting ever take only two minutes?

Whether I wanted to let them in was beside the point; it wasn't like I could leave them outside. So I opened the door and in walked a team of four. They were youngish, wearing a uniform with an eco-design logo on the breast, and the guy with long curly hair holding the laptop was quick to shake Bryce's hand. "Thanks so much. We were literally a block over, so it was great timing that you could line this up on such short notice."

Bryce shot me a look, then introduced us. The man's name was Luke, and while he looked like a surfer, I was quick to realise the guy was very, very smart. And hearing Bryce interact with him professionally, I could say the same about Bryce.

Luke's team of four buzzed in and around the now-empty space, taking pictures and using some kind of software that noted measurements and dimensions. So them being here didn't take two minutes, but it was no more than five. They were in and out, fast and efficient.

Bryce flashed me his Colgate smile. "I'm sorry for springing that on you. I called them on my way here, and Luke said he was just around the corner, so it made sense to kill two birds with one stone. I literally got off the phone to him when you got here, but then . . ." He waved me up and down. "The suit thing happened."

I chuckled. "You have a thing for suit porn, apparently."

Bryce hummed. "Apparently."

I opened the job folder. "Right. We need to get this done, or this store won't be yours."

I had a list of ten or so questions for him to help fill out the contracts. We got through them quickly, and once he was talking about his business, he was serious and articulate. "So, that just about does us," I said. "Once this is all written up, the contracts will be done. I've told Natalie I'm handing you over to her."

"You did?"

"Well, yeah. You said you thought it was a good idea that we separate work—"

"Yeah, I did." He pouted. "I just . . . now we won't get to do site inspections and make out."

I laughed. "Pretty sure that was the point."

He was still pouting. It was kind of cute. "Next time I have some great idea based on good intentions, say no."

I collected the folder and took the keys out. "Come on. I'll let you buy me lunch to make up for it."

We got to the door. "Wait," he said. He lifted my chin and kissed me softly. It was sweet and laced with emotions I wasn't quite prepared for. It stole my breath and unleashed a belly full of butterflies.

He thumbed my chin, my lips. "What time can I come over tonight?"

"Six."

"Did you originally say eight?"

"Shut up."

He chuckled. "Five it is."

"I can leave work early, but not that early," I said. "I normally work till about six or seven . . ."

"You can have an early mark for being such a good boy."

I scoffed. "Pretty sure you and I both know that would be a lie."

He ran his nose along my jaw. "Oh, I know."

Christ, he was making it hard to think. "I was going to do some laps after work. Before you got there." I sounded breathless, desperate.

"I can join you. I like swimming," he replied. "Will you wear Speedos?"

I met his eyes. "Will you?"

The corner of his mouth lifted. "Want me to?"

I swallowed hard at the mental imagery of his cock in wet Speedos. "Not if you actually want to do any swimming. But yes."

He laughed and pulled the door open. "Let me buy you some lunch. If I keep you any longer, you'll have to stay back later this evening and ruin all my plans."

"What are your plans?"

"To do you three times. I believe that was the demand from one Mr Bossy."

"You're a very quick learner."

I locked the site up, and Bryce bought me some sushi for lunch. I reminded him that I'd send through the contracts for his lawyers to go over, and with a devilish grin, he reminded me of his plans for me tonight.

Only those plans went to shit at ten to six.

My intercom buzzed and I didn't even look at the screen. I was trying to pull on my Speedos and hit the button. "You're early."

"For what?" Susannah's voice replied. I almost broke my neck turning to the screen—it wasn't just my sister. She had Mum and Dad with her too.

Oh no no no no no . . .

What the hell?

I had to find my phone, which I'd evidently thrown onto

the bed when I tore out of my suit five minutes ago. I shot a quick message to SAF.

My parents just turned up uninvited. Give me until seven. Wear the Speedos.

I pulled on my robe and grabbed a towel as I went to open the door. My parents were barrelling down the hall-way, my sister at the rear with a ridiculous grin on her face. "Come on in," I said. I didn't miss the way my mother looked at the robe and my bare feet. "Excuse the outfit. Was just about to go downstairs for a swim."

"We thought you might like to join us for dinner," Dad said.

I shot Susannah another look. She was smiling with zero shame. "Well, I would have if I'd had some notice. But I have plans."

I realised my mistake as soon as the words were out of my mouth.

"Oh?" Mum perked up, instantly interested. "Anyone we might know?"

How would it ever be anyone they knew?

"No, I don't think—"

"Oh, is this the guy you've been seeing for a while now?" Susannah piped up with a look of victory on her face.

I could feel my mother's stare zero in on me like a missile while her excitement went nuclear. There was a discernible shift in barometric pressure, I was sure of it. "You're seeing someone, Michael?"

Before I could answer, Susannah said, "Do you know his name yet?"

I glared at her with the invisible wrath of the Death Star on Alderaan. "Yes, I know his name. Christ, Susannah, you can throw me under the bus once, but there's no need to back over me a few times."

"Michael, don't swear," Mum chided. "And go and put some proper clothes on. You look like Hugh Heffner in that robe."

I looked down at my Versace robe. At my very nothing-like-Hugh-Heffner robe. I was going to argue, but really, there was no point. "Sure," I mumbled as I went to my room. "Though I would just like to take this opportunity to remind everyone here that I was going to swim a few laps before going out tonight. If I'd had some notice that you guys were coming . . ."

By the time I finished ranting, I was in my room pulling on a pair of shorts.

And then I heard the very familiar intercom buzzer. I heard Susannah say something, but it took a second to register what it was . . .

Oh my god.

Time seemed to move in slow motion, all hot and cold and pulsing in my ears, and by the time I pulled on some shorts, I almost fell over trying to get out to my living room just in time to see my dad open the door.

Bryce stood there in his Purple Rain T-shirt and jeans, holding up a pair of Speedos. "Get ready—"

His words died right then and there, and he spotted me behind my dad.

"Come in, son," Dad said. "You must be the boy Michael was just telling us about."

And I swear to fucking god, my soul left my body.

CHAPTER TEN

BRYCE

AN OLDER, very handsome man with blue eyes and grey-blond hair stood in Michael's doorway. I realised, far too late, as I stood there holding up a pair of rather small Speedos, that it was not Michael.

Then he said something like, "Come in. Michael was just telling us about you," and I happened to glance past his shoulder and saw Michael.

He looked . . . well, horrified was one word to describe it. Mortified was another. Possibly aghast. Definitely stunned and embarrassed, but mostly horrified.

"Dad," Michael squeaked.

Michael's dad grabbed my arm and pulled me inside. "Don't be shy, we don't bite."

I noticed a woman, possibly early fifties, stunningly beautiful and clearly Michael's mother. Because if I thought he looked like his father, he was the spitting image of her. And there was a younger woman, also tall, thin, and blonde. Her eyes were trained on Michael, her grin was wide.

Michael's father held out his hand. "Stephen Piersen," he said.

Stunned and blindsided, I shook his hand. "Bryson Schroeder."

He waved his hand to the two women. "And this is Reina and our daughter Susannah."

I gave a nod; my mouth was suddenly dry. "Nice to meet you."

Michael, wide-eyed and paler than usual, shook his head. He mouthed, "I'm so sorry."

Then Susannah took my hand. "Nice to meet you too," she said, clearly enjoying this far too much.

Michael intercepted us, giving his sister a death glare. "You're the worst sister ever," he hissed.

She laughed, ignoring him, and spoke to me. "I let you in. He was getting changed."

I met his gaze. "I sent you a text," he whispered.

"I didn't get it," I replied.

"They were just leaving," Michael said, loud enough for everyone to hear. "They have dinner plans, but I told them we had a . . . thing on tonight."

"A thing?" Susannah repeated, still grinning. "I bet you do."

"Michael, don't be embarrassed," his mother said.

"I need a fucking drink," Michael mumbled. He left me and walked into the kitchen, pulling the bottle of vodka from the freezer. He grabbed a glass, poured a decent amount, and drank it, straight. He shook his head to ward off the burn. Then he poured another decent swig and I was slightly worried he was going to drink it, but he pushed the glass on the counter toward me.

I went to take it but realised I was still holding the Speedos. Michael laughed, and I snorted, thought *fuck it*, and threw the vodka back in one gulp.

"Okay, we'll leave you boys," Stephen said. He shot me

an apologetic look as he led Reina toward the front door. "Nice to meet you," he called out. "Susannah, let's go."

Michael's sister, whose amused smile hadn't waned one bit, laughed. She and Michael had some silent eye-dagger argument, then she turned to me. "It's nice to finally meet you. And now I can put a face to the name . . . Well, now that we have a name. Because he has told me about you, and he gets all flustered when he does."

"Susannah," Stephen called out again.

"Bye, boys, have a good night," Reina said.

Susannah chuckled, then she gave me a wink as she walked past. "Yeah. Have a good night."

The front door snicked closed and the silence they left behind was deafening. I slowly turned to Michael, who now had the bottle of vodka in his hand. He raised it in a 'cheers' fashion. "I'm so fucking sorry." Then he put the bottle to his lips and chugged.

I pulled it from his mouth before he drank too much. He gave no resistance and instead leaned his hands on the counter and let his head drop forward. "I was wearing the robe when they turned up. With Speedos. If that's any indication of how my evening is going."

"I waved a pair of the smallest Speedos I could buy in front of your father's face," I added. "If you're wondering how my evening's going."

He looked up then and almost smiled. "Fucking hell. I'm so sorry."

I took a sip from the vodka bottle and relished the burn. "I could tell by your face. The horror-stricken, absolutely mortified look on your face told me you didn't plan this."

"Plan this?" He was back to looking horror-stricken. "I'd rather plan a colon cleanse with bleach and a toilet brush."

I laughed and took another drink straight from the bottle. "I don't know if I'd go that far."

He looked at me like I'd lost my damn mind. "I sent you a text. I told you to not come here. This whole disastrous encounter could have been avoided. Do you have any idea how impossible my sister is going to be now?"

I pulled out my phone and checked my messages. "I didn't get a text from you."

"Then who the hell did I send it . . ." He blanched. "Oh god. Who the hell did I send it to?" He patted down his body for his phone, then searched the kitchen frantically. "Where is my phone?"

I couldn't see it anywhere, so I hit Call and his phone rang from his bedroom. He ran to get it, and when he came back out, he was staring wide-eyed and ashen at his screen.

"Michael?"

He held his phone up, and no, he wasn't aghast before. He was aghast now. "I sent it to Natalie."

He walked robotically toward me, shoved his phone at my chest, and plonked himself on the couch.

I read the screen.

My parents just turned up uninvited. Give me until seven. Wear the Speedos.

And as if that wasn't bad enough, she replied. *LOL Michael I'm going to assume this message wasn't for me. Hope the Speedos were a hit.*

"Oh dear."

He shot me a defeated look. "Yeah. Oh dear." He held his hand out for the bottle. I passed it over and sat on the couch with him. He took another drink.

"It could have been worse," I tried. "You could have accidentally texted something like 'be here at seven and be ready to give me dick' or 'I want your dick so bad.' That would've been worse."

His mouth fell open. "I would have to change my name and leave the country if I did that." He let his head fall back on the backrest. "I am so sorry. No one in my family has a filter, and boundaries are something other families appreciate. Mine, not so much."

I stared at him, waiting for him to look at me. He didn't though. Instead, he put his arm over his eyes.

"Michael," I said gently. "I thought your family seemed kinda great."

That made him look at me, and I was beginning to think, from the size of his eyes, that maybe I'd sprouted a second head. "Are you insane?"

I chuckled. "Honestly, they seem like genuinely nice people. Well, I think Susannah enjoyed your misery a little too much, but isn't that what siblings do?"

"She's getting me back because when she started dating Jad and she was trying to keep Mum and Dad out of it, I one hundred percent threw her under the bus."

I laughed at that, and keeping his eyes on me, Michael smiled first, then he laughed. "Fucking hell. That was not how I wanted tonight to start, I can assure you."

Had I intended to meet his whole family? Absolutely not. But now that I had, did I mind?

No, I didn't.

"So, is everyone in your family a six-foot blond supermodel?"

He chuckled again and let out a long sigh. "My mum used to model when she was younger. And I'm technically only five foot eleven and a half inches, so no."

I turned to face him. "Still wanna go for that swim?"

"I drank a quarter of a bottle of vodka, so that's probably

not a great idea." He squinted his eyes shut and opened them again. "And you're a little blurry."

I took his hand and pulled him with me as I lay back so he was lying on top of me, his head on my chest. I fumbled the TV remote and found the comedy section. "*Gremlins,*" Michael called out as I scrolled.

I laughed but selected the movie and planted a kiss on the top of his head. "*Gremlins,* it is."

He dozed a little about half an hour into the movie, then decided sleepy kisses were in order, and we missed the rest of the movie because sleepy kisses led to sleepy sex. We ordered food sometime after nine, laughed at stupid shit on the internet for an hour, and we went for that swim in our Speedos at midnight. And then, because Michael Bossy McBosserson demanded that third orgasm, we finally got to sleep around three.

I WOKE up to a kiss on my cheek. "I gotta get to work," a voice said, warm in my ear. He smelled all shower-clean and warm-aftershave. "Pull the front door shut behind you when you go. Or stay here all day." He kissed my hair. I felt his knee leave the bed. "If you're still in my bed when I get home, I won't mind."

I cracked an eyelid, smiling. "What time is it?"

"Eight." Michael stood there, looking fine as hell in suit pants and a pressed shirt. He seemed conflicted.

"What's up?" I asked.

"Just looking at you, naked in my bed and barely covered by the sheet . . ." He shook his head. "I'm just wondering what meetings I can reschedule today."

I laughed and rolled over, facing away and tucking his

pillow under my head. "Go to work. I'm doing work things today too. Just need to nap for a little longer."

He laughed and slapped my arse, planted a kiss on my shoulder, and was gone.

I smiled into his pillow. It smelled of him, of us, and I fell back asleep for a bit. I was content and happy, and I'd be kidding myself if I didn't acknowledge that my heart was involved now.

Well, my brain and my dick had been involved since the beginning, so that was nothing new. But my heart . . . it felt full and fluttery, and I didn't care anymore. I didn't want to fight it. This feeling, all warm and fuzzy, I wanted to fill a bathtub with it and soak in it.

I showered at his place, left my Prince T-shirt on his bed, and picked out a clean shirt from his wardrobe. It was a bit tight, but I didn't care. I wanted to wear his shirt, and I wanted him to have mine. I wanted to see him in it, I wanted him to smell like me, I wanted him to have some part of me, and I wanted him to think of me while he wore it.

Was that some weird possessive shit that put some kind of claim on him as mine?

Probably.

Did I care?

Not one bit.

I smiled all the way home, and I was still smiling as I walked into the apartment, throwing my keys and phone onto the marble table before opening the fridge to look inside.

"I wondered when you'd get home," a deep voice said, scaring the shit out of me.

I shot back, clearly startled to find my dad standing near the hall. I put my hand to my heart. "Christ. Warn me next time." He almost smiled, so I took the juice from the fridge and poured myself a glass. "When did you get back?"

"Last night. Eight o'clock." He gave me a disappointed look. "I wrongly assumed you'd be here."

"I wrongly assumed your flight got in today."

He gave a tight smile and a nod. "My meetings finished early."

God, I hated that things were like this between us. I tried to be more upbeat. "So, what are your plans for today? Did you want to do lunch?"

"I thought you'd be busy," he replied. "With your new business."

He said the word like it sounded bad. "I am," I answered. "But I can make exceptions."

He considered that as though I was a child playing childish games, and he was quiet for a long moment. "So, where are your plans up to? What stage of the planning process?"

"I've got the contract for a property to lease," I said. "I've sent the paperwork to my lawyer to look over, and the design team are finalising the fit-out."

He nodded. "Moving along, then?"

"Yep."

"And the address?"

"King Street Wharf."

This surprised him, until it didn't. "Rent would be ridiculous. Are you sure that's the smartest decision?"

"Yes, I'm sure. It's a prime location."

"For a prime premium. I assume you've factored that increase into your financial—"

"Yes, Dad. I have. Jerry looked over it himself."

He pursed his lips, and if he was going to make a snide

comment, he thankfully decided not to. "So, when will work on the storefront begin?"

"As soon as we get the green light from the owner. The design team are ready to go and they sub-contract their construction guys." I shrugged. "Ideally, things will start this week."

Dad nodded slowly again. "I won't be able to meet with you for lunch," he said, almost like an afterthought. "I'm leaving for Brisbane in an hour. It should be a quick trip. I should be home for dinner on Sunday if you wanted to do something?"

I was very used to being alone, so the pang of disappointment surprised me. "Yeah, sounds good."

He stood there as if he wanted to say something more but didn't know how. I gave him a smile, trying to ease the awkwardness. "I'll order us some Greek food. That way you can come home and relax for a bit."

His smile was genuine. "That sounds nice." Then he cleared his throat. "So . . . you spent last night somewhere . . . ?"

I almost choked on my juice. "Uh, Dad . . ."

"You don't have to tell me . . . but you've been out on the town a lot. Are you—"

Oh god. "I'm not going out on the town," I said, whatever that meant. "I'm not getting hammered or wasted, Dad. I'm . . . seeing someone."

"Oh."

"Yeah. It's kind of new."

"Is it the same guy you were seeing the other week?"

"Yeah."

"I thought you said it wasn't serious."

"It wasn't . . ."

"And now it is?"

"Well, I don't know. It could be."

God, this was the worst.

"You know that a distraction is hardly—"

"He's not a distraction, Dad. He's a person."

His eyes narrowed and he snapped his mouth closed. He took a breath and tried again. "Finding yourself being drawn in several directions won't help your business. Especially when you're just starting out. I hope he understands where your priorities are."

I knew he meant well, and he only had my interests at heart. But god, this attitude got old, fast. "Yes, he understands. He supports me."

That probably wasn't as true as I made it out to be. Sure, Michael supported me. He helped me find a better venue, for fuck's sake. But did he understand that my time would be stretched thin in the lead-up to the store opening? And I'd probably see him even less once it was operational . . .

I'm sure he did understand. He was smart, and he was a business-minded person. But maybe my dad brought up a good point. I needed to be honest and upfront with Michael. I was the one who'd said that I wanted to see him, that I wanted to date him. He didn't suggest that. I did. I pushed for more, and now I'd have to remind him that starting my business was going to cut into our time together.

I just hoped he understood.

Goddammit.

"Anyway, if I'm going to make my flight," he said.

"Yeah, of course." I waited for him to collect his carryon. "Have a good flight."

"See you tomorrow night," he said, the front door closing behind him.

I stood there for a while in the silence, unsure of what to do with myself. I had a stack of work things to do, but after my brief and frustrating conversation with my father, I wasn't in the right mindset.

I took my phone and hit Terrence's number instead. "Hey, T."

"Wassup? Everything okay?"

He could always tell. "Yeah, just spoke to my dad. You know how that is."

"Ah, say no more." He proceeded to tell me all about an argument he'd had with his dad yesterday at work, and the way he spun it like he always did had me smiling in no time. "Did you want to come over for dinner tonight? Or we could have a few drinks somewhere."

"Ugh, can I take a rain check?"

"Sure."

"I just have some things I need to go through today for the store and I have dinner plans with my father tomorrow night."

"If you need me to call in a bomb threat, just text me the name of the restaurant."

I laughed. "You are a good man."

"I know."

Then I thought of something. "But you know, next weekend could be my last before shit gets real with the store, so should we plan something for next Saturday?"

"Yes!"

"That sounds great," I said, much happier now. "I'll think of somewhere and let you know."

"Bring Michael."

That stopped me cold. I almost laughed. "What?"

"You heard. Bring him."

"I don't know . . ."

"Shut up, Bryce," he replied in only the way that

Terrence could. "You have it bad for him. I know you do. It's time he met the boys."

"Oh god."

"It's not like you're meeting the parents or anything," he joked.

"Well, about that . . ."

There was a long beat of silence. "What?"

"I met his parents. It was an accident. It was horrifying and really funny, kind of. Well, more horrifying than funny." I told him about how Michael's father's first impression of me was me twirling a pair of tiny Speedos and telling him to 'get ready' and how Michael's sister kept making it worse and by then, Michael was drinking vodka straight from the bottle.

Terrence laughed for two minutes straight. He laughed so much I wondered if I should hang up and call him an ambulance. When he could finally speak, he said, "That's settled then. You're bringing him. And I know where he works. So if you don't ask him to come along, I will."

"You're a horrible friend."

"You just said I was a good man."

"You can be both."

"You're bringing him, and I'll tell the others to be on their best behaviour."

"Oh god."

"You'll be fine."

"It's not me I'm worried about."

Terrence chuckled. "Oh. You still owe me lunch. I could be free on Wednesday, twelve o'clock. Let me know where you decide we're eating."

And with that, the line went dead in my ear. I laughed as I threw my phone on the couch beside me. Terrence really was one of a kind and there was no point in arguing with him. So, if Michael was willing, we were doing the meeting-of-friends thing.

Christ almighty. How did it go from nameless hook-ups to him meeting my friends?

I dug the heels of my hands into my eyes and tried to decide if I was scared by the idea of us moving forward so fast. But I really wasn't. In fact, the more I thought about it, the more I liked the idea.

God, Bryce, you're in way over your head.

Aaaaaand that realisation didn't scare me either.

So instead of freaking out, I reached for my phone and sent Bossy a text.

Busy tonight?

His reply took just a few seconds. *Was going to try and actually sleep. You?*

Wanna come to mine? Promise I'll let you sleep.

The text bubble appeared and disappeared, then appeared again. *Sure you will but okay.*

I ignored the way my heart soared and how stupid my smile was. *Seven o'clock in the foyer. Text me when you get here. I'll come down and get you.*

Do I need to bring anything? Dinner?

Nope. We can order room service.

Perfect.

I sat there smiling at my phone for a while, then pulled my laptop over and began some actual work. I had orders of plant and equipment to confirm, shipping numbers to track, emails to reply to, and a few phone calls to make. I ducked out to grab some lunch and called into the chemist for fresh supplies of lube and condoms while I was out, then finished the marketing specs.

All in all, it was a productive day.

But seven couldn't come around fast enough.

At eight minutes to, my phone pinged with a message. *Hey. I'm here.*

I rushed to get in that elevator so fast, I almost forgot my keys. But there he was, standing to the side of the hotel foyer, keeping out of the way of everyone else. It was always busy, people coming and going, staff running about everywhere.

But I swear the world stood still around him.

He wore tight dark blue jeans, the knee ripped out in one leg. His button-down shirt was white, sharp, and over-sized down to his thighs. His hair was styled up. His flawless skin. That fucking jawline and those long, talented fingers . . .

I had to swallow but my mouth was suddenly dry.

He looked like God himself put together an angel and a devil in the one body and then, just for laughs, delivered him to me.

Michael didn't see me at first and it gave me a few seconds of uninterrupted viewing time. He was checking something on his phone and happened to look up when I was a few metres away. He broke out in a smile that set every cell in my body on fire.

I walked right up to him, stood right in close, and murmured in his ear. "The way you look right now should be illegal."

He chuckled, warm and sultry. But then he caught another look at my shirt. "Is that . . . is that BTS?"

"Yes, it is," I said proudly. "Have a problem with that?"

"Oh, no." He shook his head. "I just have to wonder about the musical journey that includes shirts from the Grateful Dead to a Korean pop band."

"That *musical journey*, as you so bravely put it," I replied with a smile, "is eclectic and diverse. And it also involved me scoring tickets to their concert in Singapore and being a fan ever since."

He chuckled. "Well, it's . . . cute."

I laughed and tucked him under my arm as I led him to the elevators. "But let me guess . . . you think it'd be a whole lot cuter on my bedroom floor."

He grinned. "Like your shirt you left at my place today."

Still with my arm around his shoulder, I pressed the elevator button. "I left that on your bed, not on your floor."

He laughed again. "Did you go home shirtless?"

"No. I stole one of your T-shirts. It's mine now. It was kinda tight on me, not gonna lie, but I made it work."

"I bet you did."

We stepped into the elevator and I still didn't take my arm from around his shoulder. If anything, I pulled him in a bit closer. I didn't care if there were other people in the elevator with us, and Michael clearly liked it, if the way he smiled at me in our reflection was any kind of clue.

When I opened the door to my home, I stood aside for Michael to walk in first. "Oh, wow," he breathed.

I looked around, forgetting for a minute what it was like to see this apartment for the first time. It was the penthouse, after all, but it was just . . . home. Well, my dad's home.

"Yes, wow," I said, taking his hand and lifting it above his head, and he turned around as if we were in some kind of dance. I got a 360-degree view. "Wow, indeed."

"You gonna add this shirt to the list you want me to open the door in?"

"Don't give me ideas," I answered, pulling him against me. "Though I was hoping you'd be wearing the shirt I left at your place."

"You wanted me to wear it?"

"Want you to, yes," I said, my voice gruff. I lifted his

chin for a quick kiss on his lips. "I want to see you in my clothes."

He leaned his body against mine, his arms tight around me, smiling like that goddamned angel-devil made just for me. "I'm going to assume your dad isn't here?"

I shook my head. "He left for Brisbane earlier today. Won't be home till tomorrow night." I sighed. "He's . . . he and I . . . Ugh, sorry. It's just . . ."

His blue eyes searched mine. "Did you have a fight?"

"Not really. He's just . . . we're very different. And we're similar in a lot of ways too, I guess. But he's so focused on some things, and he takes it too far." I ran my thumb along Michael's jaw. "I have two things to ask you."

He blinked in surprise. "Two things? Um, okay."

"Come sit with me," I said, taking his hand and leading him to the couch. He sat beside me and I kept hold of his hand. He looked a little worried, so I threaded his fingers and gave him a smile. "Okay, so here goes."

"You're nervous and it's making me nervous."

I laughed. "Sorry. It's not bad. I hope. God."

"Bry, just say it."

I smiled at that. "No one calls me Bry."

"Pretty sure I just did. And you liked it."

I chuckled, side-tracked, which I think might have been his intention. I wasn't so nervous now. "Okay, so the first thing. And this comes from my dad, but also from me. It's a fair point, and something I should bring up."

"You told your dad about me?"

"Stop distracting me."

"Sorry."

"I did, yes."

"Oh my god."

"Well, I waved Speedos in front of your dad's face, so we're even."

He laughed at that. "Good point."

I took a deep breath. "I told you I wanted to see you. I wanted to be more than just hook-up fuck buddies, whatever we started out as."

He looked worried now. "Yeah?"

"And that's still true," I added quickly. "That hasn't changed."

"Okay, good." He let out a relieved breath.

"But chances are it will." I sighed. "My shop is going to take up a lot of my time. I'm going to be busy and my free time will be almost nil to none for a while. I don't want you to think that it's a reflection on you or us. Whatever free time I have, I will want to spend with you. I still want to see you."

Now it was he who squeezed my hand. "It's okay, Bry. I get it. I understand that and I wouldn't ask you to compromise your business."

"You do? I mean, you understand that?"

"Sure I do."

"I told my dad you would, but then I thought, god, I'd just said to you I wanted to see more of you only to turn around and actually see less of you."

"And what did your dad say?"

"He just didn't want to see me get hurt, that's all. He didn't want me to lose focus on my business, but he didn't want for there to be any confusion between you and me about my priorities." I shrugged. "He's all about work, work, work."

Michael looked at our joined hands. "I get it, Bryce. I do."

"You can keep calling me Bry. I don't mind."

He smiled. "And if I have to go to your shop to spend time with you, I will. I like Singaporean coffee."

I leaned back on the sofa and stared at him. He was so goddamned pretty, and so understanding, and so very mine. "Thank you."

He turned side-on, his leg folded up underneath him. I kept hold of his hand. "Okay, well that wasn't bad or anything to be nervous about. What was the second thing?"

"Oh, well . . ." I made a face, ignoring the knots in my belly.

"Oh, this one's the bad one, right? The one you were nervous about. I get it, you don't have to say it," he whispered, pulling his hand from mine. "Though after you just said you wanted to keep seeing me, inviting me here to give me bad news—"

"What? No." I snatched up his hand again. "It's not bad. Well, you might think it is, and you can say no. They'll understand. I mean, Terrence probably won't. And he'll make my life a misery, but he'll get over it."

"Bry, the fuck are you talking about?"

"Terrence wants you to meet the guys," I blurted out. "I mean, I do too, but technically he's making me ask you and he threatened to call you himself if I didn't. But next Saturday night, if you're free, that is, you're not obligated at all, I'm meeting my mates for a few drinks and want you to come with me. To meet them."

Michael smiled. "You want me to meet them, or Terrence does?"

I laughed. "It sounds bad, because he brought it up but I agree with him. Next weekend will be my last free weekend before things with the shop get crazy."

"You should spend time with your friends if this is your last chance," he began.

"I want you to meet them," I told him, looking him right in the eye. "They know I'm seeing someone, and they know it's the guy I met at the bar when I was out with them on my first night back from Singapore. They know we didn't know each other's names for a while, and they know we see each other a lot; thanks to Terrence, that is. So maybe it's time they met you. But only if you want."

He studied me for a long, heart-stopping moment before he nodded. "I'd love to meet them." Then he made a face. "Terrence won't give me the third degree again, will he?"

"He better freaking not." I leaned over and kissed him. "Thank you."

"You were so nervous I thought it was the cliché 'it's not you' speech."

I laughed. "I'd just told you I wanted to make an extra effort to keep seeing you when things with the store get busy, and then the next sentence you think I'm going to dump you?"

"That's why I was confused."

I cupped his beautiful face and kissed him. "I was nervous because it's a big deal for me to introduce you to my friends. I've never done that before. I've never . . . I've never been with anyone long enough, I guess."

"You've never . . . ? Is this the longest you've ever seen someone?"

I felt my cheeks heat. "Well, yeah. There's been guys, of course. But it's been hard for me." I swallowed thickly. "People find out who I am and they treat me differently. They see my name and not me, and it's not easy knowing who likes me for me. Know what I mean?"

"I think I do."

"Can I ask you something?"

"Is this part of the original two questions, or are we adding a third?"

"Well, you do like it when I do things in threes."

He laughed and nudged his shoulder to mine, staying a little closer to my side. "Ask away."

"Did you know who I was?" I held his hand tight, suddenly dreading his answer, because fuck, what if he did?

"I had no clue who you were. I had a name in a job file with zero clue who I was supposed to be meeting. Someone in my office had said the name was big in the hotel division, but I don't deal with hotel brokerage so I didn't know. I mean, I've heard of Schroeder Hotels, who hasn't? It's like Hilton. But even when you walked in, it took a few seconds to connect the dots. I didn't realise it was you. Like, I didn't realise you were *the* Bryson Schroeder."

"But even after," I whispered. "It's just that you never treated me any different, so I wondered if you knew . . ."

"I wouldn't treat you any different because it doesn't matter to me. The good part about not knowing who you were when we first met was that I got to know the real you." He shrugged. "Did you want me to treat you different?"

"No! God no. I, um, I'm glad you don't. I like that you don't treat me differently. A lot of people do. You know? They hear my surname, or they find out who my dad is, and they make exceptions for me and I hate that."

"I can't imagine what that's like." He rubbed his thumb over the back of my hand. "But you're one of the most down-to-earth guys I know. Well, the car is a bit of a flex, but—"

"Hey, don't knock my car. I love that car. But if you'd prefer I sell it and get a second-hand Ford Focus—"

"No, you're not selling it, god. Are you kidding me? I love that car."

I let go of his hand, gripped his knee, and pushed him back onto the couch. I hitched his knee over my hip and kissed him, both of us smiling. Michael stared up at me, then chewed on his bottom lip. "There is something we do need to talk about, though," he said.

"What's that?"

"Dinner, because I'm starving. And your BTS shirt."

"Leave my shirt alone."

He laughed. "No, I want it. You can keep the Purple Rain one. I want this one."

"You can't have it."

"Yes, I can."

"No, you can't. It's mine."

"I'm pretty sure you'll give it to me."

"Is that right?"

He ran his hands down my back and over my arse, and he rolled his hips, grinding against me. "Yeah."

I kissed him and it would have been so easy—so very easy—to get carried away, but I remembered how he said he was starving. I pulled his bottom lip in between my teeth and let it go. "I promised you dinner."

"Mmm, is there a better offer?"

I chuckled. "You need food. And sleep."

"Sleep?"

"Yeah, you said your plans for tonight were to actually get some sleep."

"I reserve the right to renege on that," he said, his gaze going from my eyes to my lips and back to my eyes.

"Oh, no you don't," I said, climbing off him and sitting between his legs. "You don't look at me like that."

He sat up, his long legs on either side of me. His hair kind of flopped a little, his lips were wet and red. Christ, he looked so hot. "Like what?"

"Like you know damn well. Like you want to devour me. Or you want me to devour you."

"Both."

I laughed. "What food do you want? Anything you feel like."

"Anything?"

"Yep. What do you feel like?"

"I would kill for a pasta, tomato-based, with vegetables or something. No, scrap that. I want some Hokkien noodles. Where can we order that from?"

"Room service. I'll call it through and they'll make you whatever you want."

He looked panicked. "Oh, I don't want to be a bother."

That made me laugh. "It's no bother."

I lifted his leg, reached over to the side table, and grabbed the phone. I put in an order for noodles and dumplings, then grabbed us a drink each from the fridge. When I sat back down beside him, he'd taken his shoes off and put them neatly beside the couch. I handed him his drink and picked up the TV remote. I hit the Netflix button and handed the remote to Michael. "Fair's fair. I've seen your viewing history; you can see mine."

He laughed, and for the next five minutes, he scrolled through, laughed at some, asked questions about others, and was bitterly disappointed in the lack of R-rated stuff.

"I live with my dad," I replied.

"Oh, fair point." He chuckled as he took a sip of his drink. "Have you always lived with him? I mean, did you ever get your own place?"

"Nope. There was no need, really. He's never here. I probably see him maybe four or five times a month. And even then it's only for a few hours at a time."

"Oh wow."

"Yeah, even growing up I was here by myself most of the time."

"That must have sucked."

I shrugged. "Yes, and no. I went to boarding school, but the school holidays here without parental supervision was fun."

He chuckled at that. "I bet it was. Party central, right?"

"Um, more *private* parties, if you catch my drift."

He barked out a laugh. "You started early."

I smiled at him. "Then there was college, which kept me busy, and then I went overseas for two years. So yeah, I live here with my dad but I very rarely see him."

"Is that hard?" he asked quietly. "You're not close with him at all."

"I don't know any different. I don't remember much of my mother. Luckily, I was old enough to fend for myself by the time she'd had enough. When she left, I was in boarding school and didn't know for weeks after the fact that she'd gone."

Michael's mouth fell open. He put his hand to my back. "Oh my god, Bry. I'm so sorry, that must have been awful."

"Her trade-off was enough money to walk away. He basically forbade her to take me, though she hardly needed convincing. I don't think she ever looked back. She calls me on my birthday. I don't call her on hers."

"Christ."

I tried to laugh. "Listen to me, nosediving the conversation."

He rubbed my back. "You didn't nosedive anything. Thank you for telling me."

I met his gaze. "Kinda fucked up, isn't it?"

"Well, it's not what some would call orthodox."

"Which is a nice way to say fucked up."

"Pretty much, yeah."

"It's okay. I know it is. I made my peace with that. My dad's very successful and he's good at what he does. And we do get along. We just have different ideals when it comes to relationships and what they should be."

"You said before he tried to warn you out of starting something new with me."

"Not just you. It's not you. He'd say the same about anyone. So please don't think it's about you. It's not you."

He put his hand to my cheek and kissed me. "I know. Thank you."

There was a knock on the door to alert us to room service, which I'd almost forgotten I'd ordered. I jumped up and let them in, and we ate our dinner on the couch watching more of that Chinese police show. We shared straight out of the takeout containers. He sat cross-legged and I had my feet on the coffee table. It was so relaxed and fun, even.

"Oh my god, this is so good," Michael said, stuffing noodles in his mouth.

I waited until he swallowed that, then picked up a dumpling with my chopsticks and fed it to him. He fed me some noodles and we ate from each other's containers, laughing, always touching. When we'd had enough, I pushed the containers onto the coffee table, lay back, and pulled him on top of me to watch TV.

It could have so easily become sexual. He was snug between my legs, his head on my chest watching the TV. He'd slid one of his hands under my lower back, his other hand rested on my arm. I rubbed his back and stroked the hair at his temple.

Not even ten minutes later, his hand on my arm fell away and I realised he'd fallen asleep.

I wasn't even mad. In fact, I liked it. I tightened my arms around him and something warm and lovely settled beneath my ribs. My heart felt too big for my chest, as if it had grown big enough for two.

As scary as it was, as much as it took the ground from underneath me, I relished the freefall.

I loved him.

I was in love with him.

I don't know how that happened. How we'd gone from a casual hook-up, from something fun and flirty to this.

To love.

But that's where I was. That's what this was.

I couldn't deny it. I wouldn't.

I was in love with Michael Piersen.

Smiling, I held him tighter, feeling the beat of his heart against my chest, the rise and fall of his chest. I kissed the top of his head, and not wanting this moment to ever end, I let him sleep.

I must have dozed off myself because I woke when he stirred. "Come on," I whispered. "Let's go to bed."

He peeled himself off me, still half-asleep and disoriented. I got up, and taking his hand, I pulled him to his feet. ". . . go home," he mumbled.

"No, baby," I said, leading him to my room. "You're sleeping here."

My room was dark and he all but swayed when I stopped him by the bed. I unbuttoned his shirt and slid it over his shoulders, his pale skin almost illuminated in the darkness. I kissed his collarbone when I unbuttoned his jeans, and he made a happy sound. "You called me baby," he murmured.

I slid my hands under the waistband of his jeans and

pushed them over his arse. "I did," I said, kissing up the side of his neck to his ear. "Baby."

His hands were fisting my shirt at my hips, and he let his forehead fall to my chest. ". . . baby."

Needing to feel his skin against mine, I quickly pulled my shirt off. He pulled his jeans down further, stepping on the legs to try and get out of them. Skinny jeans looked great on him but they were a pain in the arse to get off. He had to sit on the edge of the bed to pull them off, and by the time he was free of them, I had mine off and the bed covers pulled back.

He crawled in and I pulled him into my arms. "I'm so tired," he breathed.

I squeezed him and kissed the side of his head. "Sleep, baby."

He chuckled, snuggling in, and a few moments later, he was asleep.

My heart was full and happy, and I smiled at the ceiling until my dreams took me.

I WOKE up to Michael stretching out beside me like a cat. He let out a husky laugh and disappeared under the covers and slid down my body until his warm, hot mouth found my cock. He settled between my thighs and licked and sucked, taking me in deep and wet.

"Fuck."

He hummed and worked me harder.

"Not gonna last," I ground out.

He grunted, then fisted the base of my cock with one hand and pulled my balls with his other. It took every ounce of self-control to keep my arse on the bed and not thrust down his throat. But he kept me fixed to the spot and worked me over in the very best of ways.

It was an exquisite form of torture.

He drew my orgasm out of my bones, drinking down every drop of me. The room spun, my mind blissfully blank to everything but the ecstasy.

Blank to everything but Michael.

He emerged from under the covers, his lips curled in a victorious grin, his blond hair a beautiful mess.

"Good morning," he said.

I pulled him in for a hug and rolled us onto our sides, burying his face in my neck. "Morning," I managed to say. "Brain's still a bit scrambled."

He laughed so I rolled him onto his back and did to him exactly as he'd done to me. After I made short work of him, I dragged him into my shower and we laughed as we washed each other. He got out first, and when I came out with no more than a towel around my waist, he was dressed in his jeans . . .

And my BTS shirt.

"Hey."

He laughed. "Told you I'd get it."

My mouth fell open. "That's not how this works."

He ran his fingers through his hair, brushing it back from his face. His grin was breathtaking. "It's exactly how this works." He picked up his shirt from the floor—the over-sized one that made him look hot as hell—and threw it at me. "You can wear that."

"You're so bossy."

"It would probably be more of an insult if you didn't smile when you said that."

"It was never an insult."

Michael's smile turned sultry and he let out a huff. "Christ, can you not flirt for one minute?"

"Flirt? All I did was look at you."

"With those eyes."

"These are the only eyes I have."

"You know what I mean," he said, his cheeks pink. "You look at me like you want to do very bad things to me."

"Because I *do* want to do very bad things to you."

He laughed, then chewed on his bottom lip. "Maybe later." He patted his belly. "I'm hungry."

"Then I'll cook breakfast for you," I said. "I'm going to make you the best omelette you've ever had."

"Are you going to get dressed first?" He looked me up and down. "Because as much as I want to see you in my shirt, naked you is incredibly aesthetic."

"Nice try," I said, pulling on some jeans.

"Going commando?"

"Easy access."

He smiled. "I like the way you think."

I slipped one arm into the sleeve of his shirt. It was tight around the biceps, then across the shoulder. "I don't think," I said, beginning to button it.

"Oh no," he whispered, finishing the buttoning for me. "It fits you so well."

It was long by design, down to my thighs, but very fitted. It looked big on him and I didn't think we were that different in size. I mean, he was lean, I was more muscular, broader across the chest . . .

"Okay, it's official. You need to wear this every day," he added. "Just like your name in my phone. You're as sexy as fuck."

I rolled my eyes at him and made him help me in the

kitchen. Not that he helped much. He picked at the tomato and ham as I was dicing it, probably eating more than what went into the omelette. But he was a pro at cracking eggs and he made toast and coffee, and it was effortless to be with him.

We snuck kisses as we cooked, and he rubbed his bare foot over mine. He stood close to me, leaning against the counter, relaxed and funny, his hand on my arm or my waist or running through the hair at the nape of my neck.

I could so easily get used to this.

We sat at the table to eat, and he looked at me bright-eyed. "So, tell me where you're up to with your shop? What's happening this week?"

"The fit-out guys want to start, which means the refrigeration and electric need to happen," I answered.

"That's exciting," he replied, and he was genuine. He was honestly interested, which ramped up my own anticipation.

"Yeah, I can't wait." But it wasn't lost on me that lazy weekends cooking breakfast and having a quiet Sunday were all about to end. My dad's words came back to me and I had to shake it off. "I believe I'm coming in to officially meet your boss."

He smiled as he chewed and swallowed his eggs. "And I believe she wants me to introduce you."

That made me laugh. "Do we act all casual? Because just so you know, my acting skills are not good. And I can't lie for shit."

"I'm glad to hear that." He smiled. "And honestly, it's going to be over so fast, she won't have time to wonder. But casual, yes. No making out in my office or grabbing my arse, if that's something to go by."

"Damn it. That's what I was hoping for."

He laughed again and finished his breakfast and placed

his cutlery on the empty plate. "I gotta say, you can make me an omelette any time you want. That was divine, thank you."

"I'd like to make you breakfast most weekends," I admitted. "But I worry there won't be much time for it soon."

He reached out and covered my hand with his. "We'll make time. And if you cook me an omelette for a late dinner sometime instead of breakfast, I won't complain."

I found myself smiling at him. "Okay."

"Don't stress over what hasn't happened yet," he added. He sipped his coffee and gave me a smile that made my heart dance. "To possibilities, remember?"

God, that gave me a whole-body reaction. My heart swooped, my belly knotted, my skin felt warm all over. I was absolutely certain this was the feeling poems and songs were about, and now, maybe for the first true time, I understood the feeling behind the words.

"To possibilities."

WE CLEANED UP AFTER BREAKFAST, and Michael insisted on doing his share. I kissed him against the sink and he welcomed it, putting his arms around me and holding me as tight as he could. It was deep and real and full of every emotion I wasn't ready to tell him with words just yet.

The way he held me, touched me, smiled at me.

I'm sure he felt it too.

And for the longest while, we just stood in a tight embrace in the kitchen. I was leaning against the counter and he just snuggled right in, his forehead fitting perfectly in the crook of my neck.

Like he was made just for me.

"I really should get going," he mumbled. "I have a thousand things to do."

"Same."

Neither of us moved.

"Are you really keeping my shirt?"

"Yes, I am. We can call it a birthday present."

I pulled back, alarmed. "When's your birthday?"

He laughed. "November eighth."

"That's seven months away."

"Then we can call it an early birthday present."

I laughed and pulled his face in for a kiss. "I'm going to get it back. One day."

He had mischief in his eyes. "Good luck with that." Then he became serious, searching my eyes for something. I don't know what he was looking for or if he found it, but it made my heart thump against my ribs. "I should go," he whispered. "Tell me to go."

I gripped his jaw hard enough to make him groan. "Or you could stay."

He groaned again, but it was a pained sound. He took my hand and kissed my palm. "I have a thousand things I need to do today."

I nodded. "Same."

He held my hand for a long moment, then put my palm to his chest before dropping it and taking a step back. "I'm going to go now," he said, so quiet I almost didn't hear it.

He turned then, checked his pockets for his phone and keys, and upon finding them, kissed me before he walked out.

I stood there, dumbfounded, my world spinning, heart racing. His touch, his smell, his smile filled my head and I was grinning like an idiot. I couldn't seem to catch my breath.

"You okay?" My dad's voice scared the shit outta me.

I clutched at my heart. "I didn't hear you come in."

"I could tell." He studied me for a second. "The look on your face wouldn't have anything to do with the young blond man I just passed in the hallway?"

Christ.

"Maybe."

"I wondered where he came from."

It was safer for me to change the subject. "I didn't think you'd be home until later this afternoon."

He took a deep breath and looked decidedly uncomfortable. It made me nervous. "I didn't like how we left things yesterday. I thought perhaps you could join me for lunch."

I couldn't hide my surprise. "Oh. Sure." I had no idea what 'lunch' entailed, but this was some kind of olive branch he rarely offered. "That'd be great."

He gave a nod, then looked at my shirt. "Though you might want to change your shirt. That one's quite ill-fitted."

"It's Michael's," I admitted.

Dad shot me a look that wasn't exactly surprised, but it wasn't entirely happy. "Do you not have enough of your own?"

I smiled, and that giddy feeling in my belly rolled right into nervous butterflies. And I don't know what possessed me or why the hell I said what I said, but once the words were out, it was far too late, and I still didn't care. "Dad, I want you to meet him."

CHAPTER ELEVEN

MICHAEL

"MICHAEL, Natalie wants to see you in her office," Carolyne said, poking her head through the door. Seeing me with my job folder and my keys in hand, she grimaced. "Sorry, I know you were about to leave."

Fucking hell.

I glanced at the clock on my computer. It was 9:27am. I had a ten o'clock appointment across town and Natalie knew this. I was just about to leave, which she also knew. And now I was going to be late.

I slid the job file on my desk and repressed the almighty sigh I wanted to unload. Plastering a smile on my face, I made my way across the office to my boss' office. Except I didn't make it all the way . . .

Because in the main office area, which was mostly admin desks and some cubicles, stood Natalie and a man I'd recognise anywhere.

Bryce.

But not like I'd seen him before.

He was wearing a full three-piece suit. A dark grey suit very clearly made just for him because that fit was like a second skin. It showed his muscular thighs, his trim waist, broad shoulders, and exquisite neck and hair . . .

I almost tripped over my own feet.

Natalie gave me an odd look, half-impatient, half-what-the-fuck, but her smile was ever professional. Bryce, on the other hand, grinned before he caught himself, settling for a polite smile. Though his eyes were glittering with humour.

I held my hand out for him to shake. "Mr Schroeder, good to see you again."

Which wasn't a lie. It really was. After all, just last night we FaceTimed each other in bed and ended up jerking off together. It was as sexy as being in the same bed as him, with his warm, gravelly voice speaking low and filthy things in my ear.

I was certain by that smirk and those twinkling eyes he was remembering that.

"Ah, Mr Piersen," he replied, smooth as silk, his lips toying with a smile. "Always a pleasure."

I stared at him and his knowing, smiling eyes.

Son of a bitch.

As it turned out, he'd just arrived that very moment. So I introduced him formally to Natalie. She apologised again for not meeting him that day, to which he replied it was no problem at all. "As it turned out, Michael found me the perfect location."

I ignored Natalie's burning gaze. "It was just a matter of right place, right time," I allowed politely. "Speaking of which—" I made a point of looking at my watch. "I have a meeting on Hyde, which I'm about to be late for. Mr Schroeder—"

"Please, call me Bryson." He smiled.

I had to bite down on my tongue to keep my reaction in

check. "Bryson," I repeated slowly. "I'll leave you with Natalie. You're in very capable hands."

His eyes lasered into mine. "Yes, I am."

I gave them a nod and turned back for my office. I grabbed the file and dashed for the elevator, seeing Bryce and Natalie had disappeared into her office. I stepped into the elevator and took out my phone, quickly finding SAF in my messages, and shot him a text.

You're in so much trouble.

I knew he wouldn't be able to reply for a while, so I pocketed my phone and focused my mind on work instead. I got through my client appointment with minimal fuss and I headed back to the office. I had a dozen calls to make, twice as many emails to get through, and budget reports to finalise.

Natalie and Bryson were gone, and I was kind of glad. Not just because he was a beautiful distraction but because Natalie was already giving me weird looks. And I needed to put my head down and get through my never-ending to-do list.

I got a reply from him a few hours later. *What kind of trouble? Naughty corner kind, or the spanking kind?*

I smiled as I thumbed out a reply. *The you're-paying-for-dinner kind.*

I ate a late lunch at my desk and managed to put a dent in my workload. All in all, it was a successful Monday. It was after six thirty, and I was organising shit I had to do in the morning before I left for the night when Natalie appeared in my doorway.

The rest of the office was empty, a lot of the lights were already off, everything was quiet. "Got a sec?" she asked.

"Uh, yeah, sure," I replied. "I was just finishing up."

I had no idea what this was about, and while it wasn't

uncommon for us to speak privately, I had a bad feeling about this. There was something guarded in her expression, as though she was about to deliver bad news.

She came into my office, sat in the chair opposite me, not quite smiling, not quite glaring, but a mix of both.

It was definitely bad news.

I put my pen down and leaned back in my chair and met her gaze. "What's up?" I aimed for casual but we both knew I didn't pull it off.

She studied me for a too-long moment. "We've always been honest with each other, yes?"

Fuck.

"Yes."

"In a professional context," she added. "Anything work-related has been straight down the line between us, and I trust your decisions."

Okay, so this was going to be worse than bad.

I had no idea what she was aiming for, but I wasn't offering anything until it was necessary. "And I trust yours," I replied.

"So would you care to tell me what went on between you and Mr Schroeder?"

I kept my face neutral, and in one second that seemed to last an eternity, I weighed up whether I should deny or confirm her suspicions. I very almost lied to her, but I had no idea if Bryce had said something to her or if she knew I'd be lying. For all I knew, she could have seen us out together. She knew something was up between me and him.

To be caught out in a lie would be worse than the lie itself.

I sighed and went with the truth. "I know him. Personally."

Her eyes hardened. "Explain."

"I'm in a relationship, of sorts, with him."

Her eyes widened before narrowing at me. "Did you secure the King Street Wharf property early because of your relationship with him? That property wasn't ready to be signed off and yet you secured it for him."

"No. Not at all."

"Michael—"

"Okay, here's the truth," I replied sharper than I intended. "I'd been seeing a guy for a few weeks on a no-name basis. It was very deliberate not to know personal details. It was purely physical and fun. I did not know his name, nor did he know mine, if you get my drift." I gave her a pointed look and thankfully didn't need to explain friends with benefits to her. "Then you called me asking me to meet your client in fifteen minutes because you were stuck in traffic. Which I did. I ran there with no more than a job folder and the name of a man I was supposed to be meeting. And who should it turn out to be? None other than the guy I had a personal arrangement with. And until that very moment, I didn't even know his name."

Natalie eyed me as if she was looking for a tell that I was lying. "You expect me to believe that?"

"I don't care what you believe," I replied. "That's the truth."

She didn't like me saying that. *If looks could kill.* "But then you showed him the King Street Wharf anyway."

"The York Street location wasn't suitable."

"The King Street property was not ready for viewing. The ink on the contract we signed wasn't dry yet."

"You told me to do whatever it takes to secure the client," I replied. "Did you not?"

She didn't answer.

"You wanted him because of his name," I continued. "I didn't even know his name."

"But you learned it that day. You gave an unauthorised site inspection of a property you had no right to show. Because you were involved with him."

"I still am involved with him," I admitted. "And I handed the contract over to you. We decided it was in everyone's best interest for us not to mix personal with professional. My name is not on any of the paperwork."

She sighed quietly and looked out the window to the city beyond. "You introduced me to him like it was some kind of joke."

"I wasn't expecting to see him this morning. I was caught off-guard." Which was one helluva understatement. "No one here knows, and I'm only being honest with you because I've never lied to you."

"You should have told me the day you took him to King Street."

"Well, between you and me, I was in a bit of shock. The guy I'd been seeing was the son of the Schroeder hotel empire."

"And you didn't know who he was?" She clearly still didn't believe me.

"Not one clue. He was incredibly down to earth. He wears vintage band shirts with holes in them. His boots were expensive though." I shrugged. "Natalie, he didn't want me to know who he was. He wanted me to know the real him before I found out his connection to the Schroeder Hotels. And honestly, can you blame him?"

She chewed on her bottom lip for a few seconds. "I still don't like how this makes us look. What if word gets out?"

"Word about what? That we went above and beyond for a client?"

"That's not how it looks, Michael."

"Show me in our job specs where I crossed a line."

She couldn't and she knew it. My name didn't appear in his job file. Sure, I'd shown him some properties, but I never signed off on anything and I received no financial gain from our interaction. And that was the critical factor.

Natalie sighed again and stared out the window at the disappearing daylight over the city. "I just wish you'd been honest with me. When you told me you took him to see the King Street property that very first day, you should have disclosed your personal relationship with him to me and you didn't."

"Because at that stage, I don't know if I would have called it a relationship. It was a casual . . . arrangement."

"But now it's not."

I wasn't sure how to answer that. "It's not . . . We agreed . . . we are seeing each other, yes."

"So your boyfriend is a client."

Boyfriend . . .

Christ.

"Bryson Schroeder is your client," I replied. "Not mine."

"He's a client of this firm."

"Yes. But he was not my boyfriend at the time he was signed." I wasn't even sure that's what he was now. "And as soon as we agreed to see each other for real, I gave the contract back to you. Honestly, Natalie, I'm not sure what the problem is. If I'd have told you I was seeing him, what difference would it have made?"

"I'm not entirely certain I would have agreed to him signing the King Street property," she replied coolly.

"That location met every criteria on his brief."

"That location would have met every criteria for a dozen of our clients."

"And if I'd met with any of those dozen clients that day, I would have shown it to them. But I didn't. You said you wanted this client to sign, that he was some big deal, so that's what I did. He made first contact with you, did he not? Not me. I didn't even know who he was."

This was just going around in circles, and quite frankly, I'd had enough.

"Natalie, if you want me to apologise, then I'm sorry. Should I have told you that first day that I knew him? Probably. I'm sorry I didn't."

She looked resigned at this point. "I just worry about the integrity of our reputation, that's all."

What the fuck? "Our integrity?"

"Yes. And how this looks to an outsider."

I glared at her, so fucking done with this. "If you're so concerned, take it to the board of directors and let them decide. Just be sure it's the company's reputation that's hurt and not your pride. Because I'm done with this conversation. I'm not quite sure what it is you want from me."

She levelled a cool stare at me. "Just honesty, Michael. Nothing more, nothing less."

Now it was me who sighed because that made me feel like shit. "I'm sorry, Natalie. Genuinely sorry that you felt I was being dishonest. That was never my intention. I wasn't expecting to see him when I walked out of my office this morning."

She almost smiled. "I could tell. It wasn't his smug smile or the hearts in his eyes when he saw you. It was your face that gave it away. And possibly the hearts in your eyes."

"I did not have hearts in my eyes."

"Yeah, you kinda did." She studied me for a while, a

half-smile on her face. "I'm happy that you found someone. He seems like a nice guy."

"He is." Thankfully, the tension between us appeared to be over. "And I am sorry I didn't tell you. I didn't think it crossed any lines. I gladly handed all contracts over so there was no conflict of interest."

"Technically it didn't cross any lines, but they blurred well and truly. And to be honest, trying to hide it was a mistake. A stone statue could have seen how you two looked at each other."

I tried not to smile. "I'll be sure to tell him."

She stood up. "Just so you know, I won't be taking it further. I won't tell anyone. But please, in the future, give me a heads up."

"I will. And thank you."

She left after that. I shut down my computer, grabbed my things, and dragged my arse home. I threw my jacket over the couch and opened the fridge door, not finding anything I wanted. I really wanted a drink, but that probably wasn't a great idea on a Monday. I was contemplating a shower when my intercom buzzed. I checked the screen and found a familiar solitary figure waiting. He was holding a white takeout bag and he looked at the screen with a smirk.

Suddenly overrun with butterflies and that warm buzz only he could give me, I hit the button and went to open the front door. He came out of the elevator smiling.

"I thought we were only doing Wednesdays and Fridays?" I said. And Saturdays and Sunday mornings, I wanted to add but didn't.

"I believe my punishment was to bring dinner." He planted a kiss on my mouth as he walked inside.

"I was just trying to decide what to have," I replied, closing the door behind him. "Food or straight vodka."

He put the takeout bag on the kitchen counter and frowned. "That doesn't sound good." Then he did a double take. "What happened?"

"Natalie happened."

He stared at me. "Did she say something to you?"

"Yep. Apparently she could tell something was up by the way I looked at you."

He laughed. "You blushed like a bride."

I shoved his arm. "A bit of warning would have been good."

"I wanted to surprise you."

"Well, she ripped me a new arsehole this afternoon. Talking about the company's reputation and integrity and how I put my boyfriend before the company."

He stopped and put his hand up. "Wait. Hang on one sec. You were reprimanded because of me?"

"No, because of me. She asked me what the hell was going on between us, so I told her." I relayed the conversation, explaining that Natalie now knew about us. "It wasn't your behaviour she had a problem with. I didn't disclose the truth from the beginning and I should have."

He made a thoughtful face as though he didn't exactly agree with me but wasn't going to argue the point. "And you said you put your boyfriend before the company." He put his hand to his chest. "Boyfriend?"

I felt my cheeks flame. "*She* called you my boyfriend."

He nodded slowly, his brow furrowed, his bottom lip between his teeth. His gaze cut through me like glass. "And how did that sound to you?"

It was suddenly hard to breathe. My heart squeezed to the point of pain. "Sounded good."

He grinned and stepped over to me, his palm found my cheek, his eyes bore into mine. "I like how it sounds too." He kissed me softly. "Boyfriends, exclusive, just you and me."

I could barely whisper. "Just you and me."

His smile was something else, something special. He pulled me in for a hard, squeezy hug before he let me go, grinning now. He even laughed a little. "Oh, dinner," he said, turning to the takeout on the counter. It smelled good, whatever it was. "Korean BBQ and this." He pulled out two small, green bottles. "Soju."

"Oh god, Bry. That is absolutely perfect."

His smile did stupid things to my heart. "Oh, and before I forget," he added, ever so casually. "I told my dad I want you to meet him."

CHAPTER TWELVE

BRYCE

"YES, WE'RE COMING," I replied into the phone. I could hear the crowd behind Terrence's demand to know where the hell we were. "Five minutes away."

"Just checking you haven't bailed on us," he replied before the line went dead.

I pocketed my phone and squeezed Michael's hand. He was so nervous about tonight, despite my reassurances that my friends would love him. He was wearing grey skinny jeans and a light grey shirt, black boots, and peacock-blue pea coat. His blond hair was styled up, his jawline was sharp, his pink lips and pale skin was so fresh we almost didn't leave his apartment.

This man did things to me . . .

I'd spent Monday, Wednesday, and Friday night at Michael's place and still couldn't get enough of him. But we'd promised Saturday night to Terrence and the boys so they could meet him, officially.

As my boyfriend.

I'd never had one of those. Not really. Not like him.

Not anyone I couldn't have walked away from anyway. And there was no way I could walk away from Michael.

I was in it with my whole entire heart.

"Do I look okay?" he asked me again, for the twentieth time.

I stopped walking and made him look at me. "You look good enough to eat. Which I fully intend on doing later, just so you know."

He didn't smile. "Bry. What if they—"

"They'll be fine. You'll be fine. You're with me and they wouldn't dare fuck this up for me. And just so you know, if they take the piss out of you, it means they like you."

He rolled his eyes but granted me a small smile.

They'd chosen a bar that was trendy, quiet enough for conversation, busy enough not to be awkward. I held his hand as we walked in the crowded bar. We were met by Terrence who took Michael's arm. "You come with me," he said, grinning. Then he shoved me toward the bar. "It's your shout."

Michael's wide eyes were the last thing I saw as Terrence all but dragged him to the table where the others all greeted him. Knowing Michael was in good hands, I did as I was told and ordered a round of drinks, and when I finally made my way to the table with a full tray of drinks, Michael was laughing with my friends. Luke was telling some story and everyone was smiling as I took my seat next to Michael.

I rubbed his back to let him know he was okay, but honestly, he was fine. Two drinks later and he was talking and laughing like he'd known these boys for as long as I had.

I knew they'd love him.

Because I did.

When Michael went to the bar for a round of drinks, a silence fell over the table and Massa, Luke, and Noah all stared at me, shaking their heads. Terrence laughed. "You're so fucking whipped, Schroeder."

I couldn't help but laugh, and I certainly couldn't deny it. "Shut the fuck up."

Massa tapped my foot under the table. "He's okay, Bryce. You picked a good one."

"Thanks." I felt a sudden rush of warmth in my chest. "It means a lot that you guys like him."

Noah drained the last of his drink. "He's good for you. I think you've smiled more this last hour than you have since I've known you."

"I've asked my dad to meet him," I admitted.

They stared, mouths open.

"Fuck," Terrence whispered. "Dude."

I laughed and shook my head. "I know." I shrugged. "What the actual fuck, right?"

They all laughed just as Michael came back with a tray of drinks. He cast me a questioning look and I smiled at him to let him know it was all good. I pulled his chair a little closer to mine and rested my hand on his thigh when he sat down. I squeezed his fingers and he nudged his shoulder against mine, giving me a smile that made my heart thump.

I was pretty sure the guys at the table could hear my heartbeat because they sure looked at me like they could. And just to prove their point, I fucking laughed, leaned in and kissed Michael right there.

"Okay, stop it. You're making me regret being single," Luke replied with a roll of his eyes. "What's happening with the new store? Things moving along?"

"Yes!" I replied, excited. "Fit-out has begun. Electric

and cabinetry is done, refrigeration is in this week, and I interviewed staff last week."

"So it's full steam ahead," Massa said.

I nodded. "Yep."

"When's the grand opening?" Noah asked.

"Two weeks," I answered, unable to stop smiling.

"That's awesome, Bryce. Proud of you, man." He raised his glass to the centre of the table. "To Bryce, for living his dream."

Everyone clinked glasses. "To Bryce."

"For kicking parental expectations to the kerb," Terrence added. "Braver than me."

I raised my glass. "Sometimes you gotta just say 'fuck it' and live your life."

They raised their glasses again to that, and both Terrence and Massa gave a solemn nod. I knew they understood. "Your support means a lot," I said.

"So do we get free kopi?" Noah asked.

"Absolutely fucking not," I shot back, and they all laughed.

I turned to Michael and he was smiling at me. The kind of smile that just radiated happiness. Or maybe that was the drinks he'd had. Either way, he was looking all kinds of fine.

"Oh Christ, would you two stop it," Luke said before swigging his drink. "I'm committed to the single life and you two are killing me. I don't need a girlfriend. I don't. Absolutely do not."

Michael burst out laughing. "Sorry." Then he took his hand from my thigh.

I pulled it back and threaded his fingers with mine, and when that wasn't enough, I slung my arm around his shoulder and gave Luke the middle finger.

"You're so fucking whipped, Schroeder," Terrence said again.

Now it was me who burst out laughing. He wasn't supposed to say that shit in front of Michael. Massa leaned in and squinted at me. "Are you blushing?"

"Fuck you," I said with a grin. "Fuck all of you."

Michael raised his glass for them to clink with his, and with a laugh, he leaned against me and waited for me to clink his glass with mine. He didn't say anything, he just smiled. And when it was my turn to buy another round, I found myself standing at the bar, positioned so I could still see the table.

I couldn't hear their conversation over the music and the growing crowd, but I could see how happy they all were, how well they fit together. Michael looked so happy, laughing so hard he leaned over and clapped his hands at whatever Noah had said. Terrence said something else and Michael had to wipe at his eyes, and Luke and Massa were both cracking up.

I didn't know what was so funny, but it didn't matter.

Terrence said something and Michael guffawed again, and something settled inside me. Something profound, something warm and lovely. Deeper than it had before, warmer and brighter.

Love was a devastatingly wonderful thing.

The barman tapped the counter in front of me. "Hey buddy, what can I getcha?"

I ordered another round, but all I really wanted to do in that moment was to go home. I wanted to have Michael to myself. I wanted to hold him, kiss him, strip him naked, and lie down with him.

I wanted to move inside him. I wanted to make love to him.

I wanted him to know.

I took our drinks back to the table and Michael met my eyes. His gaze shifted. "Everything okay?" he whispered, just to me.

I nodded. "Perfect. But I want to leave soon, okay?"

He looked concerned. "Sure."

The words were on the tip of my tongue. *I love you.* I almost said them. I wanted to, but it wasn't fair to dump that on him in front of other people.

"Hey, Schroeder," Noah said across the table. "You okay?"

I laughed. "Yeah, but this is my last drink. I'm out of drinking practice, I think."

"That's such a fucking lie," Massa added. "You're a terrible liar."

I laughed again and drained my drink in one go.

Terrence raised his glass. "At least some of us at the table are getting laid tonight."

Michael finished half his drink and stood up, fixing his coat. "On that note—" He checked his watch. "Can't fuck all night if you don't start before midnight."

Massa almost choked on his drink, and I laughed as I stood up. "Yep. I have a quota to meet."

"Okay, mister three times in one night," Terrence groused.

Michael's gaze met mine and his mouth fell open. "You told him?"

Luke and Noah roared with laughter as I put my arm around Michael's shoulder. "And on that note, we'll be leaving. Thank you for a lovely evening, dickwads."

Terrence gave me a salute. "Fuck you." Then he held his hand out to Michael. "About time he met his equal."

Michael shook his hand. "Thank you. Nice to meet you all," he said to all of them.

I pulled him toward the door and gave my mates a wave as we made it to the exit. Michael fell into step beside me and he put his arm around my waist as we walked. "That was fun," he said. "Do you think?" He looked at me, his blue eyes imploring.

I rubbed his back. "Baby, they like you more than they like me."

He stopped walking. "No, they don't. Is that why we left? Did I . . . I don't know, did I do something wrong?"

I laughed and kissed his knuckles. "Michael, tonight was perfect. It couldn't have gone better. You fit in like you've known them for years."

He sighed with visible relief. "Good, because I really like them. I half expected Terrence to give me another roasting but he wasn't too bad."

"Too bad? Did he say something?"

"Mm." He made a funny face. "He might have said something . . ."

"Was he out of line? Because that's not really like him —" I mean, Terrence was protective and he fired straight from the hip. But he would never be mean.

"No, no, not at all," he replied quickly. "Well, you might not think so."

Oh, great. So what he said was about me . . . "What did he say?"

"Nothing really," he replied, and I could see his blush even by the streetlight. "Just that he, and the others, think it's great that you finally found someone and how I must be special because they've never met any of your boyfriends before."

"Well, just so you know, they're all no longer my friends and I'm taking them off my Christmas card list," I said, and he laughed. "But I've never had a boyfriend before. Not really. So that would explain that. But you are someone special. They're not wrong about that."

He put my hand to his cheek and gave me a shy smile. "You're someone special to me too."

Christ, my heart felt like it was about to burst out my chest. Was I going to tell him? Was I just going to say it here in the street? Surrounded by darkness and streetlight and neon signs and passers-by?

He studied my eyes and cocked his head. "What is it?"

I laughed, embarrassed at my inability to speak. I put his hand to my chest instead, certain he could feel the storm behind my ribs. My heart, my pulse, my blood was thunder and lightning. I'd never said this to anyone, but he was worth it.

"Michael," I said, my voice barely a whisper. "I'm falling in love with you."

He blinked, pale skin in the darkness, his eyes wide and shining like a galaxy. "Bry . . ."

"You don't have to say anything," I blurted out. "I just wanted you to know. My friends could tell. I'm different with you. I'm better. I was at the bar, watching you laugh with them, and I just needed to tell you how I feel. So there it is. I'm in love with you, but I don't expect anything in return. That's not why—"

"I'm falling in love with you too," he said, and my entire body thrilled at his words. "I think I loved you from the first night I met you."

I took his face in my hands and kissed him, right there in the street. I didn't care who saw. Nothing in the world mattered but him. "We need to go back to your place," I murmured against his lips. "Unless we want to be arrested for a whole lot of indecent behaviours."

He laughed, carefree and sultry at the same time. He took my hand and we all but ran to his apartment complex. It wasn't far, but we were out of breath by the time we got there and it somehow added to the urgency, to the foreplay.

We fell into his apartment, kissing, laughing, trying to undress. I kicked one boot off in the living room, and almost tripped over trying to take off the other in the hall near his bedroom. His shirt ended up somewhere. Mine went with it.

I managed to get his jeans off and push him on the bed. He scooted up to put his head on the pillows while I peeled my own jeans off and crawled up the length of his body. "You're so beautiful," I murmured, planting kisses as I went. He stroked himself as he watched me, his legs spreading to accommodate me. I kissed his hip, his belly, up his chest, along his collarbone, up his neck before claiming his mouth.

He broke the kiss to slay me with just a look. "Bry," he murmured. "Need you. Inside me."

I shivered all over and he smirked. So I gripped his chin. "Something funny?"

His pupils dilated; his breath hitched. He rolled his hips and gripped my arse, grinding our cocks together. He arched his back.

Fucking hell.

I reached over and found the condoms and lube. While I rolled on the condom, he slicked his own arse, slipping a finger in. He was clearly in no mood to wait.

He writhed under his own touch, urgent and desperate, his knees raised and spread. He squeezed the base of his cock with his free hand and slipped a second finger in, groaning and desperate.

Watching him do that was mesmerising.

Beautiful.

"Bryce," he growled.

I shook my head, lost in his every movement. The fire in his eyes told me he was out of patience, so I lubed myself and lifted his legs up toward his chest. I aligned my cock-head at his hole and pressed in slowly. "Is this what you want?" I breathed against his lips.

He sucked back a breath. His fingernails dug into my back. But I didn't stop. I slid slowly into his body, deep and all at once. Until I couldn't go any further. He took all of me, and I waited for him to catch his breath before I pulled back just enough to push back in.

His eyes rolled back in his head, his neck corded, his face a mask of ecstasy. So I wrapped him up in my arms and I did it again and again. Slower and deeper, but this wasn't just sex. This was so much more.

Being with him like this was like nothing I'd ever felt before. This emotional depth, the connection.

The love.

Because that's what this was.

Michael brought his hands around to cup my face, his gaze intense and full of all the emotions I felt. Every breath, every touch, every thrust.

We made love. We held each other, grasping hands, desperate mouths. We moved as one. We became one. It was so intense, so visceral, so honest.

A tear escaped Michael's eye as he gave himself over to me. I thumbed it away and buried my face in his neck as I came. He held me as tight as I held him, whispering the sweetest words in my ear, trailing patterns on my back as I feathered back down to earth.

I rolled us onto our sides, still holding him close, not wanting to miss a second of this heavenly floating feeling. I closed my eyes.

"I love you," he whispered.

I squeezed him. "I love you too."

We fell asleep like that and woke up like it too. All giddy smiles and tender touches.

What a remarkable and stupid thing love was.

What a fucking drug. So God help me, I never wanted to come down.

I HAD A BUSY WEEK. I started at six in the morning every day to get the final stages of the shop ready—fit-out, equipment, staff, orders, stock—but it was exciting. I couldn't wait to start each day. The hours flew past. I didn't get to sleep until midnight most nights but woke up buzzing to get back to it the next morning.

I spoke to Michael every day. We chatted, texted, but I had to bail on our usual Wednesday night meet up. I missed him, which was crazy. But I did. I missed the physicality: his touch, his warmth, his smell, the sound of his laughter low in my ear, his smile against my neck.

He said he understood that I was busy, and I believed him. He explained it was probably a good thing, given he and Natalie were still on eggshells around each other so it allowed him to prove to her that he was still committed to giving one hundred percent.

On Saturday night, I got to his place around ten thirty. I hadn't eaten, of course, so he ordered pasta and we made out until it arrived. Kissing him, holding him, felt like coming home. Like I'd been homesick all week and finally walked into familiar arms.

And the crazy part?

I didn't even want sex. Okay, so that's not entirely true. I would always want sex. But I was so tired . . . I just wanted to curl up with him, kiss and cuddle, and be close to him.

That was enough. It was more than enough. It was what I craved.

I told him all about where the store was up to while I ate. We sat on his couch, he had his legs all tucked up underneath him, a wine glass in his hands. He picked at my plate, listening intently, asking questions, his free hand on my thigh, my arm, in my hair.

Always touching me.

But after I'd eaten too much, my eyelids began to droop.

I patted my belly. "Oh, carbs activated," I said. "Coma in four, three, two . . ."

He laughed and took my hand. "To bed with you."

We stripped down to our underwear, I set my alarm for far-too-early o'clock, and we crawled into bed. But this time, he pulled me close, his arms tight around me, my head on his shoulder. He rubbed my back, stroked my hair, and I was warm and content, so loved that I slept like the dead.

My alarm went off, and honestly, getting out of Michael's bed was the hardest thing I've ever done. I sat up and tried to rub the tiredness out of my eyes. "Mm," Michael murmured. "Morning."

"Stay in bed. I've gotta get going."

"What have you got on today?" he asked, barely opening his eyes.

"Cleaning the whole store from top to bottom."

He snorted. "From you to me."

It took me a second to get his joke. I laughed. "From floor to ceiling. Now all the construction's done, all the fridges are in, all the furniture's in, there's dust and shit. I have to scrub everything, sanitise it all, and set up the health and safety logbooks."

He groaned but sat up. "I can help."

"No, you don't have to do that."

"We'll get it done in half the time."

"It's your one day off," I tried to reason. "You don't have to give that up for me."

"I want to. It'll be fun."

"Cleaning, Michael. I said cleaning. Since when is cleaning fun?"

"Since I get to do it with you." He rolled out of bed and staggered into his bathroom. "Starting with a shower. We can do that together. Then we can get coffee on the way."

"Or I could make you a kopi when we get to my store."

He stopped in the bathroom doorway and turned to smile at me. "Even better. Now get that sexy arse of yours into this shower with me."

I laughed as I untangled myself from the sheets, and I followed him. "Is this how bossy you're going to be all day cleaning with me?"

He pulled his briefs down, standing before me, stark naked, half-hard with rumpled hair. "I think you'll find that while I can be bossy sometimes—" He gave his cock a long, slow pull. "—I can also be a very good boy and do everything I'm told as well."

My cock pulsed and I had to palm myself. "Is that right?"

He made a show of jerking off in front of me, making full eye contact, his tongue wetting the corner of his lips. "You're taking too long. Either tell me to get on my knees and suck you off or bend me over and fuck me. But either way, Mr Schroeder, you have some catching up to do."

My cock jerked, precome spilling from the tip. As much as I wanted to be inside him, buried to the hilt for hours, we just didn't have time. "Get on your knees and put that mouth to good use."

He grinned as he folded a towel into a well-padded rectangle and dropped it to the floor, going to his knees on it. He looked up at me, still smiling, and opened his mouth.

He didn't speak. He just opened his mouth and waited for me to get the hint. He wanted me to put something in it, so I didn't disappoint him.

I stepped in close, gripped the base of my erection, and let him have a little taste before feeding it to him.

He groaned around my shaft, his lips closing tight, his tongue hot and wet, his throat welcoming. The more I gave him, the more he moaned, and I realised then that he was jerking himself off at the same time.

He sucked me and I watched the whole show in the bathroom mirror. It was one of the sexiest things I'd ever seen.

Ever.

I was lucky to have lasted all of three minutes. He coaxed an orgasm out of me in record time and he drank down every drop before he came on the bathroom floor.

I was so lightheaded I almost fell over, and laughing, we stumbled into the shower. Ten minutes later, I was picking a clean shirt out of his wardrobe and we were on our way to the shop.

I WAS ABSURDLY EXCITED for him to do this with me, to share this with me.

"Oh my god, Bry," he whispered as he walked in. "Look at this place!"

I grinned at him. "You like it?"

He looked around, taking in every detail. The white panel walls, the white cabinetry, and sand-coloured fixtures. The service counter, the wok area for roasting, the menu boards on the bulkhead, every small detail done to perfection.

"I love it." He beamed at me. "You should be proud."

His words hit me right in the heart. "I am, thank you. I can't wait to be open. Just to begin, know what I mean?"

He nodded, giving my arm a squeeze as he walked past. "Okay, tell me where to start while you make the kopi."

I laughed and pointed to the menu boards. "Which one?"

"One of each? Just to sample them all?"

I stared at him. "If you drank one of each, you'll be hearing colours and seeing noises."

"Good to know." He laughed. "Make me your favourite."

"Two kopi-di-lo coming up."

He walked into the storeroom and squealed, excited. "Oh my god!"

"What is it?" I rushed in after him, not knowing what I was about to find.

He waved his hand at the storage shelves and containers. "All the labels. It's all so neat and organised. And the smell. I think I'm in heaven."

It smelled of coffee beans: fresh, roasted, ground.

"Glad you like my organisational skills."

"Are you kidding? It's like organisational porn in here."

I laughed and pulled one container off the shelf. "This is the one I need."

Michael disappeared into the cleaning closet and I set about making the kopi. The beans had already been roasted with butter and some hazelnuts and ground down to the powder I needed. I'd done it a thousand times by now and had it down to a fine, fast art. I had two cups poured by the time he returned with a bucket and filled it with hot soapy water. "Here, taste this," I said, suddenly nervous.

"Love the cup," he said first. "Very authentic." I loved that he knew that. Kopi was traditionally served in thick ceramic cups. Then he noticed what was printed on the outside of the cup. "Oh my god, this is your logo."

He looked around again, this time seeing the stack of takeout cups with the same logo. "Take away kopi is traditionally served in plastic pouches, but I couldn't find an environmentally friendly equivalent so I had to settle for the standard cardboard. But these are recycled bamboo and they're completely biodegradable. More expensive, of course, but . . ." I shrugged.

"It's important to you," he finished.

I nodded. "It is."

"I noticed the cleaning products are organic," he added. Then he read the bottom of the menu board. "And the coffee is sustainably sourced."

I smiled. "That was the biggest hurdle."

He met my gaze and held it. "I'm proud of you."

His words—those words—meant the world to me. "Thank you."

He took his cup and sipped the dark liquid. His eyes shot to mine. "Oh Bry, this is good."

I grinned at him. "I know, right?"

He hummed as he took another sip. "I'm going to need this all the time, you know that, right?"

I laughed. "Deal." We drank our coffees and I told him about the menu of kaya toast and pandan cakes and kueh, apam balik, youtiao. "Basically, it's glorified Singaporean street food with a twenty-first-century twist."

"Can't wait to try them. When I was in Vietnam, I had a fried bread thing with pandan custard, and I'm not saying I died and went to heaven, but I died and went to heaven."

I laughed again. "I'll have to see if I can get it for you."

"I would marry you," he replied, then stopped. His eyes went wide, horrified. A rich blush crept up his neck to his cheeks. "No. I mean, I wouldn't. Not that I ever wouldn't, because I probably would, and Christ, I can't believe I said that to you just now and yet here I am still talking." He swallowed hard and picked up the bucket of soapy water and a dishcloth. "I'm going to scrub things until my fingers bleed, so that's nice."

I burst out laughing. "Right. Fried toast and pandan custard is where it's at. Got it."

He shot me an embarrassed glare over his shoulder but began scrubbing down everything. And I do mean everything. Chairs, tables, walls, counters, fridges, cupboards. He figured out how the dishwasher worked, he mopped the floor, and we cleaned windows.

We got so much done. What would have taken me all day and most of the night only took us a handful of hours. By mid-afternoon, we were almost done.

My phone had beeped pretty much non-stop, message after message, and I had a few missed calls. I checked it intermittently but there was nothing that couldn't wait. I spent most of the day up ladders, cleaning with him and organising stock and running tests through the point-of-sale computer system.

But when it rang just after three, I just happened to catch the screen. Dad. I grabbed the phone. "Hey," I answered.

"Bryson," he said, not sounding too pleased. "I messaged and phoned. I was starting to wonder if I should phone the police."

Dramatic much? "Sorry, been busy at the store. Are you in town? I thought you were in Melbourne."

"I got in this morning. You weren't at home."

"Ah, no, I wasn't . . ."

"So, you're at your store right now?"

"Yes. Michael and I have been cleaning all day. We're almost done though."

There was a beat of silence.

"Dad?"

"Well, you're about to get your wish."

"My what?"

"You wanted me to meet him *and* see your store, did you not?"

"Uh, yes?"

"Then open the door."

Oh god . . .

I disconnected the call and shot Michael a wild look. "I'm so sorry," I whispered as I walked to the door. "I'd have liked to give you fair warning, but he didn't give me any."

He tipped the bucket of dirty water down the sink. "Who didn't?"

I pointed to the door and front windows, which were still covered to the outside world. "My dad."

His eyes almost popped out of his head, and I didn't mean to laugh but his expression was funny. I unlocked the door and opened it. My father was standing back, wearing suit pants, a light sweater under his blazer, which was casual for him. He was inspecting the front windows.

"The covers come down tomorrow," I said. "And the opening-soon signs go up." I stood aside. "Come in."

My father walked inside, just a few steps, and stopped. Michael was walking out from behind the counter, wiping his hands on a tea towel. I quickly locked the door and zipped into the space between them.

"Dad, this is Michael Piersen. Michael, this is James Schroeder, my dad."

Michael smiled and held out his hand. "Nice to meet you, sir. You'll have to excuse the pruned hands; they've been in water all day."

They shook hands and my dad nodded. "He put you to work, huh?"

Michael's smile was pure relief. "It was my idea to help."

Dad gave a tight smile, then looked around the store. "Not what I expected. Aren't all coffee houses dark?"

"This isn't an ordinary coffee shop," I replied, not entirely sure where my father was going with this.

He made a face and nodded. "I like it."

I tried not to grin like a fool. "Thank you. Can I make you a kopi?"

He seemed to consider it for a second. "No thank you."

"A tea, then? I have tea as well."

"No, it's fine. I don't need anything," he replied. "Just thought I should come take a look." He walked around, inspecting the service counter, the storeroom. "So the big grand opening is close, right?"

"Yes, Friday." I shoved my hands in my pockets so I didn't fidget. "I have staff induction this week, final stock orders, and the last of the marketing to sort out." Then I thought of something I probably should have considered before now. "Will you be in town on Friday?"

My dad gave me a smile. "I can be."

My smile was instantaneous. "It would mean a lot. I'll be busy and I'm not sure how much I'll see of you, but it'd be nice to have you here."

He gave the smallest of nods, then looked to Michael. "Well, it was nice to meet you," he said, then turned back to me. "But I do have to get going. Will you be home for dinner?"

"Uh . . ."

"If you have plans," he began.

"No, dinner sounds good."

"I'll order some Japanese for seven, then."

"Sounds good."

"Michael? Will you be joining us?"

He stared and shot me a please-help glance, and finding me as shocked as him, he went on his own. "Uh. Thank you, but I will need to get home and get ready for the working week. But thank you. Next time, perhaps."

He left and I locked the door behind him before turning to face Michael. His expression probably matched mine. Somewhat bewildered yet smiling.

"Well, shit," he breathed. "I just met your dad." He looked down at himself and it was pretty clear we'd spent the day cleaning. "I'm a freaking mess."

I went to him and pulled him in for a hug. "At least you weren't waving a tiny pair of Speedos in the air like I was when I met your dad."

He laughed. "Your dad's kinda hot."

I pulled back, horrified. "He's what?"

Michael snorted out a laugh. "If he's what you're gonna look like in thirty years, you're golden."

I threw my head back and laughed, still holding him close. "You come from a family of supermodels, so you can shut up."

He pulled back and slapped my arse. "I've spent all day cleaning for you, so you can buy me food before I go home. I do have stuff I need to do this afternoon."

"Yes, boss."

CHAPTER THIRTEEN

MICHAEL

I KINDA FLOATED through the week on a cloud. Work was good and busy; I got a lot done. Things with Natalie were back to normal. She even asked me how things with Bryce were going. "You don't even need to answer," she'd replied with a roll of her eyes. "God, the hearts in your eyes say it all."

"I don't have . . ." I couldn't even finish that because I was smiling too hard. I couldn't deny it anyway. After all, she'd wanted me to not lie to her. "Things with him are great."

"I can tell," she'd said, and our conversation quickly moved onto work.

Bryce was busy from early till late but he did come over on Wednesday night. We ate dinner and he told me all about his day, about his staff training, how the sunlight gave a whole new feel to the shop now the windows were uncovered, and how the website was already getting great traffic numbers. He had the uniforms now, and it was all starting to feel very real.

His excitement was contagious.

On Thursday after work, I called past the store knowing he'd be there getting everything in order. He grinned when he saw me, locking the door behind us, and pulled me into the shop. He led me by the hand to a woman behind the counter. "Hey, Tarini, this is Michael. Michael, this is Tarini."

She was the manager he'd hired, excitedly telling me he had the perfect person because she born in Singapore, lived in Malaysia until she was eight, and spoke the better part of three languages.

"Hi," she said, her smile wide and warm. Bryce had obviously told her about me. "Nice to finally meet you."

"Same," I replied, shaking her hand. "Getting ready for the big opening tomorrow?"

"Yes!" she said. "But I think we're almost done. Just doing one last run-through."

Bryce was grinning. "I think we're good."

"What time's opening?" I asked.

"Seven," he said, making a face. "Nerves are starting to kick in."

I rubbed his back. "You got this. You're so ready for it to be open."

He gave a nod. "Media team will be here at opening, so I have to be ready."

"Is your dad back yet?" I knew he was away somewhere —he was always somewhere else—and I knew how much it meant to Bry that he'd be here.

"Flies back in around ten in the morning," he replied. "Should be here around lunchtime."

"Good."

Bry took a deep breath and let it out slow. "You're right. I can't wait to begin."

They finished up and I made Bry pose for some preopening photos. Just corny ones standing behind the counter and one underneath his sign, and a few candid shots showing his heart-stopping smile and devastating good looks.

He really was so handsome when he thought no one was looking.

Tarini bid us goodnight, giving him a smirk at the door. "Try and get some sleep. See you bright and early."

I sat on one of the tables while Bry locked the door behind her. He smiled when he turned to face me, walking back to fit between my legs. "I know what will make you sleep," I said, pulling his shirt to bring him in for a kiss.

"Oh yeah? And what is that?"

"A big feed of carbs followed by sex. You'll sleep like the dead."

He laughed. "You know me so well." He pulled me by my knees so our fronts touched and he had to lean down to kiss me. "Let's get out of here." He pulled me off the table, my legs around his waist, and held me there for a second before letting me slowly slide down until my feet hit the floor.

As soon as he had his store locked up, he was quick to grab my hand as we walked to my apartment. "Oh, I took tomorrow off work," I said.

He shot me a startled look. "You did? Why?"

"For you. In case you need me. Tomorrow's a big day for you."

He dropped my hand so he could put his arm around my shoulder and he tucked me into his side as we walked. He kissed the side of my head. "I can't believe you did that for me."

"If you're flat out busy and need someone to run an

errand or go pick something up or to do anything, I'll be there. You can put me to work."

"I plan on putting you to work after dinner," he murmured. "I believe that was the plan, yeah?"

"Hell yes, it was. Pasta first, dessert after. And because you've been working so hard lately, I'll accept one orgasm tonight."

He laughed and tightened his arm around my shoulder. "Very gracious of you."

"I think so."

He laughed, that warm, throaty sex sound that trickled down my spine with promises of what was to come.

WHEN I SAID I'd help all day, it wasn't an exaggeration. We got there just after six thirty, and Bry made himself busy the second he walked in. Tarini pretty much followed us in, then other staff, including a man who, at first, I thought might have been someone's grandpa who'd wandered off from home, but as it turned out, Ken was a kopi master. Born and raised in Singapore for the first fifty years of his life, apparently he and Bry knew each other, speaking in a language I couldn't understand. But they laughed and smiled, side by side, as Ken got busy roasting kopi in huge woks.

The smell was heavenly.

Instead of disrupting them, I went up the wharf and found a place that made a range of toasted sandwiches. I bought a bunch for everyone and took them back. They were grateful and excited, and we snuck in a fresh kopi each before Bryce did the very grand gesture of opening the front doors for the first time.

Whatever marketing Bryce had done had worked because people started filing in, and they didn't seem to stop.

Line after line, drinks, meals, toast and hard-boiled eggs, takeaways, teas, and sweets. It was a fun atmosphere, staff and customers were excited, and seeing Bryce in his element was a sight to behold.

Then the media team turned up, and there were no two ways about it: Bryce Schroeder was his father's son. Sharp and charming, he spoke about his mission to provide a sustainable product and about awareness all while promoting his store with a killer smile.

The fame of his surname never came up. He was never asked if this was a stream in his father's enterprise, he was never asked about connections. Maybe that was very deliberate on his behalf, because he wanted to do this on his own.

And he had.

I was so incredibly proud of him.

I'd forgotten all about his father turning up. Well, I'd lost track of time was probably more apt, but either way, I was surprised when I saw him walk in.

He seemed surprised. If that was because of how busy the store was or if he was surprised by how amazing his son was—how happy he was—I had no clue. Maybe he was surprised by it all. But there was a sting of something else in his eyes too. Was it disappointment?

Was he expecting Bryce to fail?

Hoping he would?

I was grateful Bryce didn't see it.

Mr Schroeder's expression glossed over when he saw me, like he could slip on a mask at will. He smiled and made his way over. "Michael," he said. "I wasn't expecting to see you here today."

"I took the day off," I explained. "I have five years' worth of sick leave and holiday time owing."

"I never did ask where you worked."

"I'm at CREA Realty," I said, waiting for the penny to drop. "Commercial property management."

And drop it did.

His eyebrow quirked, ever so slightly. "Are you managing Bryson's lease?"

I smiled. "No. My boss is."

He didn't say anything, though I could almost hear his mind racing. And, because he made me nervous, I kept speaking.

"My boss knew who he was before I did. Though I knew this location was becoming available and thought it'd be the perfect site for him, so I suggested it. My boss handled the rest."

None of that was a lie.

It wasn't exactly the most honest truth, but it wasn't a lie.

Mr Schroeder didn't reply to that and instead focused on Bry, who was busy behind the counter, and at the still-steady stream of customers. "It looks like it's been a successful first day."

"He's been flat out all morning," I replied, smiling at my boyfriend. "He's worked his arse off to get here. I'm sure you're very proud."

Mr Schroeder's eyes hardened, and I could safely assume he didn't like me saying that. Or maybe he didn't like me . . . "Oh, yes. When he sets his mind to something . . ."

We were both quiet for a moment, and when there was a split second where Bryce wasn't directly speaking to a customer or staff, I called out his name, just loud enough to get his attention. "Bry!"

He glanced up, and seeing me and then his father, he smiled. He spoke to Tarini who quickly stepped in and replaced him, and he darted over to us. "Hey, Dad, I'm glad you could make it," he said, happiness at his father's appearance clear on his face.

"I can't stay, but I wanted to congratulate you on a successful opening."

Bryce beamed with pride. "Thank you."

It was strange to watch them. It was an awkward exchange, but I could see them both trying. I only knew Mr Schroeder through the lens that Bryce coloured him, so it wasn't fair for me to judge the man, and I knew his success on the world stage and the stress and pressure that came with it was something I'd never understand. Him raising Bryce on his own told me he was a good man, despite his faults. And he was trying, more of late, given Bryce had told me that his dad had reached out to spend more time with him recently. He was trying, and he loved Bryce; that much was very clear.

Still, it was a strange exchange.

"Need me to do anything?" I asked.

"I'm not sure," Bry replied, glancing back to his staff. "I need to start sending them all on breaks. I knew we'd be busy. Well, I'd hoped we would. I planned for it, but we've just been getting smashed since we opened."

"How about I do sink duty?" I offered.

"No, I can't ask you to do that," he replied quickly.

"You don't have to ask. It's why I'm here."

"Nah," Bry said. "I put this team together. We need to do this on our own." He clapped my shoulder and went back behind the counter, easing back into the flow of his team. He was unstacking the dishwasher, and when Tarini called out an order for more kaya toast, he was on it.

I could watch him all day.

"Um," Mr Schroeder said uneasily. He gave a pointed nod toward the door. "Have you got a moment, Michael? I'd like a word, if you will."

My heart fell through my feet and I didn't even have time to be surprised. "Oh, sure."

I followed him outside. It was a beautiful day. The sun was shining, barely a cloud in the sky. People were walking, talking, laughing. There were boats on the water, birds overhead. All in all, a perfect Sydney day.

So why did it feel like I was walking to my execution?

Because in a lot of ways, I knew I was.

Mr Schroeder stopped and ran his hand through his hair. It was brown, like his son's, just with a few strands of grey. His brown eyes glittered brown and gold just like Bry's. But they weren't as warm as his. There was a hardness lurking that I imagined would conquer boardrooms and a lesser man might shy away from.

But my years of dealing with men who knew their worth, who used their worth to play games over people they thought were inferior, I could read him like a flashing neon sign. I looked him right in the eye and held his gaze, held my nerve.

He looked away first, casting his gaze out across the water.

"He seems happy," he began. "Seeing him in there just now . . ."

Okay, so that was unexpected.

"I hope he is," I said, opting for safer ground.

"I sent him away to Singapore," he said, still looking at the boats. "I thought he needed to spread his wings and experience the world on his own. I thought he'd see that the family business could be whatever he wanted it to be."

I couldn't believe I was having this conversation with him. Why the hell was he telling me this?

"But he didn't," Mr Schroeder added. "In fact, it had the opposite effect. He loved Singapore. Enough to come back with a business plan to incorporate what he learned from his time there."

This felt like dangerous ground to me. Like a tightrope or a trap. He was pouring his heart out to me, which was baffling, but there was a fall coming. I could feel it.

And it was my fall. There was no doubt.

"And that's his choice," Mr Schroeder added. "He has to live his own life. I respect that."

"And he appreciates that," I said, not sure what else I was supposed to contribute.

"I worry for him." He looked at me then, his gaze piercing. "I worry that he has too much on his plate. And seeing him in there just now, I can see how happy he is. Maybe he was never cut out for the hotel industry. Maybe I knew that all along. Seeing how invested he is in his business . . . It was the right decision for him."

"Yes, it was."

Then that fucker looked me right in the eye. "That's why I'm asking you to walk away."

CHAPTER FOURTEEN

BRYCE

OPENING DAY WAS A HIT. Every single thing fell into place, and not even the smallest hiccups could derail it. Michael helped out bringing back dirty plates and cups, he cleared tables and put rubbish in the bins. He was a pillar of support.

And my dad turning up was the cherry on the cake. Him being there meant the world to me.

But then we got busy, staff needed breaks, and at first, I noticed Michael wasn't there but thought nothing of it. Maybe he'd gone to grab something to eat or to sit down for a while. Maybe he had some phone calls to make; maybe he needed to use the bathroom.

But then he didn't come back.

It was well after two by the time I finally got to take a ten-minute break. I shot him a text. *Everything okay?*

His text bubble appeared, then disappeared, then reappeared. *Not feeling too great right now.*

I frowned at my phone and hit Call, and he didn't answer right away. It rang a few times before he picked up.

"Michael?"

His voice was quiet, distant. "Hey."

"Are you sick? Can I call someone for you?"

Silence. "No, I'm okay. You must still be busy. Can we talk when you're done?"

I had to repeat his words in my head a few times because that sounded all wrong. "Is everything okay?"

I heard him breathe in deep. "Yeah. Um. It's your opening day. I'm just . . . feeling miserable. I don't want to ruin your day. I should go, let you get back to it. I'm sorry I couldn't be there at closing time. I wanted to be there . . ."

His voice sounded so soft, so . . . sad.

"Michael."

"It's fine, Bryce," he replied, his voice stronger now. "You need to focus on your store right now. It's your opening day. We can talk later."

"I can come see you when I'm done."

"No, that's okay. I'm probably not great company right now."

"Well, lie down and put your feet up," I said. "Feel better. I will call you though."

"Okay," he whispered.

And the line went dead in my ear.

That whole conversation was weird. It felt wrong.

Was he just not feeling well? Granted, I'd not seen Michael unwell before, and maybe he was the type of sick person who needed space and silence.

Determined I'd call him later and check on him, I pocketed my phone and went back to work. It was probably another two hours later and we were quiet enough now that Annie and Niran could clock off.

I thanked them both for a great first day. They were all smiles, but it had been a long day. And then Niran said the strangest thing. "Oh, say thanks to Michael for helping out," he said. "I was going to say something when I saw him on my break, but he looked kinda mad talking to that rich guy so I just left them to it."

He looked kinda mad talking to that rich guy . . .

"The rich guy?" I asked, though I didn't really have to. I already knew.

"Yeah. In the expensive grey coat. They were talking in here; then they were talking outside."

I nodded because it suddenly made sense.

Michael hadn't come back after my father had been here, and Dad had worn that godawful grey coat he got in France.

"I'll be sure to tell him you said thanks," I replied to Niran. "See you both tomorrow."

Tarini gave me a few minutes to finish scrubbing the stainless-steel jug to within an inch of its life. "You okay?" she asked.

"My father," I replied. "Just couldn't keep his fat mouth shut. On opening day. Today of all days."

She winced. "That sucks, sorry."

I sighed. "I'll deal with him after. Let's just get to the finish line here. As far as opening days go, it's been a good one."

Well, it had been . . .

She gave a determined nod. "Yes, it has. Let's finish it right."

And she was right. Professional until the end. I would deal with my father later. As for now, I had a business to run.

IT WAS LATE, the store was finally closed, and I had everything ready for the next morning. Tarini had gone home and I was alone and tired. Not to mention that I was pissed off at my father. Probably not the best time to call him but I didn't care. He answered his phone on the third ring. I didn't bother with pleasantries. "Do you want to tell me what you said to Michael out the front of my store today?"

"Probably best not a conversation to be had over the phone."

"Probably not best a conversation to have to have at all, but here we are."

"I take it he told you."

"He didn't tell me anything. Not yet. He disappeared and I was left wondering if he was okay, and when I spoke to him on the phone, he sounded awful. But he never said anything, no. My staff did. They saw you arguing out the front of the store." Then I shouted, "Out the front of my store on opening day! On. Opening. Day, Dad. What the fucking hell?"

"Don't swear at me, Bryson."

"Don't you dare try and act all high and mighty. Don't you fucking dare." That was crossing about a dozen lines with him, but I was well past caring. My heart was hammering, my pulse was thundering, and I was pissed off. "What did you say to him?"

He sighed as if I was some petulant child. "I explained that if he truly understood how much your new enterprise meant to you, he'd make himself less of a priority."

My blood ran ice cold and steaming hot at the same time, and I swear my vision blurred. I wanted to punch the ever-loving shit outta something. "You're lucky this conversation is over the phone and I'm not standing in front of you," I said, my voice low and seething.

"Bryce—"

"You don't get to make decisions for me! You had no right!" I thumped my hand down on the table and tried to speak more calmly. "You had no right to even speak to him. I'm going to see him now, and I swear to God, if he won't see me . . ."

I disconnected the call before I could actually threaten him.

I locked up the store and ran to Michael's apartment. It wasn't far, just a few minutes, but I was panting by the time I arrived. I pressed the intercom. "Michael, it's me."

Nothing.

"Michael, please."

He didn't speak, but the door buzzed open and he was holding the door slightly ajar when I stepped out onto his floor. "You okay? You sounded like you were being chased," he said.

He was wearing tight black lounge pants and a black-and-white striped, long-sleeve shirt. But his face was drawn and pale. He looked wounded. "I ran here," I replied. I put my hand to his chest, to his neck, and up to his jaw. "What did he say to you? What did my father say?"

Michael let the door close and his whole face crumpled. Tears welled in his eyes, spilling down his cheeks, searing me with a pain I'd never felt before. Seeing him cry, seeing him hurt and so upset damn near killed me. I pulled him against my chest, wrapping him up in my arms.

"I'm going to fucking kill him," I breathed.

Michael shook his head and pulled away. He used the sleeve of his shirt to dry his tears and he took a breath. "I didn't want to ruin your first day," he whispered. Then he started to cry again. "It was supposed to be special."

I took his hand and led him to the couch. We sat side by side but I held his hand in mine. "Tell me what he said."

He shook his head again, but not as though he didn't want to tell me. It was more that he didn't want to relive it. I dunno. He just looked so damn sad. "He said if I cared for you at all, I should understand that you need to focus on your shop."

"But that's not true," I replied.

"Isn't it?" he shrugged. "He began by telling me how proud he was of you and how he thought sending you to Singapore would make you want to work with him, but instead you came home with dreams that weren't his. He didn't say that exactly, but he may as well have. He said he could see now how driven you were to succeed and how happy you were to be working in your own business." Michael wiped at fresh tears. "He said that I should respect your drive to succeed and not stand in your way. He said given how busy and blinded you were by me, you wouldn't have the foresight to see the inevitable, so he wanted me to be the one to walk away."

I let out a slow, measured breath. "I'm going to fucking kill him."

"I told him he was wrong," Michael said, crying again. "I told him if he thought that of you, then he didn't know you at all. I told him he didn't know me at all either." His chin wobbled. "I was . . . I couldn't go back inside. I just had to leave. I couldn't let you see me."

"Why? Baby . . ."

He shook his head and tears escaped his eyes. "Because it would have proved your father right. Hell, it did prove him right. I was everything he said I was."

"A distraction."

Michael nodded again. "He wanted to make me a distraction just to prove himself right." He put his free hand to his face and sobbed. "I'm sorry."

I touched his arm, his face, his hair. "No, Michael. Don't be sorry. You have nothing to apologise for. I'm so sorry he said those things to you. I'm sorry he hurt you."

He looked at me then, nose red, eyes wet and puffy. "Bry, what if he's right?"

I shook my head. "No. No, he's not."

He pulled his hand from mine and folded his legs up underneath him, effectively putting a small distance between us. He'd sat like that with me a dozen times, but this felt different.

He wiped at his face and let out a shaky breath. "I never expected your father to welcome me with open arms. But I never expected him to outright despise me."

"He doesn't despise you," I said.

"He despises what I am to you. He wants me out of your life."

He sounded so defeated, as if he agreed with what my father had said. "Michael, please."

"I'm just . . . I'm sorry. But what he said really hurt me."

"Baby, he's not me. What he said doesn't reflect how I feel. I love you. That hasn't changed."

"I know, and I love you too."

"But?"

I knew it was coming. I could feel it.

"But I think I need a little time."

My heart beat in my chest like a hummingbird caught in a snare. "Are you . . . are you breaking up with me?"

He shook his head and fresh tears streamed down his face. "No. I don't want to." He chewed on his bottom lip.

"But I need some time." Then he let out a laugh that was half-cry. "And you know what I hate the most? It's that it makes your father right, and it gives him exactly what he wanted."

"So don't give it to him," I replied. "Give him the opposite of what he wants. If he did this to break us up, then let's prove to him that we're stronger than that. We're together, you and me, whether he likes it or not. And if he thinks for one second that he can dictate what we do or manipulate us into what he wants, then let's prove him wrong."

Michael wiped his face with his sleeve again and sighed. His gaze locked with mine, and he almost smiled. "He already doesn't like me, Bry. I don't know if poking the hornet's nest is a good idea."

"Let me tell you one thing about my father." I put my hand on his thigh. "He will respect you more if you stand up to him. I'm not just saying that so you won't dump me like he wants."

Michael snorted.

"Sure, it might piss him off in the beginning, but in the end, he'll know where you stand. He deals with all kinds of bigwigs from all over the world, and I can tell you the ones he respects are the ones who challenge him."

Michael didn't say anything for a long moment, but eventually he wrapped his hand over mine. "I don't want to lose you."

"Then don't. Don't punish me because of something he said or did."

He frowned and got teary again. "I didn't mean to. I'm sorry. I'm punishing myself too. God, why today of all days? Why would he say that to me today?"

"Because he just sees his own agenda." I shrugged. "He's been telling me for weeks that I shouldn't be distracted, that I needed to focus on my business. Because that's how he operates. It's hard to explain," I said, scrubbing my hand over my face. "My father and I have a very complex and strange relationship. I know he loves me. It's only ever been him and me and he's done a lot. He's also not done a lot, not by any fault of his own. He was creating an empire and thought paying other people to look after me was parenting."

"I'm sorry, Bry," he murmured.

"But it made me who I am. It made me independent. Always being on my own made me stronger. If it was urgent or important, he'd be there; there was always the safety net of knowing that. But for the most part, it was just me." I sighed. "So he doesn't get to act like an arsehole when it finally dawns on him that I don't need him or that I don't think like him, because I'm the product of his parenting.

"Michael, I'm sorry he said that to you. It's unforgivable, and you have every right to be mad and hurt. I don't blame you one bit. I blame him. And believe me, he's gonna know about it. I already yelled at him over the phone."

"You did?"

I nodded. "Yep. One of my staff saw you and him talking out the front of the store, so I knew he'd said something to upset you. He didn't even try and deny it when I called him."

"What did he say?"

"He said it was probably a conversation we shouldn't have over the phone. I told him he was lucky it wasn't in person. I'm feeling a lot calmer now that I've spoken to you, but I swear to God, I could have punched the piss out of him."

Michael chuckled and put his hand over his mouth. "Please don't punch him."

I shook my head and sighed. I met his gaze. "Are we okay, Michael?"

He nodded. "Yeah."

"Thank God." I brought his hand up to my lips and kissed his knuckles. "I do love you. And I'm glad we could talk this out."

He smiled, for real this time. "Me too."

I played with his fingers for a bit. "I'm still gonna let him have it. He's going to know where I stand and what you mean to me. He was way out of line today and he needs to know that."

Michael inhaled deeply and let his head rest on the back of the couch. "How did your first day end up?"

"Really good. We were so busy. It was huge. Huuuuuuge."

He squeezed my hand. "I'm really proud of you."

His words warmed my heart. "Thank you. That means a lot. I was hoping it was going to be as busy as that, but honestly, it went better than I expected. And I know it won't always be that busy once things settle down, but it was great. And Niran said to say thank you."

He smiled. "He was sweet."

"They're a good bunch. Hopefully I can keep them as excited about their jobs as they were today."

"I'm sure you will. Early start again tomorrow?"

I nodded. "Yep. Will be for a while."

"You must be tired."

"I am. But I needed to see you tonight."

Now he brought my hand to his lips and pressed my palm to his cheek. "What are you gonna say to your dad?"

"I'll think of something. I won't see him until tomorrow night, so with a bit of luck, the impulse to punch him will have passed."

Michael smiled. "Wanna go to bed?"

I nodded quickly. "Yes, please. I need to shower first."

"Have you eaten?"

I shook my head. "No. I ran straight here."

"Go shower. I'll fix you something."

I leaned over and kissed him, soft and sweet. "I love you, Michael Piersen with an e."

He smiled. "I love you too."

MICHAEL CAME to the store with me first thing. It was Saturday and he had to go to his office by eight, but him wanting to help me just reinforced to me that I'd made the right decision.

Michael and I were the real deal.

Up until yesterday, things between us had been fun and flirty, serious and very sexual. In the scheme of things, and in just a few short months, we'd fallen hard and fast, but that didn't make our relationship trivial. Our first falling out had been a doozy. My father had fucked up, big time, but Michael and I had talked our way through it. He expressed his hurt and I'd listened, and together we'd found a way to the other side.

I felt even closer to him than I did before.

We were stronger now.

Customers started to file in as soon as the doors opened, and before I had time to think, Michael ducked in behind the service counter and put his hand on my arm. "I'm off now. I'll be back this afternoon."

I met his gaze. "Thank you."

He smiled, and I knew we were good. He went to work and I got busy with customers, putting in new stock orders, checking the reports on the point-of-sale system. Michael came back around three with a sandwich that he handed to me. "I knew you wouldn't have eaten."

I grinned at him. "I haven't, no. Tarini, I'm taking five."

"Okay, boss," she said as she seamlessly stepped in.

Michael and I sat out on the ledge seat on the wharf, enjoying the sun and the sounds of the city. "Did you get everything done?" I asked, taking a bite of the sandwich.

"Yep. It was a productive day. You've been busy all day again?"

I nodded as I chewed. "Flat out."

"Good."

"I sent my father a text message," I told him.

"You did?"

"Yep. Told him I needed to see him. He said he's free this afternoon. I said I'm not. That time didn't suit me. I told him I'd see him tomorrow night."

Michael smiled. "What did he say to that?"

"Nothing. I'm happy to let him sweat on it for a bit. I want him to sweat on it."

Michael's smile twisted a little. "I don't want you to have to choose."

"I didn't choose this, Michael," I replied. "He chose to say what he said. He can deal with the consequences."

"Are you sure you don't want me to come with you?"

I shook my head. "No. I got this." I winked at him and he reached over and squeezed my hand.

"You'll come see me right after, yeah?"

"Baby, I wouldn't be anywhere else."

I ARRIVED HOME—THE apartment where I lived with my father, whenever he was in Sydney—just before six thirty. The store was closed after its successful third day, and I'd told my dad he could expect me around half six.

I almost expected him not to be there. I wouldn't have been surprised to find a note on the kitchen bench saying he'd been called to some important business matter in Kuala Lumpur. But he was home. I could hear him talking, on the phone, I presumed.

I grabbed an apple out of the fruit bowl and took a few bites before deciding it wasn't crunchy enough. I binned it and went down the hall toward my father's office. His door was open so I walked right in and sat opposite him at his desk.

I greeted him with a smile and waited for him to wrap up his conversation.

I was going for confident, and I didn't even have to put on that much of a show. I'd spent the last three days thinking about what I'd say to him and how this conversation was going to go.

My father stared at me. "Okay, Amah," he said into the phone. "I have to go. But I'll be in touch. Thank you."

He put his phone down and continued to stare at me. "Bryce."

"Dad."

He looked away first. "Look. I know what you're going to say."

"You have no idea what I'm about to say." His eyes narrowed at me and I wondered if that was how he'd looked at Michael. It fuelled my resolve to have this conversation. "You told Michael to leave me."

"No, I said—"

"You said if he loved me, he should walk away."

He clamped his mouth shut and changed tack. "I told him it was difficult for a parent to stand by. As a father, it was my duty—"

I sat forward in my seat. "You don't get to parent me now. Dad, I love you, and I respect all you've accomplished. And yes, there was always food in the fridge and a roof over my head, but you never *parented* me. Wanna know who taught me how to tie shoelaces? Julia, the nanny from Ireland. I was five. Who helped me with my homework projects in primary school? Sharline, the nanny from England. Then I went to boarding school. Oh, and who taught me how to drive? Roger." Roger had been my dad's personal driver for years. "So don't come at me with your parenting high horse bullshit."

He levelled a cool stare at me. "You're clearly still mad at me."

"Mad doesn't begin to cover it. You should have seen me on Friday night. I wasn't kidding when I said it was probably best I didn't see you face to face."

He didn't say anything for a long few seconds. "I can understand your anger. What I did was for your benefit. I'm sorry things ended between you and him, but if you want to be successful—"

"You're not sorry." The words were out before I could stop them. "What you did was cruel and unnecessary, and for no one's benefit but your own."

"That's not true. I saw how busy you were, how well your business was set up, the effort you'd put into it, and how happy that made you. If you want that to continue, it needs to remain a priority. I know that's probably not what you want to hear, but distractions at this point of your start-up could be detrimental to the business."

"What was detrimental to my business was you telling

Michael to leave me on opening day. On opening day!" I wanted to pull my hair out. He still didn't get it. I doubted he ever would. "And stop calling him a distraction. You think the only way for someone to be successful is to be alone with no distractions. Like I told you before, Michael is *not* a distraction. He's a person, a human being with emotions and a heart bigger than I deserve."

"Bigger than you deserve?"

"Yes! I love him. And I won't apologise to you for being happy. Well, I was happy. Until you fucked it up. You have just been biding your time and waiting, waiting, waiting for me to fuck something up. A successful business or a successful relationship, like they can't exist in the same universe. But I *can* have both. If it kills me, god, I will have both. But now he won't even speak to me because of what you said." That wasn't the truth, but he didn't need to know that. The plan was to make him realise the damage he'd caused.

"Bryson, it'd be a mistake."

I stood up. "Don't you dare tell me it's a mistake. Falling in love with him was not a mistake. This is not my mistake. This is *your* mistake. This is your mess. You fucked this up, and so help me, you will fix it."

"Fix it?"

I slammed my fist on the desk. "You will fix it. You will go and see him, and beg and fucking grovel if you have to. And you will apologise. Because, thanks to you, he won't see me. And unlike you, as much as I want my business to succeed, I will choose him over any of this, any day of the week."

"Bryce."

"Don't 'Bryce' me. You need to fix this because I am not you. I can give one hundred percent to my business *and* one hundred percent to Michael. Because he gives one hundred percent back to me. See, Dad, that's the thing about relationships. You get back what you put in. I'm sorry my mother left you. But she left me too." That hurt him to hear as much as it hurt me to say it. "And if that's taught me anything, anything at all, it's that I have more reason to fight for him."

"I . . . I don't know what to say," he whispered.

"You can start with an apology. To me, and to Michael. You don't just get to try and ruin the best thing to ever happen to me and walk away like it was nothing. You hurt him, and by doing that, you hurt me. I love him, and I need you to make this right."

My father swallowed hard. "I, uh, I have a very busy week and I'm out of town—"

"I'm not asking. You find the time to apologise to him. Make it happen, Dad. You need to make this right."

Dad sat there, still and silent, and I stood there in front of him. I wasn't backing down and I wasn't apologising. "I'm not even going to discuss your timing of this whole mess," I said, low and calm. "I'm going to pretend you didn't try to sabotage my opening day and my relationship just to prove your point that the two can't exist side by side. And honestly, it's not the fact that you hurt me that bothers me the most. You hurt Michael, and that's worse. So if you make no attempt to fix what you broke, I'll know that what I've said here tonight means nothing to you." I stopped short of saying that I'd know my happiness meant nothing or that I meant nothing.

I didn't need to say that. It was right there, like a third person standing beside me.

Two against one.

Still, he said nothing. But I'd said everything I'd come to

say, everything I'd told Michael I was going to say. Why did I give him the impression that Michael had broken up with me?

To make my father realise his betrayal and work for his apology. If he knew that Michael and I were okay, he'd see no reason to apologise. He'd simply brush it off as nothing lost, no damage done. At first I thought maybe Michael and I should confront him as a united force, but this worked better.

And there was no untruth spoken here tonight.

"Okay," I said, letting out a resigned sigh. "I've said all I needed to say. I'm gonna go now." I got to the door. "Don't forget to eat dinner."

"Bryce," he said, getting to his feet. "Where are you staying?"

I met his gaze. "Not here. It's not forever. I just need a few days. I'm sure you understand."

I left with my chin raised. I'd stood up to him, and I'd said what needed saying. But man, the closer to Michael's place I got, the worse I felt. He opened the door, took one look at me, and pulled me into his arms. "Oh, Bry," he murmured. "You okay?"

I nodded. "Yeah. I said everything he needed to hear." I sighed. "And now we wait."

He pulled back and cupped my face. "I love you. Let me look after you tonight. Tell me what you need."

I kissed him, soft and sweet. "I just want to cuddle on the couch. I want to lie with you, hold you close, and think about nothing." Then as an afterthought, I added, "Oh, and I want my BTS shirt back."

He grinned. "Four out of five, I can do."

CHAPTER FIFTEEN

MICHAEL

I HATED that Bryce was hurting over his father. I hated that his father had put him in this position, and I hated that his father put his own agenda before Bryce's happiness. I hated that this was all happening when Bryce's business was brand new. He had enough on his mind without all that.

Most of all, I hated that his father made him feel like shit.

He'd been so exhausted from work that when I'd pulled him onto the couch and we'd settled down, he put his head on my chest, I stroked his hair with my fingers, and he was asleep in no time at all.

I had to wake him to get him into bed, and he was restless all night. I fed him toast and juice at six o'clock and then sent him to work, and I was in the office a few minutes after seven thirty. I had a busy day ahead—it was Monday, after all. I could get more done in the hour before people started arriving, before meetings, and before the phone started ringing than I usually did in the rest of the day.

I hadn't so much as looked up from my desk when

Carolyne knocked lightly on my office door and came in. I glanced at the time on my computer. It was 8:32am. "There's a guy here to see you. He doesn't have an appointment. I told him he'd need one, and he said to let you know who he is. He said his name is Schroeder."

I frowned. "Bryce?" Because he should be busy as hell at work . . . unless his arsehole father went and made things worse . . .

She shook his head. "No, not Bryce. James. He said his name is James."

Oh, dear God.

Just then, because of fucking course, Natalie walked into my office. She was wide-eyed and a little pale. "James Schroeder is here to see you. *The* James Schroeder is sitting in our waiting room."

"Uh . . . Yes, Carolyne was just saying."

She looked between me and Natalie. "Oh, is that . . . Schroeder of the Schroeder Hotels . . . oh god." Her eyes went wide and landed on me. "I thought his shoes looked nice. And his coat. Actually, even his haircut looks expensive . . ."

Natalie was still staring at me. "Yes, that Schroeder. Just one of the richest men in Australia, actually. Property mogul extraordinaire, sitting in our waiting room. Waiting, Michael. You don't keep James Schroeder waiting."

"Actually, I think we should. Let's take bets to see how long he'll wait. I've got twenty bucks on five minutes . . . no, four minutes. I'll give him four minutes before he walks out."

Carolyne was clearly confused. She leaned in and whispered, "Why are we making him wait?"

"Because he's an arsehole," I replied. "And arseholes can wait."

"Oh," Natalie breathed. "I see." She put her hand to her forehead. "Michael, we're not letting our personal relationships affect our professional reputation, are we? That's what we agreed on. Now, I don't know what he did, but please don't make this—"

Carolyne was still lost. "I'm so confused."

Natalie pursed her lips. "I'm assuming that meeting the father-in-law didn't go as planned."

Carolyne's eyes and mouth were all perfect circles. "Oh."

I sighed. "We're hardly at that point."

She pointed toward the door. "Michael, you need to get your arse out there now. We don't keep client's waiting."

"He's not a client and he doesn't have an appointment," I replied, knowing how childish I sounded. I checked my watch. "Has it been four minutes yet?"

Natalie made a whispering, seething sound that was a little scary. "Michael."

I stood up. "Fine. I'll go speak to him. I just wanted to make him sweat a little." And honestly, I also needed to steel my nerves and remember what Bry had told me.

I walked out of my office and buttoned my jacket as I strode into the waiting room. Bryce's father sat, looking incredibly expensive. Carolyne wasn't kidding about the coat and shoes. "Mr Schroeder," I said, as professionally as I could.

He stood. "Michael. Thank you for seeing me. I understand you're probably busy, but I was hoping you could spare a few minutes."

"I have a meeting at nine," I said. Which wasn't untrue. It was just a staff meeting, but I didn't care. I had four other meetings today, but I could guess that he probably had ten meetings to get to, in three different cities. I gestured toward my office. "Come this way."

I led him into my office and waited for him to walk in so I could close the door behind him. I sat in my seat and he sat, rather uncomfortably, across from me. "Nice view," he said, nodding to the city outside. "You've obviously done well for yourself."

I gave him a tight, almost polite smile. "I'm good at my job."

"Bryson speaks very highly of you." He swallowed hard. "He's a very good judge of character."

"Mr Schroeder," I began.

He raised his hand. "Please, let me speak. What I said to you the other day was wrong. I shouldn't have said that. I shouldn't have implied I knew what was best for him, because as it was made very clear to me last night, I do not."

Holy shit.

"Bryce was very upset with me," he continued. "Actually, he wasn't upset. He was angry. And he had every right to be. I was out of line and I've come to apologise."

I nodded slowly. "You were out of line. But I accept your apology. Thank you for coming to see me."

He almost smiled, and god, he looked so much like Bryce right then, any anger I felt toward him dissipated. "I tried to protect him," he said. "But I went about it the wrong way. What I should have said was that I don't want you to leave him; I want you to support him. His new business will be a priority, but if you support that, then that will help him." He grimaced. "I think that still sounded wrong. I don't know. I'm trying here."

I had to bite the inside of my lip so I didn't smile. "I want him to be happy too. And successful. I want those things for him as well. And I'd like to help him as much as possible."

He looked out the wall of glass again before meeting my gaze. "He told me, in no uncertain terms, that I had to fix the damage I'd done. But I'm not just saying this to you so he'll forgive me. I want him to be happy. And apparently you make him happy. Please don't think bad of him because of me." He grimaced then. "So if you could please tell him that I tried to right my wrongs, I'd appreciate that. I know how stubborn he can be, and once he makes up his mind . . ."

Mr Schroeder had clearly suffered enough, so I put him out of his misery. "I'll let him know you came to see me. I will tell him you apologised. I'm sure he'll be relieved."

He visibly relaxed and even managed a smile. "Thank you. I appreciate that."

"Mr Schroeder," I said. "Bryce loves you very much. And he's a great man. He's driven, focused, and he's a lot of fun. All he wants is your approval and for you to be proud of him." I shrugged. "When you took him for dinner the other week, he talked about it for days."

"He did?"

I nodded. "And I would never assume to tell you how to parent, but maybe when you're in town and you haven't seen him in a bit, you could take him out for dinner again. I think he'd like that."

He smiled and nodded, then he got to his feet, signalling that our meeting was over. "Thanks again." He looked pointedly to my phone, turned screen-down on my desk. "I know you're busy. Actually, I think your phone buzzes more than mine, so I'll let you get back to it." Then he got to the door. "And Michael, if Bryce and I go out for dinner, you might like to join us."

I grinned as I stood. "I'd like that. Thank you."

He gave a final nod, opened the door, and disappeared. I collapsed back into my chair and put my hand to my hammering heart. Both Carolyne and Natalie appeared in my doorway. "So? What happened?" Natalie asked, walking in.

"You might want to clear the pigs for landing," I said. "Because hell just froze over."

She cocked her head. "What?"

I laughed, relieved. "He came to apologise." Checking the time, I realised it was almost nine. I picked up my phone and found SAF's number. I shot him a text message as I stood and walked to the staff meeting.

Your dad just left my office. Apology received and accepted.

I knew he wouldn't be able to reply for a while, so I pocketed my phone and walked into the staff meeting. New clients, old contracts, addendums, legislature, conveyancing . . . it was a blur until Carolyne knocked on my office door. "Lunchtime," she said. "Want me to grab you something?"

I grinned and stretched my aching shoulder muscles. "No, thanks. I'll be ducking out for a bit. Won't be long."

To save time, I cabbed it to the wharf and smiled at the line of customers in Bryce's store. There was a new staff member behind the counter and a familiar face. Tarini smiled brightly at me. "He's out the back. I had to make him take a lunch break." I laughed because that sounded familiar. "Just go on through. He'll see you on the security camera."

"Thank you," I said as I ducked behind the counter. And sure enough, the office door opened as I got to it. He had half an eaten sandwich in his hand and wore a huge grin.

"I just read your text. It's the first time I've sat down all day. So, he did it, huh?"

I sat him back down in his seat and parked my arse on his desk. "He was very gracious and embarrassed. He was humble. And I even got an invite to dinner."

Bry laughed, covering his mouthful of food. "Well, shit." He swallowed and nodded. "I'm glad. I was pretty sure he would, but I'm still happy he did the right thing."

"Me too," I admitted. "You know, I was still mad at first, but I could see how hard it was for him and how honest he was. There is so much of you in him. I couldn't be mad."

Bry shoved the rest of his sandwich in his mouth, threw the wrapper into his bin, and stood up. He pulled me in for a hug, standing with a foot on either side of my legs, and he held me while he chewed and swallowed his food. "Thank you," he said; his voice reverberated through where my ear was pressed to his chest. Then, still with one arm around me, he called his father. "Dunno if he'll pick up," he murmured before I heard a tinny voice from his phone. "Oh hey, Dad," Bry said. "I'm just calling to say thank you. ... Yeah, he's here right now. We sorted everything out. ... Yeah, I think so." His voice was so soft and sweet it made me pull back and look up at him. He was smiling, his eyes met mine, and he even blushed a little. "Okay. See you then. Have a safe trip."

He disconnected the call and put his phone on the desk before cupping my face and kissing me. "He likes you," he said.

"I'm a likeable guy," I replied.

"Yes, you are."

"You were supposed to say I was lovable."

He laughed. "You're that too."

I sighed. "Should we feel bad that we kind of lied to him?"

"Nope," he said, then kissed the tip of my nose. "And we didn't lie to him. Not exactly."

"We led him to believe we'd broken up."

"No, I led him to believe you left here and didn't want to speak to me. That much was true."

"I only didn't want to see you because I would have burst into tears as soon as I told you what happened, and it was your opening day. You needed to be here."

He cupped my face, his eyes sincere. "Please don't hide from me again. You never have to hide anything from me."

I melted into him a little. "I know. I just didn't want to ruin your day."

"You didn't. He did. But that's behind us now. He learned his lesson and he apologised. Plus, I got to say some stuff to him that probably should have been said years ago." He kissed me softly. "I think we'll be better for it. He's flying out to Singapore this afternoon. Wants me to email him a list of anything I might need him to bring back . . . for the store, that is. And said we should do dinner when he gets back."

I ran my hand up his chest, marvelling at his smile. "I'm glad it all worked out, Bry. I look forward to getting to know him better."

"Same," he said with a laugh. "Maybe now he's stopped seeing me as a kid, we might talk some more. I think he was trying . . . before. Who knows. But I've got a good feeling."

"I'm glad. And speaking of multiple good feelings," I said suggestively, "what time will you be finished tonight?"

He caught on immediately. He gave me a kiss with a wicked grin. "I can be at your place by seven thirty."

"Excellent. Because you're behind on your orgasm quota and you really need to catch up. So, I'll provide dinner. You provide the rest."

He laughed. "You're so bossy."

"And you love me for it."

"Yes, I do." He kissed me with smiling lips. "I really do."

EPILOGUE
MICHAEL

Twelve months later

SO, here we are at the end. Remember how at the very beginning I was going to explain how this all went down? Well, there you have it.

But before I tell you how this panned out, I want to explain something real quick.

Sex for the purpose of just sex is a thing that happens. Uncomplicated, no-strings-attached, mutual-physical-gratification kind of sex. As long as it's consensual, safe, and satisfying for all involved, everyone wins. Right?

Only now that happens to other people.

Because now sex was a wondrously complicated, highly emotionally connective, intimately private thing. Sure, sometimes we still fucked like rabid bunnies. But it's so much more now.

I know, I once said that not everyone needs an emotional connection to enjoy sex. Sometimes that emotional connection just complicates matters, and who needs complicated in their lives?

I once said that I certainly didn't need that complication and that I had neither the time nor the inclination for complications.

I was so wrong.

I got absolutely blindsided and mowed down by a man called Bryson James Schroeder, and it wasn't gloriously and spectacularly bad at all. The train wreck analogy might have been an over-exaggeration. I never said I wasn't melo-dramatic.

But had my life been derailed?

Yes, it had.

Bryce was, without doubt, the best thing to ever happen to me.

I was a different man now. I was different because he loved me. Yes, yes . . . that sappy bullshit where I say stuff like that is where I'm at. I told you last-year-me wouldn't even recognise today-me, and that was a very good thing.

So here we are, twelve months later.

I stood behind the service counter, wearing a staff uniform, complete with an apron and a huge grin. I was up to my elbows in soapy water, laughing at something Ken had said.

I still had my corporate real estate job and probably always would. Bryce had asked me to join his team, but I'd declined every time. Sure, I helped out a lot when I could, but the separation of professional and personal was a good thing.

Work was work, home was home, and never the twain shall meet. Yes, we lived together and had for several months. He basically lived at my place anyway, so it had made sense to make it official. So having work/home separa-tion was a very good thing. Another upside was our now-shared wardrobe. I had access to all his band T-shirts and he could wear any of my tight-fitting tailored shirts. It was a win-win, honestly.

But getting back to work . . . Today I was helping out because today was special.

Why was it special?

Because Bryce was opening his second store.

We'd found the perfect location in Bondi, and opening day was huge. We got hammered; the stream of customers just didn't seem to stop. So there I was when the store was finally closed, washing up for the fiftieth time that day, when I could feel eyes on me. I looked up to find Bryce and James at the end of the counter, both watching me.

They were smiling: Bryce's with an edge of adoration and James' with a hint of amusement. I pulled the tea towel from my back pocket and threw it at Bryce's father. He caught it and shot me a look. "If you're just gonna stand there," I said, "I'll put you to work. Don't have time to just stand around."

Bryce laughed. "Told you he was bossy."

But, as a surprise to everyone, James took the tea towel and began to dry. Bryce laughed, his eyes wide, and I stood up, stretching my aching back. "Wanna swap? Got time to laugh, Schroeder, you got time to wash up."

Bryce just laughed some more and went back to the point-of-sale terminal to do his end of day sales report, and James gave me an approving nod as he dried the first tray. "Glad you're still keeping him in line."

I snorted. "As much as I'm able." I wiped my biceps against my forehead as I scrubbed a canister. "This work makes me appreciate my desk job, I can tell you that much."

He chuckled and had to get out of the way for one of the staff carrying a box of some cakes to restock the fridge.

"It is a good reminder," he said, still smiling. "Has he thought any more on branching out in Melbourne?"

"I think it'll happen," I replied. "He'll let this place get settled in first. He's very cautious about overstepping his capital."

James smiled proudly. He and Bry had come a long way, and James had accepted me being an important part of Bryce's life. We weren't on par with the Brady Bunch or anything, but it was pretty sweet.

"What will you do if he has to go to Melbourne for a while?" James asked me. There was no malice in his tone, just concern.

"We'll be okay," I answered confidently. "No matter where he is or where I am, we'll be fine. And if I have to take a few days leave to go help him or just be with him, then I will. It's just what we do."

He nodded and smiled, more to himself this time. "I'm glad he has you."

I pulled the plug in the sink and wiped it down. "I'm glad I have him too."

"Okay, we are done!" Bryce called, holding his hands up in a victory crow. "Opening day complete."

His staff all cheered and even James clapped and laughed. Bryce put his arm around my shoulder and kissed the side of my head. "Couldn't have done this without you."

I held up my very pruned and wrinkly hands. "You owe me a manicure."

"Since when do you have manicures?"

"Okay, well, then you owe me dinner."

"That I can do."

Bryce ordered celebratory pizza for everyone and we sat around eating, our tired feet up on stools, smiles wide. It had been an awesome day. Everyone had really pulled through, and even though Bryce was exhausted and there was the added pressure of starting his own franchise, he was proud. And so he should have been.

Bryce thanked his staff and told them he was grateful and proud, and when the last of them had left and the doors were locked, he ran his hand through his hair and looked around his store. "What a day," he said. "What a bloody day."

"Exceeded your sales projections?" James asked.

Bryce grinned. "Far exceeded. Far."

"I'm proud of you," I said.

"I'm proud of you too," James added, a rare and high praise.

"Thank you," Bryce replied. "Both of you. I love you both. Your support means the world to me."

I hugged him and he leaned heavily against me. "How about we get you home? You're just about dead on your feet."

"Sounds good." He straightened up and looked at James. "Thanks for helping out, Dad."

"It was my pleasure. And congratulations on launching your own franchise. You'll be coming for my title soon."

Bryce rolled his eyes. "Not likely, but okay." It had been a very long few weeks to get to this point and he really was exhausted.

"Hand me your keys," I said to Bryce. "I'm driving. You're too tired."

He pouted. "You're so bossy." But he handed his car keys over and stood there, taking a last look around his new store. "Still can't believe this is real."

"You'll believe it when your alarm goes off at five in the morning again," I replied. James laughed and Bryce groaned.

He slung his arm around me. "Take me home."

We said goodbye to Bryce's dad and I slid in behind the steering wheel. I didn't need an excuse to drive Bry's car, but it sure was nice. He sat kind of side-on to face me, smiling but oh so tired. "Today has been a really good day."

"I'm so happy for you," I said.

He reached for my hand and he didn't say much on the ride home. He just stared at me and smiled, all dreamy-like. And he was looking at me like that when we got to our apartment. He just looked at me with a dopey smile.

"Everything okay, Bry?"

He nodded and even chuckled a bit, his cheeks flushed with colour. *That was weird.*

"Do you need anything else to eat? Or just want to have a shower and go to bed?"

He shook his head. "Neither. Can I ask you something?"

"Yeah, of course."

He held his hand out, so I took it, curious now because he was acting weird.

"I couldn't have got to today if it weren't for you," he said.

"Yes, you would have. You would have found a way."

"No," he said adamantly. "You push me to do better, and to be better. But for the right reasons. You want me to be happy."

"Of course I do. It's the one thing I want more than anything."

His smile became serene. "You know, when we first met . . . I never dreamed I'd be here with you now. Like this. I can't imagine my life without you."

I put my hand to his cheek and studied his beautiful

face. He was tired, but he looked so peaceful. "You don't have to. I'm not going anywhere."

He closed his eyes, still smiling. "No matter how busy I get, no matter what new crazy business idea I decide on next, you never doubt me. I'm so blessed that you love me."

Okay, this was getting weirder. "You're so tired you're delirious. Let's get you into bed, 'kay, baby?"

But he didn't move. His smile faltered a little. "Michael," he murmured, holding my shirt so I couldn't leave. "If I asked you to love me forever, would you?"

Forever . . .

"I will already love you forever," I replied, still unsure what he was getting at.

"No, if I asked you if you'd be with me forever . . ." His tired brown eyes met mine. "Would you be with me forever? If I asked. Because I'm asking. Love me forever. Say you will. Because I will only want you until the day I die. There is no one else for me. There's nothing else for me but you. Forever. Michael."

Oh my fucking god.

"What are you asking, Bry?"

He took my hand—my left hand—and kissed my knuckles before meeting my gaze. "I didn't plan this. I don't have anything to make it official. I don't even need it to be official. Just look me in the eyes right now and tell me you'll be mine forever."

"I will love you forever," I whispered, my heart thumping in my chest. "I promise you."

He sagged with relief and joy. His eyes became glassy. "I promise you too. I will love you forever. I'm sweaty and gross. I'm tired as hell, and I smell like a coffee grinder. But I couldn't wait . . . looking at you tonight, I just had to ask. Marry me or don't, it doesn't matter. If you want a ring, I'll buy you whichever one you want. Whatever it takes to make this real for you. Michael Piersen with an e, I love you now and I will love you forever."

I nodded, a little teary. This was the last thing I expected. My heart felt like it'd doubled in size and it took my breath away.

Once again I was completely blindsided by him. Bryson Schroeder just barrelled me from all angles, and I fell in love with him a little bit more. I cupped his face and kissed him. "We can talk about rings when you're not falling asleep."

He chuckled sleepily, pulling me close and leaning heavily against me. I held him up and helped him walk to bed. I mostly undressed him, then myself, and he lay down with his arm out, waiting for me to climb in. I snuggled into him and he sighed. "You made me so happy," he mumbled.

"Maybe now you can change my name from Bossy to Michael in your phone."

"Mm-mm. No way."

I chuckled, and with a deep sigh, he was already asleep.

SO THERE YOU HAVE IT. The crazy tale of how an agreement for uncomplicated sex became a true story of a forever love.

Yes, I was completely blindsided and foolish for thinking complications with Bryce would ever be a bad thing. Complications could sometimes turn into the best thing to ever happen to you. Sometimes it was a train and you were stuck on the tracks and it was gonna hurt like a bitch. And sometimes that train wore vintage band T-shirts and a beautiful smile and derailed your life anyway.

Like I told you before, meeting him and falling in love with him was highly traumatic and life-changing. With a dash of possibly wonderful.

And I wouldn't have it any other way.

THE END

ABOUT THE AUTHOR

N.R. Walker is an Australian author, who loves her genre of gay romance. She loves writing and spends far too much time doing it, but wouldn't have it any other way.

She is many things: a mother, a wife, a sister, a writer. She has pretty, pretty boys who live in her head, who don't let her sleep at night unless she gives them life with words.

She likes it when they do dirty, dirty things... but likes it even more when they fall in love.

She used to think having people in her head talking to her was weird, until one day she happened across other writers who told her it was normal.

She's been writing ever since...

ALSO BY N.R. WALKER

Blind Faith

Through These Eyes (Blind Faith #2)

Blindside: Mark's Story (Blind Faith #3)

Ten in the Bin

Gay Sex Club Stories 1

Gay Sex Club Stories 2

Point of No Return – Turning Point #1

Breaking Point – Turning Point #2

Starting Point – Turning Point #3

Element of Retrofit – Thomas Elkin Series #1

Clarity of Lines – Thomas Elkin Series #2

Sense of Place – Thomas Elkin Series #3

Taxes and TARDIS

Three's Company

Red Dirt Heart

Red Dirt Heart 2

Red Dirt Heart 3

Red Dirt Heart 4

Red Dirt Christmas

Cronin's Key

Cronin's Key II

Cronin's Key III

Cronin's Key IV - Kennard's Story

Exchange of Hearts

The Spencer Cohen Series, Book One

The Spencer Cohen Series, Book Two

The Spencer Cohen Series, Book Three

The Spencer Cohen Series, Yanni's Story

Blood & Milk

The Weight Of It All

A Very Henry Christmas (The Weight of It All 1.5)

Perfect Catch

Switched

Imago

Imagines

Imagoes

Red Dirt Heart Imago

On Davis Row

Finders Keepers

Evolved

Galaxies and Oceans

Private Charter

Nova Praetorian

A Soldier's Wish

Upside Down

The Hate You Drink

Sir

Tallowwood

Reindeer Games

The Dichotomy of Angels

Throwing Hearts

Pieces of You - Missing Pieces #1

Pieces of Me - Missing Pieces #2

Pieces of Us - Missing Pieces #3

Lacuna

Tic-Tac-Mistletoe

Titles in Audio:

Cronin's Key

Cronin's Key II

Cronin's Key III

Red Dirt Heart

Red Dirt Heart 2

Red Dirt Heart 3

Red Dirt Heart 4

The Weight Of It All

Switched

Point of No Return

Breaking Point

Starting Point

Spencer Cohen Book One

Spencer Cohen Book Two

Spencer Cohen Book Three

Yanni's Story

On Davis Row

Evolved

Elements of Retrofit

Clarity of Lines

Sense of Place

Blind Faith

Through These Eyes

Blindside

Finders Keepers

Galaxies and Oceans

Nova Praetorian

Upside Down

Sir

Tallowwood

Imago

Throwing Hearts

Sixty Five Hours

Taxes and TARDIS

The Dichotomy of Angels

The Hate You Drink

Pieces of You

Pieces of Me

Pieces of Us

Tic-Tac-Mistletoe

Free Reads:

Sixty Five Hours

Learning to Feel

His Grandfather's Watch (And The Story of Billy and Hale)

The Twelfth of Never (Blind Faith 3.5)

Twelve Days of Christmas (Sixty Five Hours Christmas)

Best of Both Worlds

Translated Titles:

Fiducia Cieca (Italian translation of Blind Faith)

Attraverso Questi Occhi (Italian translation of Through These Eyes)

Preso alla Sprovvista (Italian translation of Blindside)

Il giorno del Mai (Italian translation of Blind Faith 3.5)

Cuore di Terra Rossa (Italian translation of Red Dirt Heart)

Cuore di Terra Rossa 2 (Italian translation of Red Dirt Heart 2)

Cuore di Terra Rossa 3 (Italian translation of Red Dirt Heart 3)

Cuore di Terra Rossa 4 (Italian translation of Red Dirt Heart 4)

Natale di terra rossa (Red dirt Christmas)

Intervento di Retrofit (Italian translation of Elements of Retrofit)

A Chiare Linee (Italian translation of Clarity of Lines)

Senso D'appartenenza (Italian translation of Sense of Place)

Spencer Cohen 1 Serie: Spencer Cohen

Spencer Cohen 2 Serie: Spencer Cohen

Spencer Cohen 3 Serie: Spencer Cohen

Spencer Cohen 4 Serie: Yanni's Story

Punto di non Ritorno (Italian translation of Point of No Return)

Punto di Rottura (Italian translation of Breaking Point)

Punto di Partenza (Italian translation of Starting Point)

Imago (Italian translation of Imago)

Il desiderio di un soldato (Italian translation of A Soldier's Wish)

Confiance Aveugle (French translation of Blind Faith)

A travers ces yeux: Confiance Aveugle 2 (French translation of Through These Eyes)

Aveugle: Confiance Aveugle 3 (French translation of Blindside)

À Jamais (French translation of Blind Faith 3.5)

Cronin's Key (French translation)

Cronin's Key II (French translation)

Au Coeur de Sutton Station (French translation of Red Dirt Heart)

Partir ou rester (French translation of Red Dirt Heart 2)

Faire Face (French translation of Red Dirt Heart 3)

Trouver sa Place (French translation of Red Dirt Heart 4)

Le Poids de Sentiments (French translation of The Weight of It All)

Un Noël à la sauce Henry (French translation of A Very Henry Christmas)

Une vie à Refaire (French translation of Switched)

Lodernde Erde (German translation of Red Dirt Heart)

Flammende Erde 2 (German translation of Red Dirt Heart 2)

*Vier Pfoten und ein bisschen Zufall (German translation of
Finders Keepers)*

*Ein Kleines bisschen Versuchung (German translation of The
Weight of It All)*

*Ein Kleines Bisschen Fur Immer (German translation of A Very
Henry Christmas)*

Weil Leibe uns immer Bliebt (German translation of Switched)

Drei Herzen eine Leibe (German translation of Three's Company)

Sixty Five Hours (Thai translation)

Finders Keepers (Thai translation)

CPSIA information can be obtained
at www.ICGtesting.com
Printed in the USA
LVHW090200160321
681659LV00008B/53